Mercy and Justice Myst

Fourth Printing, October 2021

Contact: mercyandjusticemysteries@gmail.com

Cover Photo: Adobe Stock Photos

Cover: Millie Godwin

Editing: Anna Palmer Darkes

The Penitent Priest

The Father Tom Mysteries, Book 1
By
J. R. Mathis and Susan Mathis

Also by J. R. Mathis and Susan Mathis

One

It has always struck me as odd that people believe that priests don't have pasts, that they are somehow born full-grown men with Roman collars around their necks.

People don't think this about their accountant, or their lawyer, or their doctor. But they assume their priest knew he had a vocation from the moment he was born, and grew up in some kind of preschool seminary before actually landing on the steps of their local parishes.

Of course, the truth is completely different.

No man can even enter seminary until he is at least 18 years old, and it's rare that any do so that young. Most have probably tried some sort of illegal drugs, almost everyone has driven too fast, gotten drunk at least once, and disappointed his mother on numerous occasions. One or two may have spent time behind bars, perhaps even outside the country.

It's also fair to say that many—if not most—are not virgins, though there is no record kept concerning this. Most of those who are not have slept with women, though a few have slept with men. The requirement is chastity from the day you choose this life—or more precisely, decide to see if God has chosen you for it—going forward, no matter what you have done in the past.

But a few of us, like me, don't have to be asked for details. The fact is right out there, because we have been married before.

Yes, I am one of the few people now on earth who, at the end of my life, will have received all seven sacraments of the Roman Catholic Church—assuming someone's around to give me last rites, which I certainly hope they are. But it's not really the kind of thing you can plan for too much.

Because people assume that we don't have pasts, people also assume their priests don't have emotional triggers—events that cause them flashbacks or discomfort. But of course we do. There are priests who still get a little sentimental about a song on the radio, or some for whom the smell of a certain food brings him back to Mother's house.

For me, being back at Saint Clare's today is one of these triggers.

1

The last time I was here I was not standing behind a font but instead, in front of a casket, that of my much loved, much too young wife, Joan, who had died in my arms just a few days earlier.

Today could not be any more different than that dreadful day, for while then it seemed that my life was ending—and in a way a part of it was—on this day the life of little Benedict James Reynolds is just beginning, and it is my job to welcome him in to the arms of the Holy Mother Church.

And that's what makes me nervous.

To make bad matters worse, little Benedict himself is something of a trigger, clad as he is in a family heirloom baptism gown. It's not unlike the one my mother passed on to me when I took my first fiancée to my family home in Florida to meet her. Strangely enough, Mom didn't ask for it back when that engagement ended in a heated argument in a cheap apartment, instead of sacred vows in front of an altar. Instead, she waited until after I did marry—and lost—Joan, with the child who might have worn that gown, to ask for it back. Of course, by then, my sister Sonya had had numerous pregnancy scares and, as Mom said in her usual way, "You've already lost two women, Tommy. God only knows if you'll ever find anyone else."

Apparently God did know, because I never did find anyone else. Instead, I found Him and a very surprising vocation to the priesthood.

That is why I am standing before this altar now, about to pour holy water over the forehead of this squirming infant in the arms of his proud mother.

We get to the part I have been dreading, as I carefully take little Benedict James from his mother and hold him over the font. I pick up the silver shell, dip it in the water, and pour the water over his head. The little boy is still and peaceful, looking at me with wide-eyed wonderment. I have worried for days that he'd scream the entire time, and prayed that he wouldn't. Fortunately my prayers are answered, and I hand Benedict back to his mother, breathe a sigh of relief, and turn to the assembly.

"Let us welcome Benedict James Reynolds into God's family."

The crowd applauds, punctuated by the cries and screams of the dozens of children in the pews.

The 10:30 a.m. Mass is a lively, well-attended one. From what I can tell, the church is full almost to capacity—primarily with young families, though all ages are represented. I recognize some of the people from years ago. Anna Luckgold, my mother-in-law, is here, third row from the front. Glenda Whitemill, the parish secretary, sits in the front row studying my every move.

She was also at 8:00 a.m. Mass.

I make it through this, my first Mass with more than an audience of five since—well, ever. Everything is fine until the end. I have just finished the prayers before Communion when I see movement out of the corner of my eye. Glenda Whitemill has left her seat and moved to the altar with the other Eucharistic Ministers.

Instead of lining up with everyone else, Glenda comes right to my elbow and whispers, "Remind the parents to keep their children in the pews."

"What?"

"They only come up if they're old enough to receive Communion. Otherwise they have to stay put."

I look at her and shake my head slightly. "I'm not going to do that. The parents can bring their children up for a blessing if they want to."

"But Father Anthony—"

"Is not here," I say, firmly. "Now, please go back with the others."

She looks at me, her eyes burning with indignation.

"Yes, Father," she says quietly. She walks back and stands with the others. After the final prayers, I say, "Please be seated for just a moment."

The congregation sits down, mothers and fathers wrestling reluctant toddlers and older children back into their seats.

"Before the final blessing," I say, "I just want to say how happy I am to be here at Saint Clare's. I look forward to the next four months with you, and please know that my door is always open if you have any need or concern. I'll do my best, but I'm not planning on making any major changes, since I've never been in a parish on my own before, so please bear with me as I find my way."

I hear a wave of murmurs through the church, intermingling with the sounds of fussy children. I try to read people's faces. I think they look approving—except, of course, for Glenda Whitemill.

I let the murmuring die down. "Most of you are newer to the parish." I pause before going on. "Some of you may remember me from—from my previous life here in Myerton."

Glenda jerks her head up at that. I hear more murmuring and think I notice a couple of signs of recognition. "I look forward to renewing old acquaintances and making new ones in the short time I'm here."

That's not true. My real hope is that my brief return to Myerton will be quiet and uneventful. I am only at Saint Clare's because Archbishop Knowland ordered me here to fill in for Father Anthony. I have no more desire to stay than I had when I left everything behind fifteen years ago.

I give the final blessing, the final hymn starts, and I proceed down the aisle with the altar servers, led by a pair of very serious young men who look so much alike they must be brothers. Back in the vestibule, I thank everyone, introducing myself to Vincent Trent and his younger brother, Dominic.

Vincent shakes my hand firmly and informs me, "Father Greer, this is my last Sunday here before I leave for college, but Dominic is well trained and completely up to taking my place as head altar server."

I say casually to Dominic, "Is altar service a family apostolate for you?"

He surprises by answering me with complete seriousness, "It was at first. When Vincent started out, he and I were about the only little boys in the church. It's only been in the last ten years or so that the Lord has blessed us with so many young families. Father Anthony brought to the parish a wonderful combination of orthodoxy and family support."

With this piece of information ringing in my ears, I go outside.

***

The day is one of those sunny, clear days in mid-September that have the last taste of summer and the first taste of fall. It is warm, but with a cool breeze that makes being outside in full Mass vestments tolerable.

I place my hand against one of the six white marble columns that line the portico. Saint Clare's is an imposing structure, said to be one of the largest churches west of Baltimore. The white Ionic building was constructed in the 1850s to replace the earlier brick parish that had burned. Funded by the small donations of Irish immigrants who had made their way into the Allegheny Mountains to work on the railroad, as well as the larger ones of the Myer family who employed them, the church has seen untold numbers of baptisms, as well as weddings and funerals.

Joan and I stood under its soaring vaulted ceiling the day we married. She wore white, looking impossibly beautiful, her veil covering her chestnut brown hair and her lace-covered shoulders. Father Anthony, whose place I am taking, officiated that day, and then said her funeral mass just a few years later.

People begin coming out. Children run past, chased by frazzled moms hastily saying, "Thank you, Father," as they hurry by. I shake hands, saying, "Thank you very much," to people who say, "We're glad you're here" and "Good homily, Father." I am surprised at the number of people who pass by whom I have no memory of. Then, a large man about my age stops. With him are two twin teenage boys. Leaning on a cane, he extends a beefy hand. I laugh, grasp his hand, and give him a hug.

"John Archman," I say, "how are you?"

"Good to see you, Tom," says this big bear of a man. "Or maybe I should say Father Tom?"

"Tom's fine. I didn't know you were still living in Myerton?"

John nods. "Chloe wanted to raise the kids here; it's near her parents. And I like it, too."

"So, what are you doing now?"

"Consulting," Archman says. "The new Tech Center outside of town."

"Bit far from D.C. for consulting, isn't it?"

"Internet, teleconferences, you'd be surprised how little face-to-face time is required in IT consulting." John turns to his boys. "John, Mark, say hello to your godfather." The twins say hello, then ask their dad if they can hang out with their friends until it's time to leave.

"Don't make me come look for you," John says as they run off. When he turns back to me, he grimaces.

"You OK?" I ask.

"Yeah," he replies. "My leg still gets to me sometimes. I'll have to get back into physical therapy."

Soon after 9/11, John enlisted in the army. He served two tours in Iraq. During his second tour, an IED exploded as his squad was on patrol. He was the only survivor and was himself severely wounded.

"So," he says, looking me up and down. "You're a priest now. I've gotta tell you, I didn't see that one coming."

"You're not the first one to say that to me. Is it that remarkable?"

"No, not remarkable, it's just—I remember what you and Joan were like together. You were inseparable. I envied you two that. Chloe and I—I've never seen two people in love as much as you two were—I know how devastated you were after her—" John pauses. "Joan was special," he whispers.

"Yes, she was," I say quietly.

"Then you left and didn't tell anyone where you were going. No one heard from you for a while. Then when Anna told us—none of us could believe it. " He pauses. "So how did it happen?"

It is a question I hear frequently, especially when people learn how old I was when I was ordained. Granted, most priests don't discern their vocations when they are in their late 20s. Even fewer receive the vocation after they are married. But my situation was different. So, I keep getting the question, one I am getting kind of tired of being asked.

"It's kind of a long story," I reply. "I don't want to get into it right now."

He holds up his hands "OK, OK. No problem. But you say you weren't in a parish before here? What have you been doing?"

"I've been the archivist for the Archdiocese since my ordination, so I've been at the main office for eight years."

"Well," he says smiling. "It is good to see you. Chloe will be sorry she missed you. Home with a sick kid. Hey, we'll have to have you over for dinner. Catch up."

I hesitate. "Maybe when I get the time. But give Chloe my best."

John's smile fades. "Sure, sure Tom. When you get the time. I'll tell Chloe you send your best." I watch as John, leaning on his cane, goes off to find his boys.

"So you've seen John," Anna says, having come up behind me. I turn.

"He's missed you," she says. "You were his best friend."

"And he was mine."

"He could have used a friend like you over the last few years."

I look at her, puzzled. "He hasn't had an easy time since you left," she explains.

"He seems fine to me, except for the cane."

"Looks are deceiving. He's struggling. Chloe tells me these last few years have been hard."

I remember how John was after he came home. The physical wounds were slow to heal. The emotional wounds festered. Joan and I were as supportive as we could be, but after a while, John just withdrew.

I look at her. I don't know how to answer.

"Anyway," she smiled. "Good job. Everyone seemed really pleased."

"Except Glenda."

"Oh," she waves her hand, "don't worry about Glenda. She's had the run of this place for years. It's about time someone stood up to her."

"I didn't want to cause a scene."

"You didn't. You did what Father Anthony should have done a long time ago. But Father Anthony isn't inclined to confront her. And Glenda is—"

"Yes, she certainly is."

The day I arrived, Glenda Whitemill made it very clear what she thought of me.

"I don't know why the Archbishop sent you," she had said. "Father Anthony's coming back. He doesn't need to be replaced."

"I'm not replacing Father Anthony," I said. "I'm just here for four months while he . . . rests."

"We can get along just fine having a priest show up for mass," she went on like I hadn't said anything. "When I spoke to the Archbishop—"

"You called the Archbishop?"

"—I told him we didn't need a resident priest. I asked him just to send one around for mass on Saturday nights and Sundays. He gave me some hogwash about a parish needing to have a resident priest. I told him exactly what I thought."

She went on like that, all the while showing me through the rectory, a two-story house sitting next door to the church. A walk from the front door led to what I assumed was the side door of the church. Another path led to the sidewalk. The first floor had a living room, dining room, kitchen, guest bedroom and what would be my office and Glenda's office. Upstairs were two bedrooms—Father Anthony's and another guest room, where I would be staying. The furnishings looked like rejects from Mike and Carol Brady's home, frankly hideous in shades of brown, yellow, and that tried and true staple of the 1970's color scheme, avocado.

There was a worn and threadbare quality to the whole place, much like Whitemill herself.

I realize I have not seen Glenda coming out of the church. Not knowing where she is makes me nervous. I look around in the crowd and finally spot her. She is standing on the corner, speaking to a man about my age. He is also about my height but wears a pullover hoodie and jeans that hang loosely about his frame, showing he is quite a bit skinnier than I am.

"Who is that?" I ask Anna.

She turns. "Who?"

"That guy over there talking to Glenda." They are too far away to hear, but she is shaking her right finger in his face, and he is shaking his head emphatically.

"Hmm," Anna says. "I'm not sure. I know Glenda has a nephew, and that could be him, but I can't say for sure. Not sure I've ever seen him."

The man storms away from Glenda, who just stands there looking after him.

"He's not a member of the parish?"

"I don't know—he could be. Maybe he just comes to the earlier Mass or only shows up at Christmas and Easter, I really can't say. I don't know everybody, Tom."

Glenda turns. She looks upset. Looking around to make sure no one had observed the scene, she walks quickly down the sidewalk to the Rectory.

The crowd has thinned out so there are only a couple of small groups talking to each other, their children running up and down the steps. Some have started an impromptu game of tag on the grass between the church and the parking lot. Two brown-haired twins start wrestling for reasons only known to them. A young woman, trailed by a little girl with brownish-blond hair, rushes to the two boys and pulls them apart. They're soon joined by a large, muscular man who takes both boys by the arm and leads them away, either for a firm talking-to or for a more painful exhortation.

"Why don't you come over for lunch?" Anna says. "Nothing fancy, just sandwiches."

I hesitate. "Anna, I'm kinda tired—"

"I'm going to see her this afternoon," Anna goes on. She pauses to let that settle in.

"It's been a long day," I say. "I'm really drained. Maybe another day."

She looks at me, but says nothing. I see the accusatory look in her eyes and brace myself. Then, she smiles.

"It's OK, Tom," she pats me on the arm. "Some other time." She begins to walk away, then turns and says, "I'm sure she likes them."

"Likes what?"

"The carnations," Anna says. I shake my head. "The peppermint carnations?"

Peppermint carnations. Joan's favorite flower.

"What about peppermint carnations?" I say, thoroughly confused.

"You really don't know what I'm talking about?" Anna asks. "You haven't been sending peppermint carnations to her gravesite once a month?"

"No, it wasn't me," I say. "Sorry."

Anna sighs. "Oh. I just assumed. Guess it's one of her friends." She begins to walk away.

"For how long?" I say after her.

"It's been a long time. Almost fifteen years," she says over her shoulder. "I thought it was you. Guess I was wrong."

With that Anna walks away. I walk back into the church. In the sacristy, I take off my vestments and turn the lights off.

I look around. The only light comes through the stained glass windows and from the candles. Incense still hangs in the air; I can also smell the oil on my hands from anointing the Reynolds baby.

The building is at peace.

I am not.

Two

Monday is a parish priest's traditional day off. Since arriving at Saint Clare's I have not had the time to learn about the parish, so I decide to spend it in my office. There are files on the desk, put there by Glenda, I assume, that I need to go through. After my first cup of coffee and Morning Prayer, I sit down at the desk and begin to familiarize myself with my temporary assignment. I know I will have a couple of hours of silence because Glenda is out.

After thirty minutes, my eyes begin to glaze over. I've never had much of a head for numbers, and trying to make sense of Saint Clare's financial statements is taxing my limited powers to the utmost. I can't tell if the parish is running a deficit, has a surplus, or is breaking even. From what I know of other parishes around the Archdiocese, the truth is probably somewhere in the middle.

I plow ahead with another folder labeled "Baptisms and Confirmations." While Saint Clare's does not have a lot of money, it is rich with people. Since January, ten babies have been baptized into the Church; also, four adults entered the Church the previous Easter and five more are preparing to join the next. The folder on religious education also shows healthy numbers.

Whatever is going on at Saint Clare's, it is good.

The doorbell rings. I don't get up at first, because I think Glenda will get it. By the third ring, more insistent this time, I remember she is still out. I open the door to find the man I saw Glenda talking with the previous day.

He seems surprised to see me. "Good morning," I say.

He doesn't speak at first. He looks like he is in a daze. I can't tell if he is high or just confused.

I try again. "Can I help you?"

"Huh?—Oh, yeah, sorry, Father," he finally says. "Is, ah, is—is Glenda here?"

"No, she's out right now. She should be back soon. Would you like to come in?" I open the door wider to make it more inviting.

"No, no, no, that's—that's OK, Father. I'll, ah, I'll just call her later—"

"—Is there something I can help you with?"

"You?" He seems shocked by the question.

11

"It's kind of what I'm supposed to do, help people. Comes with the collar." I smile, hoping the joke will put him at ease.

It doesn't work. "No, no, I'll just get Glenda later. Sorry to bother you." He turns and walks off, looking back over his shoulder at me.

"What's your name so I can tell her you stopped by?" I call after him. He doesn't answer me so I just stand looking after him before going back to my desk and picking up where I left off.

I have only been back at work for about a half hour or so when the doorbell rings again.

"Some day off," I mutter as I go answer the door.

This time, there is a woman at the door, one I recognize.

"Hello, Chloe," I smile.

Chloe Archman smiles the smile of a person who has the choice of either laughter or tears, and chooses laughter only because it isn't as socially awkward.

"Hi Tom—Father Tom," she said.

"Tom's fine, Chloe. Please, come in." We hug, and I show her into the living room. She sits on the edge of the couch, hands folded in her lap. I sit opposite her in an ugly seventies-brown armchair. A spring pokes me in the back.

"Sorry I missed you at Mass," I say. "John told me one of the kids is sick. Are they better?"

"Oh, yes, she's doing much better. A twenty-four hour thing. The kids are at home. We homeschool but someone comes in to watch them a couple of mornings a week. I teach one class per semester at the college."

"So you're back teaching? English lit, isn't it?"

"Yes." She pauses. "So, how have you been?"

"Fine, fine."

"Good, good."

There are a few moments of silence while we just look at each other.

"Can I get you something to drink? Water, coffee?"

"No, I'm fine." She sighs. "Sorry, this is harder than I thought it would be."

"What is?"

"Coming here. Seeing you—my best friend's husband—for the first time in fifteen years. You know, I thought about what I'd say when I finally saw you—oh, I had some choice words in mind for you. Leaving without saying good-bye. Not coming back even one time. Not a card, not an email, not so much as a text. The only thing we ever heard was from Anna—we couldn't believe it when she told us you'd been ordained to the priesthood—so at least we knew you weren't dead. I am so, so angry, with so many things to say. But I can't say any of it now because you—" she gestures with both arms "—are now a priest. Worse, you're my priest. So, is it a grave sin to be angry at a priest?"

"No graver than being angry at anyone else," I answer.

"Oh, OK, well—I'm angry at you, Tom. Really, really angry. You left Anna, you left John, you left me. You were the only connection I still had to my best friend. I was devastated when she was murdered. I was devastated when you left. But you know what, not nearly as devastated as John."

"John?"

I can see tears beginning to form in her eyes.

"Oh, Tom!" She cries, and buries her face in her hands. I grab a nearby box of tissues and hand it to her. She takes out a couple and wipes her eyes.

"Anna told me he's had some problems."

"Not just some problems, Tom. Oh, you don't know, but then how could you—you weren't here."

"Well, I'm here now. Tell me what's going on."

She exhales. "After he came home from the hospital, he seemed to be doing well—I guess as well as could be expected. He was still in pain, but the physical therapy was helping and he was working hard at it. He got stronger, he was seeing a therapist to help him process what happened, he was becoming the John I knew again. Well, you remember how he was."

"I remember. After a while, he seemed like the old John."

"He was doing so well," Chloe says. "Then, he began to change. He became withdrawn, spending more and more time by himself. He didn't want to see anyone or do anything. He spent all his free time either locked in his office or taking long walks by himself." She pauses and wipes her eyes as the tears return.

"Oh, and by the way, you and Joan were not much help," she continues, rage now strengthening her. "It seemed like every time we wanted to do something, Joan was too busy with her new business."

What she says is true. Joan was busy back then, trying to get a new design business off the ground. But I also remember a few times when I tried to get John out for a boys night, only to have him turn me down. There were also plenty of times they cancelled plans with us. In the months before Joan's murder, we spent very little time with the Archmans.

I am wrestling with these thoughts while Chloe continues, now in the voice of spent, rather than active, rage. "Not long after Joan's death, his leg began bothering him—he reinjured it somehow, he thinks when he tripped on the back stairs while taking the trash out."

"That's why he uses the cane," I say.

Chloe nods. "But before that," she goes on, "his mood changed. His depression got worse and he began having nightmares. He started drinking. When he reinjured his leg, he couldn't get around without the cane. He's been in pain ever since. He won't do physical therapy anymore—says it's voodoo, doesn't work. I don't know when he decided that—just takes painkillers and drinks." A tear snakes its way down her cheek. "But I can handle the physical pain. That doesn't worry me as much as the other."

"What other?"

"The moods. The depression," she said. "He'll be happy one minute, then screaming with fury the next."

That doesn't sound like the John I knew. "Has he ever hurt you or the kids?"

"Oh no, no, he's never laid a hand on us. He has the presence of mind to go scream in the garage when he's really angry. I think he knows I'd leave if he ever did anything like that."

"He needs to get help, Chloe," I say, "before he hurts someone."

"I'm more concerned about him hurting himself. When he's really down, he begins to talk about how he's responsible. That it's his fault people died. He says he's a coward, how he should have done something to help instead of hiding, about how he betrayed them, about how the wrong people always die."

"But that makes no sense," I say. "He received a commendation. There's no way any of that in Iraq was his fault."

"I know. But he's been carrying a big load of guilt for a long time."

Guilt. I cringe at the very word. It seems like most of my life has been shaped by things I could have or should have done. But Chloe doesn't know that, can never know that, and anyway, this isn't about me, it's about her.

"Is he seeing anyone?" I ask, trying to apply what we're taught in seminary about dealing with parishioners suffering from depression.

"No, not anymore," she said. "He did for a while, saw both a therapist and a psychiatrist, right after he came home. It was helping." She shrugged. "Then he stopped."

"Why'd he do that?"

"Well, he told me he doesn't need to go anymore, but I don't know the real reason." She sits back and sighs. "I'm about at the end of my rope and am hoping you can talk to him.

"I'll try," I say. "But I don't know what I can do."

"You were—are—his friend. He used to listen to you. I've run out of ideas. Besides, you're a priest."

"That's true, but still, he'll have to want to talk to me, he'll have to want help. Do you think he does?"

She thinks for a moment, then, "I don't know. I really don't know."

I sigh. "OK, Chloe. I'll try talking to him. In the meantime, I'll keep you and your family in my prayers."

She smiled, a real smile this time. "Thank you, Tom. Thank you so much."

After she leaves, I settle back into my study with another folder, this time on the Knights of Columbus, when I hear the front door open. What sounds like two people come in.

"There's no reason to bother the Father about this," Glenda says.

"I just want to ask him if he would mind if we had one this year," a young woman replies.

"Father Anthony has said no each year for the past five years," Glenda continues. "It would be just too disruptive."

"Well Father Anthony's not here, and it will not be disruptive. We're just talking about a small, simple production—"

"You will not talk to Father about this because—"

By this time, I am standing in the doorway. The young woman with Glenda is one I recognize from the 10:30 a.m. Mass sitting with her husband and three children, a girl and twin boys.

"Glenda," I interrupted. They look at me.

"Oh, Father," Glenda says. "I was just telling Miriam that—"

"Thank you, Glenda, but why don't you let Miriam talk? Miriam, you have something you want to ask me?"

"Well—yes, yes, Father Tom," Miriam says. "I want to ask—well, some of the other moms in the parish think—you see, Christmas is in a few months—"

"Yes, that seems to happen every year," I say. Smiling, I add, "What would you like?"

Miriam takes a deep breath. "We are wondering if you would allow us to organize some of the children to do a Nativity pageant."

"You mean with the children playing the various parts? Mary, Joseph, shepherds, kings? A few toddlers dressed as sheep?"

Glenda interjects. "I told her it would be impossible, Father."

"Really, and why is that, Glenda?" I ask.

She seems stunned that I would question her statement. "Well . . . well—it just would be. The Advent and Christmas season is already so busy, and the children would disrupt everything."

"Now Glenda, if Saint Clare's could survive being used as a hospital during the Civil War, I think it can survive a small Nativity play." I turn to Miriam. "Sounds like a fine idea, Miriam—what is your last name?"

"Conway. Miriam Conway. Thank you, Father, thank you so much. Now we thought maybe Saturday, a week before Christmas?"

"Actually I have an idea. Isn't there a Christmas Eve Vigil Mass, Glenda?"

"Yes, at 5:00 p.m."

"Good. Why don't you do it at the Vigil Mass?"

Miriam smiles. "Really?"

"At the Vigil Mass?" Glenda is not smiling.

"Yes. I would think that Mass would have a lot of children attending, with parents wanting them to get to bed early. It would be fun for them. We'd do it instead of the homily. What do you think, Miriam, do you think everyone would go for that?"

"Absolutely! Thank you, thank you, Father. This means a whole lot to us—more than you can know."

Miriam shakes my hand, looks at Glenda, and leaves. After she is gone, Glenda turns to me.

"Father Anthony—"

"Is not here, Glenda. Let me ask you, just between you and me, did he ever actually tell the ladies he didn't want a Nativity play?"

Glenda hesitates. "Well, well, not exactly—"

"I thought so." I pause. "Glenda, I understand that you spent a lot of time acting as Father Anthony's gatekeeper. I'm sure he appreciated it. But you don't need to do that with me."

"You cannot spend your time talking to every parishioner who wants your attention."

"I know, but I can speak to most of them," I say. "From now on, I'm available for anyone who wants to talk to me during office hours."

"Father Anthony didn't keep office hours. People had to make an appointment."

"Well, they can still make an appointment, but if they stop by and I'm here and I'm not in the middle of something critical, I'll be available to them. Understand?"

Glenda stiffens. "Yes, Father. If you'll excuse me, I have to put the groceries away and start dinner. You're having chicken tonight." She grabs her bags and storms out.

"Oh, Glenda," I call. She stops in the doorway and turns slightly. "Someone stopped by to see you."

"Who?"

"I don't know his name. I saw you talking to him yesterday after church. Anna thought it was your nephew."

The blood rushes from her face. "He . . . my . . . he stopped by the Rectory while you were here?"

I furrow my brow. "Yes, it was while you were out. Is everything OK, Glenda?"

"What—yes," she said, squaring her shoulders. "Oh yes, Father, everything is fine. I'll call him after I finish lunch. I'm sorry he bothered you."

"It was no bother, Glenda. Does your nephew live with you?"

"Yes, yes. Roger, he's my sister's son," she says quickly. "He's staying with me while he works a construction job at the college. I'll call him in a bit."

She has just cleared the doorway when the phone rings. I look at the clock. It's just 11 a.m. I have to be in the church by 11:30 a.m. to get ready for the Noon Mass.

"Lot more lively place than I thought it would be," I mumble to myself. I pick up the phone.

"Hello, Saint Clare's Rectory."

"May I speak to Father Tom Greer, please?"

"Speaking."

"Oh, Father Greer, good. My name is Nate Rodriguez. I'm a freelance documentary filmmaker."

"What can I do for you?"

"I'm hoping I can interview you for my next film project."

"Me? Why would you want to interview me?"

"Well, you see, my project concerns the unsolved murder of Joan Greer."

Three

"I know this was short notice, but I really appreciate you agreeing to talk to me," Nate Rodriguez says.

"Let me be clear, Mr. Rodriguez—"

"Nate, please call me Nate."

"OK, let me be clear, Nate," I say. "I have not agreed to anything. I only said I would meet with you."

Only two hours after he called the Rectory, I find myself sitting across from this very earnest young man with auburn hair at The Perfect Cup, a little coffee shop across Main Street from Myer College. The stone archway people consider the main entrance to the campus is just opposite where I sit.

Dominating the scene is the statue of Winthrop Myer, founder of Myerton and the College. Myer had arrived in the western Maryland mountains having gained and lost his first fortune in Baltimore. On the frontier, he built another on lumber and the railroad. He dreamed of the mountain town rivaling Baltimore or Pittsburgh in size and wealth, with Myer College becoming the Johns Hopkins of the Alleghenies.

I look at the young boys and girls, books in hand, backpacks on their backs, walking to class or back to their apartments. It was at a spot very much like it, but at another college campus a couple of hours east of where I sit, where I met the first woman I ever loved.

***

I was finishing my sophomore year at the University of Maryland. One day in early March, I was walking along, not paying attention to where I was going—I was reading something, don't remember what—when I walked into a young woman, knocking her down and sending a large stack of books flying out of her hands. Worse than that, there was a three-ring binder in the stack, and it broke open on impact, allowing the pages inside to blow in every direction.

"What the hell is wrong with you?" she yelled, "Are you blind or stupid or both?"

19

"I'm sorry," I said, before deciding to try to get back the moral high ground. "It's just that I haven't seen too well since that tear gas went off near me."

She froze at this and said, "Wait, what?"

"Yeah," I continued, warming to my story. "I was protesting poverty in Baltimore, and some fascist counter-protesters attacked us. The police had no choice, I understand that now. But still . . ."

I started staring over her shoulder blankly, even as I reached my hands out toward her. She quickly grabbed them, grasping one of my fingers particularly hard. She began to bend it back when I said, "Wait, it's a miracle. I can see."

She let go, laughing in spite of herself. "I'll help you get them back," I said sheepishly.

"Damn right you will," she replied as she began chasing after her notes. I follow after her, grabbing notes of various types cartwheeling across the lawn, all the while keeping my eye on this woman.

Unlike most of the female students and faculty on campus, she didn't wear jeans; instead, she wore a long straight denim skirt that coyly accented her delightfully round figure. That day she had paired it with a red turtleneck. Her black curly hair was pinned up and a few stray curls framed her soft face.

But it was her eyes that caught my attention.

They were like no eyes I'd ever seen before, blue sapphires floating in shining bowls of white.

We managed to get the papers gathered up. As I handed her my stack, I said lamely, "I hope they're OK."

She didn't take any time to look at them but instead just shoved them into the space between the binder's covers. "I sure they are," she said over her shoulder as she began to rush off.

I just stood there on the sidewalk, students passing us on their way to or from classes, looking after her. Then, I called out, "Are you hungry?"

She turned. "No, but I am late," she yelled back, then hurried on to wherever she was going before we collided.

That was the last I heard of her until the following fall, when I found myself comfortably seated in a class that had just started when she rushed in. If anything, she was even more beautiful than she had been in the spring. The next class, I got to the room early, took a seat near the door, and placed my backpack in the seat beside me. When she arrived, late again, I was ready.

The rest was—or more precisely, should have been—history.

It took me two weeks to work up my courage, but I finally asked her to lunch.

We wound up at Marlowe's, a restaurant in a small Victorian house not far from campus. She had the Cobb salad. I had the tomato bisque and four-cheese grilled cheese.

We were engaged six months later, and parted ways a couple of years after that. I never saw her again.

They say you never forget your first love, and for all that I loved my wife dearly and would give anything to have her back, no, you don't forget.

***

"I'll be glad for any help you can give," Nate says, bringing me back to the present.

"Let's just slow down a bit," I reply.

"Sure, sure, OK."

I stir my coffee. "So, you make documentaries?"

"Yes, that's right."

"Anything I might have heard of?"

He shakes his head. "No, no, nothing—well, actually, I've only done a few small projects for my classes at Myer, so this is the first big project I've worked on."

"I see," I reply. "You went to Myer?"

"Uh-huh, graduated two, three years ago. Got my degree in journalism."

"Are you working for the Myerton Gazette?"

"Ah, well, not exactly." He takes a drink of coffee. "I actually work here."

"Here," I repeat. "At The Perfect Cup. As a—?"

He shrugs. "Whatever my uncle tells me to do—wait tables, bus tables, barista. Listen, Father, can we get on with this? I only get thirty minutes for lunch."

I wonder even more what I am doing there. "Let me see if I understand correctly," I say. "Your project is to investigate—"

"OK, well, investigate is probably too strong a word. I'm not really investigating your wife's murder—can I call her your wife, I mean, with you being a priest?"

In spite of myself, I hesitate. It's been so very long now since she was my wife. I've been without her longer than I was with her but, yes, she is still my wife. She just lives somewhere else, with Someone who will not fail her like I did.

"Obviously I was not a priest when I was married to Joan," I say. "You can call her my wife."

"OK, OK, well, your wife. So the project isn't to try and find who killed her—though I gotta tell you Father, that would just be so cool." He stops himself when he sees the expression on my face. "I'm sorry, I don't mean cool-cool, just, you know, finding justice after all this time—"

I hold up my hand. "So what exactly is your project?"

He takes a deep breath. "I was looking for a project for my next film and was doing research in the files of the Myerton Gazette when I came across stories about the murder. You know, Myerton is a pretty small town. Murders don't happen every day. The way it happened, no one was caught—it got a lot of attention."

I nod. He is right. At the time, Joan had been the first person murdered in Myerton in almost a year. The paper covered it extensively and reporters from as far away as Baltimore came to do stories for a few days afterwards.

"So it got me thinking," Nate continues, "about what happens after the news cameras leave and the paper stops writing articles. What about the people left behind? How do they cope? How did it change them? I mean, in your case—"

"Yes, yes, I see what you're getting at."

"So I've already done several interviews, researched the case, looked at the police file—"

"You got a copy of the police file?"

"Oh yeah, you can get almost anything through a Freedom of Information request. There's some portions blacked out, but it's been helpful. So I have that."

"Who have you interviewed?"

He pulls out a notebook. "Let's see, some people who knew her from college, her mother—"

"You interviewed Anna?" I wonder why she hasn't given me a heads up about this guy.

"Yeah, Mrs. Luckgold was great—very helpful. Gave me some great pictures and videos to use." He looks through his notes. "The owner of the gallery up the street, The Painted Lotus, did an interview."

"Bethany Grable's still in town?" She was a friend and colleague of Joan's from Myer's Fine Arts Department.

"Yeah, she gave me all sorts of insights about who she was."

One name is conspicuously absent. "Did you interview Chloe Archman?"

Nate sighs. "No. She refused to talk to me."

"Really? Did she say why?"

"No," he shakes his head. "She just said she doesn't want to talk to anyone about Joan Greer."

I find that very odd. They were best friends, after all. Practically inseparable. Chloe was Joan's matron of honor at our wedding, like John was my best man. If Anna would agree to participate, why wouldn't Chloe?

And if Chloe didn't, why should I?

I take a sip of my coffee. I've let it get cold.

Putting my mug down, I say. "Nate, I wish I could help you, but—"

"Oh please," he says, looking at me anxiously. "Don't say 'but.' Look, I've done a lot of work. It's good, I mean I think it's good, but there's a big hole in it. That's why I was so glad when Mrs. Luckgold called and told me you were back in town."

"Anna told you I was back in town?"

"Yes, and I am so glad. I have tried to track you down, but after you left Myerton, you kind of disappeared for a while."

"Yes, I wanted it that way."

"So then you came back here, and I thought, wow, just in time, he's exactly what I need to really finish this. The victim's husband. The man whose arms she died in."

The night is a blur. Joan lying in my arms, gasping. The blood. Cold steel against my forehead. A painful throbbing in my temples. And the sound.

Click. Click. Click.

"I really, really need you for this, Father Tom," Nate concludes.

I shake my head. "No. That night is not something I want to talk about. If you have the police report, you have my statement. I can't help you." I get up to leave.

Nate stands. "Father, please, just think about it. You know, there's one thing I keep coming across. Everyone I've talked to says how much they need closure, how her murder not being solved never gave them any. What if this film, well, maybe jogs someone's memory? Maybe it could give the cops a lead? Who knows, maybe this film could help finally solve your wife's murder?"

I look at the young man. "No," I say quietly. "I gave up that hope years ago. Her murder will never be solved and her murderer will never see justice in this life."

"Are you so certain of that?"

"Yes, I am," I say. "I have to get back to Saint Clare's now. Good luck with your project."

"Father," he says as he stands up. "Just think about it. If you change your mind, please call me."

I look at him and nod.

"OK, if I change my mind. But I'm not going to."

***

Walking back to the parish, I call Anna.

When she answers, I say, "I just spoke to Nate Rodriguez."

"Oh, he got in touch with you?"

"Yes. Why didn't you tell me about him? Why didn't you tell me he interviewed you?"

"Because if I had, you probably wouldn't have spoken to him."

"I would have appreciated a heads up."

"I'm sure you would have."

"So why didn't you give me one?"

"Because you wouldn't have talked to him."

I'm not sure what Anna is trying to do with this circular argument so I decide to go forward.

"Well, it doesn't matter. I heard him out, but I'm not going to talk to him."

Anna doesn't say anything.

"I don't want to talk about Joan's murder. Not with him, not with anyone. It's not like it would do any good."

"What do you mean?"

"Anna, it's not going to bring her back, it's not going to help find her killer—her killer is never going to be found. It was just a senseless, random crime. The guy tried to rape her, I got there before it got too far, there was a struggle, the gun went off, Joan was shot, then she died. That's it."

"There's no need to shout, Tom."

I stop. I have forgotten where I am. I don't realize I've been yelling into the phone. I look around, but no one seems to have taken notice. Surprising, considering you don't see a priest yelling into a cell phone every day.

"I never knew there was a struggle," Anna says.

"Huh?"

"You said there was a struggle. I never knew that."

"Yeah, yeah," I say. "There was a struggle. I thought I told you that."

"You've never told me anything about that night."

"Oh, I'm sure I have."

"No, not a word. The police told me Joan was killed. They didn't say anything about a struggle. And I always thought you two were together when she was attacked."

I hesitate before answering, and when I do, I don't answer her question. "Everything happened so fast, I was in shock—listen, I don't really want to talk about this right now."

"OK, OK," Anna says. I hear resignation in her voice. "By the way," she says, "Bethany Grable called me today. She heard you were back."

"Nate said he interviewed her about Joan."

"Really? I didn't know that. Anyway, she still has Joan's things."

"What things?"

"You know, her art stuff. Joan had a studio there, remember?"

How can I remember something I didn't know about? If Joan had a studio at Bethany's, this is the first I'm hearing about it.

Instead of saying this, I say, "Why didn't she give it to you in all these years?"

"She tried. I told her you'd be back."

"For fifteen years?"

"I can be very persuasive. Besides, she loved Joan."

"I'll give her a call. Thanks."

"How about coming to dinner on Wednesday?"

I hesitate.

"I thought I'd invite Chloe and John," Anna prompts.

"I don't think so, Anna," I say. "Not right now. I'm still trying to get settled in. Can I have a raincheck?"

"Of course," Anna says with evident disappointment. "Any time. Maybe Sunday afternoon. Can't imagine you feel like cooking after two Masses."

"By the way," I say, wanting to change the subject, "did you know Nate Rodriguez tried to interview Chloe and John?"

"Of course. I put Nate in touch with them."

"Why didn't they do it?"

I hear Anna sigh. "I don't know. Joan told me before she was killed that things were strained between them. She never told me why. Chloe won't talk much about her. As for why John won't talk, you'd have to ask him." She pauses. "Please think about it, Tom. Doing the interview."

"Anna, why are you doing this?"

Slowly, she replies, "Because Joan deserves not to be forgotten."

I'm not sure what she means by that, if she means it as a criticism or just a general observation, that other people should remember she was murdered and no one brought to justice. I don't believe she thinks I have forgotten Joan. I haven't forgotten about her. How could I? I have just decided to forget about her murder. I don't see why that has to be remembered, especially since remembering it is not going to bring her back or bring her killer to justice. Nate and Anna can cling to the belief that someone might have their memory jogged, that someone out there might remember the One Clue that would lead to her killer.

I can't do that.

I won't do that.

All I want is peace.

Four

Thursday afternoon, I am sitting at one of the outside tables at The Perfect Cup, finishing up my coffee and one of their famous chocolate doughnuts, when I hear my name. I turn just in time to be embraced by a flood of fabric.

"I thought that was you," the flood says. Engulfed in a paisley hug, I catch a familiar whiff of incense. I know who it is.

"Hello, Bethany," I say as I return the hug.

After a moment, she breaks the hug and kisses me on both cheeks. Bethany Grable has always been physically demonstrative, a heady combination of earth-mother and shrewd businesswoman. She is artistic, but not artsy. She takes her art very seriously and makes sure she is well paid for it. She is probably very comfortable, but her outfit looks like it has been thrown together with thrift store and fabric shop rejects. Bethany is one of those rare souls who is both older and younger than she appears. When she was in her fifties, when I first met her, she looked to be in her sixties. Now that she is in her sixties, she has all the appearance of a woman in her forties.

"I have been meaning to come see you," she says, tugging on the canvas tote bag slung over her shoulder.

"Anna told me you called about Joan's studio."

"Yes, but not just that," she says as she calls Nate over to the table. "Nate, dear, bring me a chai tea, please." Nate scurries off and Bethany settles back, looking me over.

"I can't believe it's been fifteen years," she says. "A lot's changed."

I nod. "You look the same."

She laughs. "Oh, Tom, you always were a charmer. I'm doing OK, a little older, a little fatter, a little more arthritis, but I'm good. And you're a priest."

"That I am."

She folds her arms. "How exactly did that happen?"

"It's, ah, complicated."

"I bet it is. I'd like to hear the story some day."

"Someday I'll tell you." Nate brings her tea. "So how's the gallery?"

"Oh, the gallery, really good. I had a show last week for a couple of new local artists, made some good sales, made a good commission on each. My own art sells now and then, but these days I'm content to make money off of people who're younger and more talented." She sighs. "Like Joan. She had so much talent. It's just a shame."

"I know she enjoyed painting. She didn't do too much of it after we married, just the occasional canvas. Joan was too focused on teaching and trying to get her business off the ground."

She looks surprised. "You didn't know, did you?"

"Know what?"

"She kept painting," Bethany says. "That's why she had the studio."

"I thought it was for her design business?"

"Well," Bethany says, "She did do some of that. But mostly she worked on her own art."

I nod. That explains a lot.

"And you've kept all her things?"

"Oh, yes. I've had to rent out the space, but I kept everything she had. I meant to contact you about it, ask you what you wanted to do with it, but by the time I was going to get around to it, you had gone. I mentioned it to Anna, but she put me off, saying you'd be back." She sips her tea. "Just as well. I don't think she likes me very much."

This is true. While she was consistently very civil and polite to her, I always got the impression when I saw Anna interacting with Bethany—which was very rare—that Anna was jealous of Bethany's friendship with Joan. I thought Anna saw the flamboyant artist as a rival for her daughter's affections, something I couldn't understand, given how close Joan and Anna were.

"Would you like to see her things? I'm not busy now. I was just headed to the thrift store to see if I could find something interesting when I spotted you."

I hesitate. Memories of Joan are not something I want. Not today.

"Unless you're too busy this afternoon," she says. "We could make it another day."

I have nothing the rest of the day, and to say otherwise would be a lie. After I tell her I'll meet her at her gallery, I walk back to the Rectory to get my car. The gallery is just up the street from The Perfect Cup but I figure I'll need the car to haul everything in. Also, it buys me a little time to think.

About ten minutes after we part, I pull into a parking space next to Bethany's car in the alley behind her gallery. She is standing at the back door, fumbling with her keys.

She finally gets the door open and I follow her in. "Joan's studio is up this way," Bethany says as I follow her up the narrow flight of stairs leading to the second floor. She leads me down a hallway, saying, "Be careful," as she lets me into one of the rooms. "He's into industrial; don't trip over something. It's either junk or his next piece."

I can see what she means. The brightly lit studio, with sun streaming through the windows, is dominated by a large object that resembles a wrecked automobile. Looking more closely, I can see that this is exactly what it is—a wrecked automobile. Only this one is covered with Barbie dolls painted red.

I look at Bethany. "He calls it 'American Carnage.'" She shrugs. "Someone will buy it, I guess."

Picking my way through the room, being careful to not trip over the numerous objects scattered on the floor, I follow Bethany to the back of the studio.

"I put her things in this storeroom," she says, unlocking the door. "I've kept everything safe."

She pulls open the door and reaches in to flick the light on. I peer inside. Shelves line one wall and the back of the room. I see it is mostly covered with paints and Joan's sketchbooks—she always seemed to have a sketchbook with her, though until this moment I never realized where they all were—with a few bankers boxes. I also see a small pink suitcase I recognize as her laptop.

"How long did she have the studio?"

Bethany thinks for a moment. "Hmm, she had just graduated from Myer with her bachelors and was starting her MFA. She asked me if she could rent the studio space. I asked her why, since students in the MFA program were given their own space at the college, but she said she wanted a private space to work. I didn't ask any questions, and I didn't charge her anything."

She had the space before we met. "Did anyone else know?"

"I doubt it," Bethany says. "She really wanted her privacy."

A bell rings. "That's someone downstairs," she says. "Take whatever you like and close the door behind you."

After she leaves, I walk further into the room, to the shelves. I peek inside the banker's boxes. At random I take one of the sketchbooks off the shelf and open it. Joan had dated it. She started it a month before her murder.

I flip through it rapidly. Some are pencil and charcoal, others pastel, all things that had caught her eye or potential studies for paintings. The book was only about half full.

I flip to the middle. Stuck in the center is a folded piece of paper, about five inches by eight inches, the kind traditionally used for letters.

I smile. I'd often leave Joan notes, little things saying "I love you" or "thinking of you." I open it, wondering what I had written her on what day.

But I hadn't written it.

My grip on the letter loosens and it floats to the floor. My knees buckle and I grab onto the shelves for support. There is a chair nearby and I collapse into it. I can hardly breathe. I pick the letter up off the floor and stare at it, reading it over and over.

It takes me a few minutes to catch my breath. I shake all over and look up at the other boxes. Jumping up, I grab one, tear the lid off, and begin rifling through the contents, pulling handfuls of papers out and flipping through them, looking for the same notepaper, looking for more letters. I take a second box, then a third, repeating the same process. I go through all the boxes in the same frantic manner. But I find no more letters. Joan was a pack-rat, usually unwilling to get rid of anything. The papers were a mix of old bills, receipts, student lists from her classes at Myer. But no more letters on cream-colored note paper.

I shake my head. It must have been a letter from a student of hers who had developed a crush on her.

In my haste, I drop a plain manila envelope, unsealed but clasped. I peek inside. I can see it is a marriage license. I smile and pull it out.

My smile quickly turns to a frown.

It isn't our marriage license. It has her name on it. But not mine.

I collapse back in the chair, a wave of nausea passing over me. There is a sink with a mirrored cabinet over it. I make it just in time.

I rinse the sink out and splash my face with cold water. Looking around for a towel, I open the cabinet.

There are three prescription medicine bottles. I pick one of the bottles up. The date is fifteen years old.

Joan's name is on it.

***

I get back to the Rectory about an hour later, slipping inside with a box and Joan's laptop, before carefully closing the door.

Glenda calls from the kitchen, "Is that you, Father?"

I stop dead in my tracks. "Yes, it's me."

"Just in time. I didn't know where you had gone. Your dinner will be ready in ten minutes."

"OK, thank you," I say, walking to the kitchen and peering inside. She is at the counter, working with her back to me. I have to admit, it smells good even though I'm not very hungry.

"You have some phone calls to return," she says. "The messages are on your desk."

I furrow my brow. "Calls don't go to voicemail?"

She turns to look at me. "Yes, they do. I check it and give you the messages. Or if I'm here and you're not, I answer the phone and take a message. Parish secretary. It's my job."

On this, I have to admit she's right. "Thank you," I say, "I'll return them after dinner."

I walk away before she can say anything else. I go to my room, put the box and laptop on my bed, and go back downstairs to the kitchen. Glenda is putting food on my plate as I walk over to the refrigerator and get a soda.

"Anything I can do to help?" I ask.

She turns and looks at me with her 'what is this strange life form' look. "No, I've got it," she says with a tinge of irritation. Then, "Thank you," she adds as an afterthought. She walks to me with the plate in one hand and a knife, fork, and napkin in the other.

"Since you're here," she says, handing them to me. I stand there as she washes and dries her hands. Glenda notices me still standing there. "Anything else?"

I shake my head. "No, no, this is fine. It looks and smells really good, thank you." It seems rude to tell her I'm not hungry.

"I will see you tomorrow, then. Good night, Father," she says as she walks past me out of the kitchen. When I hear the front door close, I put the silverware back in the drawer and the plate in the refrigerator. If she asks why I didn't eat anything, I'd come up with an excuse.

I go back up to my room and look at the box, then at the time. I need to say Evening Prayer. I pull out my phone and open my Breviary app. Usually, I'd go into the church. Tonight, I don't want to go anywhere. Instead, I pray with a confused and distracted heart.

I finish Evening Prayer and look at the time again. It's only 7:30 p.m., but it seems like midnight. I am drained from the last few hours so I change into my pajamas, move the box to the floor, and crawl into bed, lying for a moment looking at Joan's picture, in a small frame on my bedside table.

When we were married, I always made sure she was the first thing I saw in the morning and the last before I turned out the lights. After her murder, I framed this picture, because it showed her as I always wanted to remember her—the laughing eyes full of life, the flowing chestnut hair, the red lips whose feel I still remember. For fifteen years, I've told her I love her every night and every morning, just as I did when she was alive.

Tonight, I just turn the light out and roll over.

***

As tired as I am, I can't go to sleep. Instead, I keep thinking of Joan. And that night.

I have run the entire scene in my head hundreds—thousands—of times. Tonight is no different. I replay everything that happened again and again. I can't stop it, no matter how much I try. It is as if I am forcing myself to relive it over and over again to punish myself. The only way it stops is if I sleep.

Tonight, though, other thoughts run through my head.

Questions I have no answers to.

Questions I'm not sure I want the answers to.

I get up, turn on the light, and go through my bag, pulling out a bottle of sleeping pills filled six months ago, a 30-day dose. There are still 20 pills in the bottle. I open it and look at the pills. I put the lid back on and the bottle back in my bag.

Not tonight.

Instead, I decide to read, since reading usually relaxes me. I get my e-reader and pull up one of Chesterton's Father Brown mysteries.

Forty-five minutes later, I am no closer to sleep. I put the e-reader on the table and just lay in bed, staring at the ceiling. When I close my eyes, I think of the box, feeling it pull at me, call to me to open it, to look inside.

I don't want to, because I don't want to know anything else.

After another 30 minutes, I give in. I sit up and pick up the box, placing it on the bed beside me. Opening the lid, I pull out the pill bottles.

Lithium, Risperdal, Lexapro. To my knowledge, Joan hadn't been on any medications. I don't know what these were for. A quick internet search answers the question. They are all treatments for bipolar disorder and anxiety. I have no idea why Joan would have these.

I toss them back in the box and pull out the manila envelope, unclasping the flap and reaching inside to pull out the one piece of paper it contains: a marriage license.

From the date, Joan would have been sixteen. There's her name, Joan Luckgold. And a man's name. Randy Earl.

Who was Randy Earl?

I just sit on the edge of the bed, staring at the official piece of paper in my hand. Joan had been married before. She had never told me. It didn't come up in our premarital counseling sessions with Father Anthony. What did it mean? Why didn't she tell me? Was our marriage even valid? Or was everything—the wedding Mass, our lives together—a sham?

I lay the envelope on the bed beside me and pick up the folded cream-colored note. I open it and read again the short letter to Joan, in handwriting I don't recognize but know isn't mine.

My love, I don't know why you won't return my emails, or answer my calls. Don't you realize yet I'm the only man for you? Haven't I sent you enough notes and cards, pouring my heart out to you? You don't love him. You couldn't. He's nothing like me. I'm the right one for you.

Maybe I haven't done enough. Maybe I need to do more.

Maybe I need to show you.

Five

Maybe I need to show you.

I read the words over and over again, trying to figure out what I'm looking at. Had Joan been having an affair? Was there another man? I can't see how. We were so happy.

Or were we?

Had I missed something? Was what I thought was a happy marriage in fact a lie?

I look at the box. Joan hadn't told me she was on medication. She hadn't told me about being married before. So there are already two lies I knew of. Now three. But a lie about what?

I read the whole note. There is a tone of desperation and longing mixed with a vague hostility and threats.

It is stalkerish.

Was Joan being stalked? Had she become the target of a deranged person? Who had sent this? The letter is unsigned, the handwriting tight and precise but I can't place it.

One thing I am certain of though, even fifteen years later.

She had never mentioned this to me.

At all.

Why?

Why had she kept this from me?

Maybe it was just a one-off, I think.

But the note refers to other cards and notes. This was the only one I have found. Are there more?

A few moments later, I am looking at the login screen of Joan's laptop. Fortunately, Joan always valued ease of memory over security. I type "Password 1," and her desktop comes up.

Her background image is a picture of us, one from our honeymoon. She has photo editing and design programs for her design business, along with the standard word processing and spreadsheet software. There are also folders on the desktop related to the classes she taught at Myer as an adjunct. The summer before her murder she taught a still-life class. Her design business was supposed to help pay the bills, but she really loved teaching.

I click on her email icon and see the last opened email, the one I sent the day of her murder.

I got the reservation. You wanna just meet me there? It was about dinner that night.

There is another email, right below it. The subject line catches my attention.

Why won't you talk to me? The email address is "artluver57@myer.edu." Whoever sent the email was at the college. Was it a student, a colleague? "Artluver"—art lover. Someone in the Fine Arts department? But who?

I scrolled through her inbox. In the month before her death, there were about fifty emails from artluver57. I clicked on the first one.

Did you like the flowers I sent you?

Joan had responded, *I told you, you need to leave me alone.*

I don't care if you're married. I love you. Can't you see that?

I'm telling you, please stop this. I thought I made that very clear to you.

What is clear to me is you don't know me very well, you don't know my heart. I'm gonna show you. Then you'll see. You'll fall in love with me.

You know I love Tom. There is no way that's going to happen.

We'll see.

That was the last of that thread. There were dozens of others after that, none of which Joan had opened, except for one with an attachment.

Why can't you be this happy with me? It reads. *Why don't you smile that way at me? I want you to smile that way at me.*

I click on the attachment. It is a photograph, taken at some distance, of Joan and me. We are walking across the commons at Myer. I must have said something funny, because her head is thrown back and she is laughing.

The date of the email is a week before her murder.

None of the other emails, up to three or four per day, were opened. One says, *You're not answering my calls. Why? Please talk to me.* Another says, *I can't believe you're ignoring me for him! If he wasn't around, you'd have time for me. Maybe I need to do something about that. What do you think?* The next one, sent ten minutes later, says, *I'm sorry, please don't be mad. I don't want to hurt anybody. I just get so desperate. I love you so much, I need you so much. Please, please just talk to me.*

The emails alternate back and forth between pitifully pleading for her attention and veiled threats.

But not against Joan.

All his threats are against me. And Joan had just ignored the emails—even the one with the photo of us. She never told me about them and I can't figure out why. Had she told anyone or did she just think they were something she could ignore, that whoever it was would go away, or was just saying things?

Then two thoughts burst into my mind.

What if Joan's murder wasn't random?

What if he meant to kill me?

I stand up and start pacing—I often pace when I am trying to figure things out.

What do I have?

I have a letter from an unknown man, one Joan had not told me about, that was vaguely threatening to me, and definitely showed an obsession with her.

I have unsigned emails, probably from the same person. I pick up the letter again and study it closely. There was no clue who wrote it.

I look at the prescription bottles again. And her marriage license.

Joan hadn't told me about any of it.

What else hadn't Joan told me about?

As I pace, I realize I don't know a lot about Joan's past. I know her mom, of course. I know her father had died when she was in her early teens, but she never told me how. I know she entered Myer a year late, but she had alluded to taking a gap year to travel. I know her grandparents, aunts and uncles lived out of state—I only met them at the wedding—and she had cousins she didn't particularly care for.

To be fair, I hadn't shared much about my family. She did question why I didn't invite my mother to our wedding, but not very deeply, sensing correctly that my mother was a topic I didn't want to talk about.

But does any of this tie into her murder? I put my head in my hands, the question turning around and around as I feel tears welling up in my eyes. I replay the scene in my head, trying to remember the look in the man's eyes. Through fifteen years of time and grief, I try to focus on his eyes, and try to remember the look. What was there?

Suddenly I know.

It was anguish.

Had he said something? Had he screamed, "No!"? I can't remember. It is all so foggy. Then he put the gun to my head and pulled the trigger.

Click. Click. Click.

I don't remember much else after that. I came to, he was gone and Joan was dead beside me.

I push the box to the floor and collapse back on the bed, finally drifting off to sleep.

***

A ringing phone wakes me with a jolt. .

I grab my cell phone and see it's just after midnight, but that isn't the source of the noise. As the fog lifts, I realize it is the Rectory phone. If someone is calling for a priest at that time of morning, that can mean only one thing: someone has died.

I lift the receiver and say, "Saint Clare's Rectory, Father Greer speaking."

"Tom?" says a woman with panic in her voice. It's Chloe.

"What's wrong?" I ask.

"I don't know," she said. "It's John. He . . . he's not home yet. He should have been home hours ago. I've tried calling his cell phone but it goes straight to voicemail."

"Have you called the police?"

"He hasn't been missing for more than 24 hours so they won't do anything. They did tell me no accidents have occurred involving him. I called the hospital and he's not there." She pauses. "He used to do this all the time, but it's been a while. The last few days, though, he's been . . . different."

"Do you have any idea where he might be?"

She sighs. "One. But he promised me he'd never go there again."

Six

The Hoot-n-Holler is off of Highway 62, north of Myerton. The sign out front advertises all-you-can-eat boiled shrimp and a crab cake po' boy. I doubt many of the pickups and sedans in the parking lot belong to people there for the food, not at 1 a.m. The place has the heavy smell of beer, liquor, and desperation. The polished wood bar parallels a mirrored wall, with shelves holding dozens of bottles—tequila, whisky, scotch, bourbon. Behind it stands a man in his late thirties, wearing a t-shirt pulled tight across a muscular frame, pulling a mug of beer heavy with foam while country music plays from the loudspeakers. John isn't at the bar so I look around the half-filled room and spot him alone in a booth, nursing a shot of something.

I walk up to him and stand at the table for a minute. He doesn't appear to see me, or at least he doesn't acknowledge my presence. "John," I say.

He glances at me, then back at his drink. He picks it up and downs it in one gulp. Then he looks back at me with eyes heavy with intoxication, his hair mussed, his tie undone, his suit rumpled. He has a plate with the remnants of the boiled shrimp.

Apparently, some do come for the food.

"John," I say again.

He looks at me and smiles, but not in a 'glad to see you' way. "Well, hello there, Father Tom. If it isn't Father Tom, used to be just Tom, not a priest or even much of anything."

"Come on, John, it's time to go."

He stares at me then goes back to picking through the plate, looking for more shrimp. Then he holds up his glass, shouting at the bartender, "Hey, Steve, another one. And one for my friend."

"No, thanks, I'm good," I say over my shoulder. Turning back to John, I say, "Look, Chloe's worried about you—"

"—I know she's worried about me. I know better than *you* she's worried. I even know *why* she's worried."

A young woman with her red hair pulled back in a ponytail, wearing tight jeans and a tight low-cut t-shirt from Luray Caverns, brings him the

40

drink, placing it and a cocktail napkin on the table. John says, "Thanks. Put it on my tab."

"Uh-uh," the woman says. "Tab's closed. Pay up."

"Aw, cummon, Lola—"

I say, "You've had enough, John."

"Listen to your friend," she says. "Cash or card?"

"This," John points to me, "is not my friend, at least not now. He is my priest!"

"Listen, I don't care if he's the President," Lola replies. "He's right, you've had enough, now pay up." She crosses her arms. "Or am I going to have to get Steve over here?" She indicates the heavily muscled guy behind the bar.

John puts up his hands. "OK, OK." He fumbles for his wallet and pulls out a card. "Here."

Lola takes the card and John downs his drink. "Well, I guess I'm going. You gonna drive me?"

I nod. "We'll pick your car up later."

He reaches into a pocket and pulls out his car keys, tossing them on the table in front of me. Lola comes back with his card and receipt. "You need a pen?"

"Do I look like I need a pen?" He fumbles in his coat pocket and pulls out a silver ballpoint. He adds a tip and scratches out his signature. Putting his card back in his wallet and his pen in his pocket, he says, "OK, lead on, Padre."

I've seen John drunk only a couple of times but I don't remember him being an angry drunk, more quiet than anything else. I don't like this side of John, and I realize I don't know him anymore at all. I have been away too long.

He is only a little unsteady on his feet, leaning on his cane, so I only have to help him navigate around a few tables, chairs and bodies before getting him outside. I walk him over to my car and get him in the passenger seat. He fumbles for the seat belt, but I reach in and buckle him in place. I get in the car and soon we are heading south to Myerton.

We drive in silence for a few moments and I think for a time he has fallen asleep. Then I hear John say, "Chloe shouldn't have bothered you."

"It's no bother," I say. "Glad to be of help."

"I guess it's your job now, helping, right?"

"I'm not doing it because it's my job," I say. "You're my friend."

"Friend," he says, letting out a short laugh. "Yeah, I'm your friend you haven't seen or spoken to in ten years."

I have nothing to say to that. "I know," I say after a minute, "But I'm still your friend and still care about you."

"Save it for Sunday, Padre."

"Now look—" I stop myself and drive in silence while John sits leaning his head against the window.

After a while, John speaks again. "Why'd you come back, anyway?"

"I was assigned to Saint Clare's for four months."

"I know, I know, that's what you say. But why did you come back?"

"I had no choice. When the Archbishop makes an assignment, you can't say no. He's like my superior officer. You were in the Army, you know that."

"Yeah," he says quietly. "Yeah, I know that." He looks out the window. "So why did you leave?"

I sighed. "Does it matter?"

John looks at me. "Yeah, Tom, it does, to me and a lot of people. You know, you left so suddenly—people had a lot of questions. Rumors flew around for a while."

I look at him quickly, then back to the road. "Rumors? What rumors?"

"The kind of rumors that your friends spent a lot of time putting down. Rumors like you had gone crazy with grief and had checked yourself into a mental hospital. Rumors that you had killed yourself—that was a good one. Rumors about some coed at the college. There were some whispers that you were responsible for Joan's death and you had run before you could be caught."

"What?"

"You heard me," John says. "That the whole story of the attempted rape, that you made it all up to cover the fact that you killed Joan. Didn't help that the police started asking questions."

"What kinds of questions?" I grip the steering wheel as my face gets hot and beads of sweat erupt on my forehead.

"The kind of questions the police ask about a husband and wife when the wife winds up dead."

I am quiet for a few minutes before slowly asking, "Did they question you?"

"Me? Oh, yeah. I'm your best friend, remember?"

"What did you tell them?"

"That you and Joan were the perfect couple, the absolutely perfect couple, without a flaw or problem in the world. You know, the truth." He snorts.

"John, you make one really mean drunk."

"That," he says, "is why I don't drink at home."

"I don't remember you drinking at all, well, not like this."

"Lot's changed," he mumbles. "A whole lot's changed."

"What's changed for you?"

He looks out the window. "I don't want to talk about it."

"You can talk to me."

He shakes his head. "Nope, not interested."

"I'm your friend," I press. "And as you pointed out, I'm your priest."

"What do you want me to do?" John says, turning to look at me. "Confess my sins to you, so you can absolve me?" He turns back to the window. "No thanks."

"Nothing like that, just talk to me, tell me . . . "

"Just drop it."

"But John—"

"I. Said. Drop. It."

We drive in silence, then suddenly John says, "Tell me something—tell me about the night Joan was murdered."

I don't say anything. "Thought not," he says, then closes his eyes and leans back against the window.

I turn my attention to the road. We have just passed back into town and I make the turn on the street that will take me in the direction of his house.

"Tell me something," John says.

"What?"

"Why did you become a priest?"

I sigh. Not this question again. "It's complicated."

"How complicated could it be? You were a married man. Your wife died. Now you're a priest. I just want to know what happened between the wife dying and becoming a priest."

"It isn't that simple."

"Was it grief? You couldn't live a normal life without her, so you went into the Church? Guilt, like you had to do penance for something you did or didn't do—"

"Drop it, John."

"I'm just asking—"

"I said drop it." I say it louder and more forcefully than I mean to.

John just looks at me. "We're not that different. You have your pain, I have mine. We keep it private. I drink, you pray."

I say nothing the rest of the way to his house. When I pull in the driveway, Chloe is waiting. I get John out of the car and he walks to her, steadier on his feet than I thought he would be. I guess that the alcohol is finally wearing off.

"Do you need help getting him inside?" I ask Chloe.

She shakes her head. "No, I've got it from here. Thanks again."

I nod. "John, take care." As I turn to walk off, he touches my arm. "Hey Tom?"

"Yeah?"

"I, uh, you know—sorry. Thanks."

I smile and pat him on his shoulder before turning and walking back to my car.

By the time I get back to the Rectory, it's about 3 a.m. As I begin to walk up the path to the door, I have a sudden sense that someone is behind me. I spin around, and in the dim light from the streetlamps, I think I see a figure dart behind the corner of the Rectory.

"Hello?" I call. "Is someone there?"

No one answers so I continue up the path. Then I hear leaves rustling, even though there is no wind.

I turn again.

No one.

I am at the door and putting my key in the lock when I hear the plod-plod of running feet. I turn in the direction of the sound and see a hooded figure running down the sidewalk away from the Rectory.

"Hey! Hey!" I call, running after the figure.

Why I run after them, I don't know. But by the time I reach the edge of the yard and look down the sidewalk, they're gone.

Seven

The next day, Friday, is a busy one. In the morning, I visit the hospital and give communion to some parishioners who are there, then go over to the nursing home and do the same thing. After Mass, I have meetings with three parishioners. The evening is taken up with a facilities committee meeting where the discussion of painting the classroom areas takes up more time than it should have because Glenda keeps insisting that the rooms don't need to be painted, that they were just painted five years ago, and we really should wait until Father Anthony comes back so he can weigh in.

"What she means is," one of the committee members whispers to me, "is so he can agree with her."

"Does that happen a lot?" I ask.

He nods. "Eventually, he always agrees with her."

Saturday morning is the first time I am able to call and check on John.

"He's better," Chloe says. "Slept most of yesterday, still asleep now. He sleeps a lot," She pauses. "Thanks again for going to get him."

"It was the least I can do. Don't mention it."

I hesitate for a moment. "I want to ask you something."

"Sure, what is it?"

I take a deep breath. "You and Joan were close, right?"

"I like to think we were."

"You two talked about things?"

She doesn't answer right away. "Yes, we talked about a lot of things."

I decide to dive right in. "Did she say anything about anyone giving her unwanted attention?"

Slowly, she says, "I'm not sure what you're talking about. What do you mean?"

I tell her about the letter and the emails, the tone. "I just want to know if she mentioned anything about them to you."

"Did she mention them to you?"

"No," I answer. "That's why I'm asking you."

"Why do you think she'd say something to me when she didn't mention anything to you about it?"

"I don't know, I just thought because you were her best friend—"

"And you were her husband," she interrupts. "I don't see why you would think she would mention them to me when she didn't say anything to you."

I'm getting a little exasperated as I say, "I told you, Chloe—since you were her best friend, I thought she might have said something to you when she obviously didn't feel comfortable telling me about it."

"Tom," Chloe says, "did it occur to you that she didn't tell you because she didn't want you to know?"

"Well, obviously she didn't want me to know. I just want to know why."

"No, you don't," she says, then stops herself.

"Why?"

"No, Tom. I can't say anything. I promised her I would never—"

"She's dead, Chloe. It doesn't matter now. And it might be important."

"How?" she whispers.

"Because—because I'm beginning to think her murder wasn't random. That whoever sent those letters was responsible."

After a minute, Chloe answers, "That's not possible."

"Why? Why isn't it possible?"

Chloe hesitates. "Because it just isn't, OK? You need to trust me on this."

"For heaven's sake, Chloe—"

"—Please, Tom—"

"—don't you care about finding Joan's killer?"

"It was a long time ago," Chloe says, her voice suddenly hard. "Besides, when did you get so interested? You left town. You got on with your life. Some of us had to stay here with it."

I don't respond, but hear something in the background.

"I'll be right there," Chloe calls. "One of the kids needs me," she says. "I've got to go."

"Chloe—" But she has already hung up.

***

I hear confessions that afternoon. Business is brisk; apparently, people have been saving up sins. There is a line of about four or five people, all young moms, waiting when I arrive. The benefit of being new is that I haven't had time to really learn who people are, which I think helps people feel comfortable confessing to me. I have no doubt business will drop off.

The confessions are pretty standard. "Yelled at my children too much." "Yelled at my husband." "I was gossiping about her." "I lusted after him." "Used the "f" word in talking to my mother-in-law." "Used the "f" word talking about my mother-in-law." One penitent, an older man from the sound of his voice, tells a long story about himself, his brother, and a fishing boat that apparently began ten years before and is still a problem between them. I tell him for his penance he needs to sell the fishing boat and give his brother half the money. Apparently, that is the wrong answer, since he leaves before I can give him absolution.

I look at my watch. 3:45 p.m. Fifteen minutes, then I have to get ready for the 4:30 p.m. Mass.

All's quiet for a few minutes. Then, I hear the door on the other side close and I open the screen.

I can only see a shadowy figure on the other side. "Let us begin," I say, "this sacrament of God's mercy in the name of the Father, the Son, and the Holy Spirit."

I hear nothing from the other side of the screen. For a second, I think I have made a mistake, that the door hadn't closed. Then I hear a sigh.

"Do you want me to hear your confession?" I prompt.

Still nothing. I have never experienced anything like this.

"Take your time," I say. "I'm here when you're ready."

But there is still no sound coming through the grille. Suddenly, I hear movement, the door opening, and footsteps on the marble floor leading away from the box.

I shake my head. *I guess they changed their mind*, I think.

Looking at my watch, I see it is just after 4:00 p.m.. I leave the confessional and check the penitent's side to turn the light off, when a glint catches my attention.

A gold ring lays inside. I pick it up and look at the inscription.

It's my wedding band, the one I left on Joan's headstone the day I left Myerton.

Eight

I spend a restless Saturday night tossing and turning, pacing in my room, reading the notes and emails over and over again for some clue—any clue—to the sender's identity. But there is none.

I have no proof that the person who wrote the letter and the emails is in fact the person who came to the confessional. But that person left my wedding ring there, which means they had taken it from Joan's headstone.

Sunday mass is a fog as I find myself looking out over the congregation and wondering, *Are they here? Are they watching me?*

As I stand on the steps greeting the parishioners as they file out, I sense a change in the mood. As people speak, I hear sympathy in some, pity in others. I see little clusters of people speaking in whispered tones, with occasional glances in my direction.

I know what they are talking about. Myerton is a small town and there are enough people in the parish who remember what happened. As much as I might wish it, Joan's murder was never going to be a secret for long.

Anna stops and says, "You're a big topic of conversation, Tom."

I sigh. "I can guess why. Everyone's heard the story by now."

We start walking back through the church towards the sacristy. I have many questions for her about Joan, but I don't know where to start. Or how.

"I wouldn't worry about it, Tom," Anna says. "It was a straightforward random crime."

"That's what I told the police," I say.

Anna stops. "Was it something else?"

I look at her. "No," I say quickly, "No, of course not." I pause. "John told me the police asked about me, after I left?"

She nods. "Yes, they did. I don't think they ever took you seriously as a suspect. But after you left so quickly, I guess they wanted to cover all their bases. And it's not like anyone thought it was you. Everyone knew how in love you two were."

"Things weren't perfect," I say slowly. In the sacristy, I take my Mass vestments off. "We had our problems."

"What young couple doesn't? Drew and I fought constantly the first two years we were married, and we stayed together until the day he died." She pauses. "And I only thought about killing him once or twice."

Drew. Joan's father. I decide to probe a little. "I wish I could have known Drew. Joan always talked about how they would do everything together."

She smiles. "They were pretty much inseparable. She was only thirteen when he died and she took his death very hard."

"I don't think Joan ever told me how he died. He was rather young, wasn't he?"

"Yes, he was," she says, a guarded expression passing over her face.

"What was it, an accident?"

"Yes," she says quickly. "It was a hunting accident. He was out in the woods deer hunting when he fell over a fallen tree and his gun discharged. Killed instantly."

I am shocked. "Joan never told me her daddy hunted. That must have been awful."

"Yes," she says, "But it was a long time ago. Oh, look at the time. I'm sorry, Tom, I have to take a casserole to one of the new moms. We'll talk later, OK?"

She walks quickly out of the sacristy. So now I have another mystery about Joan, her father's tragic death. Yet another fragment of her life that floats in my mind.

***

It was Sunday afternoon that I decided to go to the police. Which is why I'm sitting in my car Monday morning in front of the Myerton Police Department.

I think I have enough to interest them in taking another look at the case. But what do I really have?

I have a letter and emails from an unidentified person who showed an obsession with Joan, but no explicit expression of violent intent.

I also have Chloe's cryptic statements, but I can't bring her into this yet.

The only solid thing I have to go on is the mysterious person in the confessional—and I cannot mention them.

And the ring.

But the more I think, the more I doubt that I'm doing the right thing, or even just the sensible one. I think about driving back to the Rectory, tossing the emails in the trash, and just getting on with my life, like I have tried to do for the past fifteen years. My coming back to Myerton has stirred things up enough. People in the parish now know about Joan's murder. Nate Rodriguez's documentary is floating around out there. Going to the police will just stir things up more.

If I let it alone, it might just go away. I'll be gone in four months, away from Myerton, away from Saint Clare's, away from the memories of that night.

Away from Joan.

On the other hand, if I do nothing, the police might never have a chance to catch her killer. Don't I owe it to Joan to find him?

But I have to wonder what exactly I owe this woman who shared my life for four years, but never told me she'd been married before. Or that she had some sort of mental health issue. Or that her father had died suddenly and tragically. What do I really owe her?

I am pondering this when I hear a baby cry. I look up, startled, to see a woman lifting a small pink bundle out of a stroller, clutching the baby to her and singing softly as she shifts to push the stroller with one hand while holding the baby with the other. This scene is enough to remind me what my duties truly are to the dead.

I take my keys out of the ignition and get out of my car. I walk across the parking lot to the front door of the police station.

***

The Myerton Police Department is a concrete and glass structure with all the charm typical of mid-20th century Brutalist architecture. It could have been a professional office building for doctors, lawyers, and dentists. The only thing that sets it apart are the metal letters that spell out "Myerton Police Department" over the concrete-covered walkway leading to the glass doors.

The inside is no more appealing than the outside, white walls contrasting to a white and black speckled floor of formica tiles. While the walls look like they were painted relatively recently, overall it doesn't look like much has been done since the original was built.

A uniformed officer is behind an elevated horseshoe desk in the lobby. To his left is a metal detector and x-ray machine of the type that have become ubiquitous in government buildings at all levels in the years since 9/11. There was much talk just after the attacks about the need to install better security, and no small amount of controversy in town, if I remember correctly. The city council had voted to install them temporarily but they have since become a key part of the decor.

I'm wearing my clericals, thinking that a priest in a collar will get a little more attention, if not respect, than someone dressed as a civilian. The officer looks up from the computer screen that has been occupying his attention. We both have an instance of recognition.

"Oh, Father Greer," the officer says, breaking into a smile. "Good morning. What brings you here?"

I don't know the name, but I recognize him as a young father of three from 10:30 a.m. Mass, the husband of the organizer of the Nativity play. I return the smile, "Good morning, Officer, er—" I can't read his nameplate.

He laughs. "Conway. Dan Conway. I'm one of your parishioners. You know, 10:30 Mass, the three brown-haired maniacs, right side rear pew."

I chuckle. "I know, I just didn't have the name. How are you? How's the family?"

"All good. Just found out number four's on the way. Miriam's thrilled. I'm hoping for a promotion. You know, just the basics."

"Four," I say. They all seem to have no problem having multiple kids, I think with a surprising pang as I remember for a second how Joan and I struggled to conceive.

"Well, congratulations. I'm sure Father Anthony will be glad to have another baptism."

The smile fades a bit. "Yes," he says. "Father Anthony's a good man." He pauses. "Anyway, what brings you here?"

I clear my throat. "Who would I talk to about the Joan Greer case?"

"Joan Greer—Oh!" he says. "Of course, Father, of course."

"It probably happened before you were on the force."

"Yes, fifteen years ago, right? I was in the Marines in Iraq, actually. Only heard about it the other day."

I nod. "It wasn't going to remain a secret forever. Anyway, who would I talk to?"

"That'll be Detective Parr. She's the chief detective—well, the only detective."

"What's she like?"

"Detective Parr? Well, she's a really good detective, been here for a couple of years. Tough, but good. Can be a little—difficult, let's say. She was a detective in D.C. Pretty high up from what I understand."

"Oh? What's she doing here?"

"Well, I don't really know. I've heard things. But gossip is a sin, you know."

"Venal at worst," I smile.

I would usually not want to hear rumors or gossip, being the current target of both myself, but something tells me that I need as much information about Detective Parr as I can get.

"Well," he leans forward. "Apparently, she clashed with higher-ups about a sensitive high-profile investigation. She raised a ruckus, and they got rid of her."

"Fired her?"

"Not exactly. From what I've heard, the Chief of Police in D.C. is an old friend of our Chief. They did a transfer, so to speak. She didn't take it too well. The first six months or so she was here, she'd take her displeasure out on the nearest person. But she's settled down a lot since then. She and I get along really well, but I've learned how to handle her. Trust me, she is not a woman you want to cross. When she gets riled up—I'll tell you, Father, she reminds me of some drill sergeants I knew."

"Thanks for the warning. Can I see her?"

"I know she's in. Let me check with her." He picks up the phone. "Yes, Detective Parr. Officer Conway at the front desk. I've got someone here who wants to see you about a cold case."

Conway pauses as Parr speaks on the other end. "The Greer murder," he says. Another pause. "It's—" he looks at me "her husband?" Short pause. "Yes, sorry, Detective, I'm sure it's her husband."

There's a long pause as she says something to Conway. Finally, he says, "Uhm. OK. Ah, when? Sure, let me check."

Looking at me, the officer says with a tinge of embarrassment, "Ah, Father, Detective Parr says that she can meet with you tomorrow morning at 9 a.m. Will that work for you?"

"Sure," I say, not at all happy that after psyching myself up to finally do something about this, I'm going to have to wait until tomorrow.

Conway nods, then says into the phone, "He says that's fine. OK, thank you."

When he hangs up, he says, "I'm sorry about that, Father."

I shake my head. "It's OK, Officer—"

"Dan," he says. "Please, Father Greer, call me Dan."

"OK, but you need to call me Father Tom," I say. "Like I was saying, it's fine. It's been this long. I doubt one day's going to make a difference at all."

***

I'm back at the station at 8:45 a.m. and Dan's again at the desk. "Hi, Father," he says. "Listen, about yesterday, I don't want you to think Detective Parr was avoiding you or anything. Apparently she had some errands she needed to run because she left right after you did. In fact, she was gone the rest of the day."

At Dan's thoughtful look I ask, "Is there a problem?"

"No, it's just that I cannot remember a time Detective Parr took a day off. She's pretty much a workaholic, if you ask me. Single. No family. No relationships of any kind really. This job's her whole life."

He shakes his head, then picks up the phone. "Detective, Father Greer is here."

Hanging up, he says, "She'll see you now, Father."

I walk past the front desk and down a short hallway, taking a right into a longer hallway. As I walk, I hear an oddly chipmunk-like voice coming from an office. It's uncharacteristically loud and I catch, "new dress and shoes, wow," as well as "you look great," and "must be someone special."

Just then a young woman in a wheelchair comes out of an office at the end of the hall and rolls toward me. Her hair is the most shocking shade of blue and she wears turquoise-rimmed glasses. I can't even describe the dress she's wearing, except that it looks like something from a 1960s catalog.

She stops when she sees me and just stares, forcing me to squeeze past her as she rolls to one side and turns. As I walk past, I hear her say softly with a sigh, "Oh, it all makes sense now."

I reach the door that has "Helen M. Parr, Detective" on the nameplate. I hesitantly knock.

"Come in," the Detective says from the other side of the door.

That voice. It—it sounds—she sounds like—

No, it's impossible.

There is no way it could be.

Still I hesitate, pushing the impossible thought out of my mind,

I turn the knob and open the door. "Detective, th—"

I stop in my tracks.

It's just not possible. But, there she is, standing in front of me.

For a moment, time freezes and then speeds backwards twenty years, to before I was a priest, before I loved and lost Joan, to a time when I was still young and this woman before me was a girl of 22. The last time I saw her, her stunning blue eyes were ringed in red, caused by hours of arguing and crying between us. She was thinner then, but still soft and gently round, as she is now, clad in an emerald green dress that is in harmony with the sapphires in her eyes and the rubies on her lips. I catch myself before I can wander any further, as she looks up at me and I see a look of amusement at my shock.

"Hello, Tom," she says, sitting back in her chair, with a tight smile on her lips.

"Helen?"

We just look at each other. I don't know what to say next. There are so many possibilites.

"So, you're a priest?" she says, breaking the silence.

I nod. "Yes," I reply. "You're a detective?"

"That's what it says on my door," she says. "What are you doing here?"

What am I doing here? *A good question,* I think. *Maybe I should just leave before this goes any further.*

"Tom," she says. "Did you hear me?"

"Oh," I say, shaking myself. "Sorry, yes, what am I doing here?"

She leans back in her chair, and folds her arms before saying with a laugh, "That's my question." She indicates a chair in front of her desk.

I sit down and say, "I'm here to talk to you about the Joan Greer case."

The detective looks at me for a moment. "She was your wife?"

"Yes, I was married to Joan at the time of her murder."

"I am so sorry," she says with a softness not in keeping with her current reputation. "That is a terrible thing to go through."

"Thank you."

"So obviously, you weren't a priest then."

"No, I entered holy orders after her death."

"Why?" Her puzzlement seems genuine.

"It's complicated."

"Hmm," she says. Her fingers dance across the keyboard.

"So I take it Parr's your married name," I say. "Congratulations. How long?"

She stops and looks up from the keyboard, then keeps typing. "Two years," she says quietly, "but I'm not married now."

"I'm sorry," I say.

"So am I," she replies, sounding strangely distant.

"Any kids?" I ask.

"No," she says, "no kids. OK, let's see. Greer, Greer—here it is, Joan Greer, assault, attempted rape, murder, case still unsolved—not a lot of those around here." She moves her mouse and clicks.

Helen stands, and I avert my eyes as she walks to a file cabinet and pulls out a file. She's in her early forties, but her figure—

"OK, Joan Greer, let's see what we have," Helen says as she sits down, opening the folder. She flips through some pages, takes out a photograph and looks at it, flipping through some more pages, pauses and looks up at me, then back down and reads another page.

"We haven't done much with this in almost ten years," she says. "I've got notes here that Detective Keifer looked at the file a few times, but the last case notes are dated about eight months after her death." She looks up at me. "That was about two months after you left town?"

I nod and prepare myself for further interrogation, but she moves on. "And now you're back, and you say you have new information. Tom, why don't you share that with me?"

"This," I say, pulling out the letter and printouts of the emails and handing them to her. I tell Helen how Joan had not told me about receiving them, how I thought maybe the person who sent them had something to do with her death.

She takes the stack, reads through it, then places it back on her desk. She says nothing but instead just looks at me.

"Is this all?" Helen finally asks me with just the slightest hint of irritation.

"No. I also found out Joan was married before she met me." I show her the copy of the marriage license I have found.

"She never told you she was married before?" Helen asks after she looks at it. "Never mentioned this Randy Earl? Never said anything to you about it?"

I shake my head. "Never."

"Let me see if I understand you," Helen begins as she leans back in her chair. "You have an anonymous letter and emails your wife didn't tell you about. Your wife also didn't tell you she had been married before you met." She pauses. "Look, I don't want to be unkind, but I have to wonder how well you actually knew your own wife."

The question stings. But it is one I've started asking myself.

"At one time, I would have said well, but now, I really don't know." I look at her now, anxious in spite of myself to hurt her like she has hurt me. "Of course, this is hardly the first time I've not understood the choices of a woman I love."

If this barb hits home, she doesn't say anything. Instead, we just look at each other across the four feet of desk that separates us. But I know that isn't the only distance between us.

No, it is time. Time and the decisions we had made.

"Well, what do you think?" I finally say to break the silence.

"What do I think? What do I think?" she repeats. Then she looks at me with a wry smile. "Well, if this were a *normal* situation, based on the history of the parties involved, I might think that you are using this situation with Joan as an excuse to make contact with me."

"Excuse me?" I reply, infuriated at her bluntness. But I shouldn't be surprised. Her bluntness in the past had led to more than one fight between us.

"You heard me," she says. "Though listening was never your strong suit—but I guess you've had to learn that, huh?"

Ignoring the jab, I say, "Helen, the last I knew you were going to be a lawyer in a big firm in New York or D.C. or somewhere. I had no idea you'd become a detective, much less that you moved to Myerton."

"Well, since you're a priest now and I'd doubt you'd lie to me, I'll choose to believe you. Still, Tom, this 'evidence' you have is useless. There's nothing here."

"You don't think—"

"—no, I don't think the incidents are interesting or relevant at all," She leans forward. "What I see here are notes from a man—presumably a man—who seems to have had a serious attraction to your wife. Stalkerish? Yes. Creepy? Definitely. Evidence of murderous intent? Not by a longshot."

"But her marriage—"

"So she was married before? What are you saying? That this Randy Earl wrote these to your wife, that he was still in contact with her? There's nothing to tie this to him—or anybody."

"There's a Myer College email address."

Helen shrugs. "A student, faculty member. It was fifteen years ago. Unless you think Randy Earl enrolled as a student just to stalk her."

She leans back and picks up a pen, drumming it on the desk. "You know, on second thought," she says. "I do find something interesting."

"What's that?"

She stops drumming her desk. "I find it interesting that you claim you never knew about any of this."

"Why is that interesting?" I ask. "It's the truth, just like I told you."

"Yes," she says with a touch of sarcasm, "I know what you told me. You told me that after having been away for fifteen years, you return to town—why did you come back?"

"I'm assigned temporarily to Saint Clare's."

"I see—you return. You get a bunch of stuff out of her former art studio. You find a letter stuck in a sketchbook and a marriage license in a box. You find these emails on her laptop. And from them," she concludes, "you get the idea that they're connected to her murder." She pauses. "Am I missing anything?"

I look at her. My idea—what had been my idea?—had been to show the notes to the police and get them interested in giving the case another look. That clearly is not going to happen with what I have shown Helen.

"Well, Tom?" she prompts.

I reach in my pocket and finger my wedding band. I hesitate, then pull it out and hold it up.

"There's also this," I say and place it on the desk in front of her.

She looks at it, but doesn't pick it up.

"Your wedding ring?" she asks.

"Yes."

"What about it?"

Slowly I say, "When I left Myerton, I left it on Joan's headstone."

"How typically dramatic of you," she says. "OK, so how did you get it back?"

I exhale. "Someone—gave it to me."

"Someone gave it to you," she repeated. "Who?"

"I—I don't know," I say. "I found it."

Helen sighs. "This conversation brings back so many memories," she says wearily. "Where did you find it?"

"At Saint Clare's. In the church."

She picks it up and looks at it. "So let me see if I understand you. You're telling me that you left this ring on Joan's headstone when you left fifteen years ago."

I nod.

"And fifteen years later it turns up at Saint Clare's."

"Yes," I say, smiling. "I know it sounds strange."

Without further comment, she hands the ring back to me. "Anything else, Tom?"

Taking the ring, I shake my head. "No," I say.

She slowly nods her head. "OK," she says. "Let's go over this again. You claim you knew nothing about these," she holds up messages.

"No, absolutely nothing."

"Nothing about a student or faculty member making unwanted advances."

"No."

"Joan didn't mention being followed or stalked."

"Not a word."

"Didn't tell you she had been married."

I shake my head.

She pauses. "Just out of curiosity, did you ever tell her about us?"

I look at her, then off to the side. "No," I say. "I never told her about you."

She considers this for a minute, then asks, "Were you two close?"

"Yes, very close. We had been married just over three years when she died. We were inseparable. Ask anybody."

"If you two were so close," Helen goes on, "then why didn't she tell you?"

"I really don't know. I've been asking myself that."

"Can you think of a reason she wouldn't want you to know?"

"No, honestly, not one."

"Were you the jealous type?"

"Jealous? No, I don't think so."

She looks at me. "Come on, remember who you're talking to," she says bitterly. "We both know better. Shall I review that with you?"

She doesn't need to.

***

In a flash, we are back at her apartment, the last time I ever saw her before today. She was insisting that we could make a long distance relationship work, that we could see each other every weekend, that she loved me and was committed to our future together.

And what was I saying?

Oh, how I wish I could forget.

I was accusing her of losing interest in me, of wanting to find someone else before she turned loose of me for good.

"After all," I screamed, "why else would you be holding out on me? If we're getting married anyway, why aren't we sleeping together?"

Her face went completely white at this. "Tom," *she said, quietly,* "*I thought we were on the same page, that we agreed with the teachings of the Church.*"

"*No, I never agreed. I just went along with what you said because I figured, if you really loved me, you'd give in.*"

"*Really loved you? Is that your only barometer, Tom Greer? How soon will I sleep with you? So that other girl, back home in Bellamy, you were really in love with her?*"

"*Well, no, but we were in high school. Everybody was doing it. It didn't matter.*"

"*Didn't matter? Well, maybe not for you but it did for me, and for the guys I dated.*"

"*Oh, yes, how could I forget the marvelous young men of Future Monks of America who showed up once a month for a dance at St. Monica's School for Girls? You mean none of them ever tried to make a move?*"

"*Not more than once,*" *she growled.*

"*Well, Helen, since that's obviously what you want in a man, I sincerely hope you find it at Duke, though I wouldn't hold my breath if I were you. Unless, of course, that's what turns you on.*"

She slapped me then, hard. I knew I deserved it but I didn't care. I turned and walked out the door. As I closed it, I heard a clink of metal hitting metal.

Her engagement ring.

She had taken it off and thrown it at me.

***

When I don't answer her question, Helen says, "From my experience, if a wife doesn't tell her husband that another man has expressed an interest in her, it's for one of two reasons. Either her husband is prone to jealousy and would react badly, possibly violently, against her or the other guy, or the attraction is mutual. So tell me, Tom, which was it?"

I sigh. "Look, Helen, I see where you're coming from, why you'd think I'd be that guy. But you know I would never hit a woman, especially one I loved."

Wistfully, she says, "Yes, I know that, Tom."

"As far as the attraction being mutual, that is one of the things I guess I'm most afraid of."

"I can understand that."

I want to ask her if that's what ended her marriage, and then, for reasons I can't explain, I want to hunt down the guy in question and hurt him badly. But instead, I continue, "I can't tell you which it was, since I have no idea who sent those."

"These, and," she picks up the printouts, "cards, notes and flowers. Pretty big expressions of his feelings, don't you think, and she didn't tell you. Could she have been having an affair?"

"I don't know!" I answer sharply, causing Helen to raise an eyebrow. I calm down and say, "No, I'm sure she wasn't having an affair."

"With all due respect, you didn't know about any of this. How can you be sure?"

"Because I knew my wife."

She looks at me. "Apparently not, Tom," she says quietly. We sit in silence until Helen finally says, "Is there anything else? Because if not, I do have other cases, ones that I can do something about."

"I do have one more thing," I say quietly. "I'm sorry about how I left things between us all those years ago. I was the one who was too immature to deal with everything. You didn't do anything wrong."

"Look, Tom, it just wasn't meant to be," Helen says, shaking her head. "We're fortunate that we found out when we did."

"That's certainly true, though I doubt we'd have made it through pre-Cana." I say the latter with a smile because I know better than she does what that would have entailed.

"I doubt I would ever have gotten you to go." She pauses, and then says with an expression that I quite can't decipher, "Did you go with Joan?"

"Yes," I say, "she wanted to get married in the Church."

"Oh, so she was Catholic?"

"Yes, uhm, but not like you." Why am I telling her this? It's none of her business.

"Oh, I see," she says with a smile. "Obviously she had more influence on you than I did."

In spite of myself, I say, "No, not really. We married in the church because that's what she wanted. But we didn't really go to Mass, mostly just Christmas and Easter." I swallow the lump in my throat, and add, "Her funeral of course."

"Then how did all this happen?" she says, waving her hand at me.

I smile sheepishly. "That's a long story. But, after her death—not right away, but after I left—I found God again. Or I guess I should say, God found me."

Something occurs to me, and I sit back, thinking I'm about to gain the upper hand. "I've been here two Sundays, and I haven't seen you at Saint Clare's."

She nods. "I don't go to Saint Clare's. I go to Saint Aloysius near Frostburg. I will admit, John wasn't much of anything by the time we met. He'd been raised Catholic, but had stopped going years ago for . . . various reasons. We were married in the Church, and I'd go by myself occasionally, but while he was—we were together, I fell away from my faith."

"I'm sorry to hear that."

"Well, after . . . everything happened with John, I started going again. I'd go to the Basilica of the National Shrine of the Immaculate Conception in D.C. on Sundays, and there was a parish near police headquarters where I'd go to daily Mass when I could."

"But why don't you attend Saint Clare's?" I ask. "It's not far from here, and we do have daily Mass, you know?"

She sighs. "A friend of mine from D.C. lives in Frostburg, she attends the parish. When I moved here, I started making the drive to go with her. I have nothing against Saint Clare's, Tom. Sergeant Conway and his family attend, and speak highly of the parish. But other than them, I don't know anybody, and frankly when I first got here, I wasn't planning on hanging around very long."

"Well," I say quietly, "you know someone now."

She says nothing for a moment, then says, "Do I, Tom?"

I open my mouth to speak, then realize I'm not at all sure what to say. I want to tell her she does, that I'm the same person she knew over twenty years ago.

But we both know that's not true. I'm very different than I was, as she probably is.

And besides, what does it matter anyway where she goes to Mass? It's not like I'm going to be here after December.

I suddenly realize that I have lost track of why I came here today and say, "As far as Joan's case is concerned, you're not going to do anything, are you?"

"No. There's nothing to do."

I sit back and stare at her. She stares back.

"Helen, please—"

"Is there anything else, Father?" she repeats.

I smiled ruefully. Standing, I say, "No. I guess not. Thank you for your time. I'll let you get back to your bike thieves."

I leave her office, struggling to keep calm.

Inside, I'm a mess.

I can't believe how she dismissed my concerns, then turned around and talked so pleasantly to me. She doesn't believe I didn't know, she doesn't believe it when I say Joan didn't have an affair. But beyond that, she isn't going to look into Joan's case. Nothing I have said or could say has moved her.

I hope our past isn't coloring her judgment, but I suspect it might be.

I drive back towards the Rectory, arriving with just enough time to get ready for the Noon Mass. Once in the sacristy, I yank off my coat, fling it on the table and quickly pull on my vestments.

As I walk past the table, I see that my phone fell out of my pocket. I pick it up to put it back in my coat when I stop. Opening the call log, I scroll down until I see Nate Rodriguez's number. I look at the time. I have just enough. I touch the number and hear the phone dial.

"Hello," the voice on the other end says. In the background, I hear people talking and dishes clattering. Apparently, Nate is at work.

"Nate, this is Father Tom Greer. Listen, I have to go into Mass, but I've thought about it some more."

I take a deep breath. "I'll do the interview for your documentary."

Nine

"I can't believe this," Nate says as he looks through the emails. "This is great! You see this, Father?"

When I called Nate and told him I'd do an interview, he was happy. When I told him about what I had found and Helen's response, he was practically speechless. Meeting him at The Perfect Cup the next day and showing him copies of the emails, he is jumping up and down in his chair like a little boy on Christmas morning.

"Don't you see, now this has everything. It's not just a cold case of a senseless murder," Nate goes on, holding up the emails. "This is a cold case of a planned murder. She was stalked, and whoever was stalking her killed her—"

"Now, really, we don't know that," I interrupt.

"—and we have the police doing nothing when new evidence is shown to them." He inhales and exhales. "Now we have a story."

"I thought you had a story before?"

"We did," he answers. "It's a better story now. And you'll do an interview on camera?"

"Yes," I say, "but who's we?"

"We," Nate repeats. "My partner and I."

"What partner?"

"My partner in the film," he replies. "Oh, did I forget to mention her? She's meeting us—oh, here she is now." Nate stands and waves at someone. I turn around to see who.

She is young, blond, pretty, and earnest. Very earnest. I recognize her from one of the local stations in Baltimore. She does those human-interest stories that really interest nobody. She leans into Nate and gives him a quick peck on the cheek.

"Katherine Shepp," Nate says, "Meet Father Tom Greer."

She smiles and extends her thin, well-manicured hand. "So nice to meet you, Father," she says, her voice as silky as her hair. I take her hand as she covers mine with her other hand and looks into my eyes.

"I'm really looking forward to working with you," she purrs.

I settle down to my usual coffee with cream and two sugars as she sips on her decaf soy latte. Nate is there until his uncle comes over to remind him that his break is over.

After he excuses himself, Katherine says, "I'm glad you've agreed to help me with the story."

Me? "Yes, I decided that Joan's story needs to be told."

She smiles, showing perfectly white teeth behind her expertly colored lips. There is no lipstick on her cup so it is either very good lipstick, or she has had her lips tattooed.

"When Nate told me about the story of your wife's murder, I was just so . . . so . . . moved, I guess is the word I'm looking for. And then when he told me you came back, and you are now a priest, well, that's just wonderful."

"I guess an unsolved murder is a bit of a change from doggy beauty pagents."

She guffaws. "Yeah, that. Not why I went to J-School, that one. I tried to sell my boss on an animal cruelty angle, but he said no one would believe that dog owners who spend $500 on a custom tailored tuxedo for their pedigree German Shepherd were guilty of abusing their pets. I guess he's right. But this is my ticket out of that crap and into real, hard-hitting stuff."

"I don't know how hard-hitting this is," I say. "Nate's tells me you're working on the human interest angle, how her murder has affected others."

"Well," Shepp says with a slight eye roll, "Nate and I disagree a little on our view of the project."

"What's your view?"

She sits back with an air of triumph. "I intend to solve the case."

It is so ridiculous I have to laugh a little. She frowns, and I clear my throat. "Sorry, Ms. Shepp—"

"Please, call me Katherine."

"OK, Katherine. Why do you think you'll be able to solve a fifteen-year-old murder when the police haven't been able to?"

Her eyes narrow. "Because I'll have your help." Then she leans forward. "Nate told me about the new information you have. The emails the police ignored. I'm not going to ignore them. I'll figure out who sent them. Are these the emails?" she says, picking them up.

I drink my coffee and watch her read through the stack. The further she gets, the more she smiles. Katherine puts the papers down and drinks from her latte. "OK, Father, yes, I definitely think that there is a connection between those emails and your wife's murder."

I smile in spite of myself, swept up in her enthusiasm and flattered that someone is finally taking me seriously.

"Now," she goes on, "we've got work to do. I'll need to lay the groundwork."

"I've told Nate I'll talk about that night on camera."

"Well, yes, of course we'll need that, but there's more, too."

"What do you mean?"

"I want to get the background, you know, the story behind the story," she says. "I want to learn everything you can tell me about Joan, your relationship, the days and weeks leading up to her murder. Did anything stand out in her behavior? Did anything unusual happen? Was there tension between the two of you?"

"Now wait—"

"I'll need to talk to Joan's mother and her friends."

"I thought Nate already interviewed them?"

"He did," Katherine nods.

"Then why—"

"Well," she leans towards me, conspiratorially lowering her voice, "if I can be candid, Father Tom, Nate's really a behind-the-scenes person. Not an on-camera one. Oh, he's sweet and technically really good, but he doesn't have the," she pauses looking for a word, "presence that someone who's on-camera all the time has."

"Someone like you," I say.

"Yes, someone like me," she says, leaning back and tapping the table with her nails.

"I have the copy of the police file Nate got," she continues. "It's so redacted it's practically useless. Fortunately, I know someone who can help get more information on what the police have."

"How?"

Katherine smiles. "Old boyfriend. He's an officer and married now, but I think I can, you know, persuade him."

I squirm. "Listen, Katherine, I'd rather you didn't do anything—"

"Oh," she waves dismissively, "I'm not going to break any commandments, Father. Maybe bend a little, but not break." She drinks. "Besides, you want the truth, right? Sometimes getting to the truth means getting your hands a little dirty. Sometimes the truth itself is dirty. In fact, it usually is." She paused. "I'm not sure people know what they're going to get when they say they want the truth. I think they'd be happier if they never knew the truth."

"I want the truth," I say with more certainty than I felt. What if she is right? What if the truth—the whole truth about Joan's murder, about Joan, about our relationship—is messier than I imagined?

She smiles the same white-veneer-perfect smile. "Now, when can I get you on camera?"

I return the smile, even as one thought runs again and again through my head.

What am I getting myself into?

***

A few days later I am standing in front of the restaurant where we were eating the night of Joan's murder. It is still a restaurant, but the name is different. It had been La Petite Maison and served French food; it is now called Pasta Primo and serves Italian. The decor is also completely different and the exact table we were sitting at is no longer there, but I can still see the area of the restaurant where it had been. The table for two was by the windows overlooking Main Street. It was the same table in the same restaurant where I had proposed to her a few years earlier.

I turn away from the window. Nate has set up a camera on a tripod and is looking through the viewfinder. He looks up, telling Katherine "All good here."

She nods and looks at me. "You can start whenever you're ready, Father."

I exhale, having been holding my breath unconsciously until that moment. I am nervous, more nervous than I remember being the Sunday of my first homily.

What are you doing? I think. *You've spent years avoiding talking about that night. And what are you going to do? Talk about that night. On camera. Your every word recorded. Everyone will hear what you say, and see how you look when you say it. And for what? What are you hoping to gain from this?*

"Peace. Justice," I mumble to myself.

Are you sure? You don't really want to talk about it. You know why.

I shake my head to still the thoughts.

You know why.

"Where should I begin?" I ask.

Nate presses a button on the camera and looks through the viewfinder. He adjusts a knob on the sound recorder slung over his shoulder, listening as I speak into the lapel mike. I am dressed in my clericals at Nate's suggestion.

"Wherever you're comfortable starting," Katherine says. "Why were you at the restaurant that night?"

"That night," I repeat. "That night was a special night."

"What made it special?"

I smiled. "It was the anniversary of our first date. Which was also the anniversary of the night I proposed. We sat at the same table where we sat when I proposed to her, in this restaurant—well, not this restaurant, it was La Petite Maison back then."

"So it was a happy night."

"Yes, very happy. But it got happier."

"How?"

"Joan had been to the doctor that day," I continued. "We had been trying ever since we got married to have a baby. But things hadn't gone well. She had problems getting pregnant. There were a couple of miscarriages along the way. We had just about given up, talked about exploring adoption, even IVF—she was an only child and I just have a sister, so we wanted to have a large family. I was looking forward to being a dad." I pause a moment.

"Anyway," I continue, "a few days before, Joan had taken a home pregnancy test. We'd had false alarms before so she scheduled an appointment with her doctor for a more accurate test. She told me what the doctor said over dinner."

"What had the doctor said?"

I smile, even as I feel a lump in my throat. The beginnings of tears sting my eyes. Even fifteen years later, the memories of that night bring up huge emotions in me. I swallow and clear my throat. "That we were going to have a baby."

"How did you feel about that?" Katherine asks quietly.

"Feel? I was ecstatic. I knew that there would be a time when it could all go wrong—we'd been down that path before, like I say—but at that moment I was the happiest man on the planet."

"What was Joan's reaction?"

"She—she was happy. But guarded, looking back. She had been through a lot. I guess she didn't want to get too excited, not while she could still lose the baby.

"What did you two do then?"

"I ordered champagne, and then realized that it needed to be sparkling cider. We laughed over that, that joyful kind of laugh you do when the whole world seems bright. While we ate, we discussed baby names, how to decorate the nursery, talked about whether we were going to need a bigger house. We had started looking at places; at the time we were living in a two-bedroom apartment that was adequate but we knew we'd need a bigger place for kids. We wanted a place with a backyard and enough space for lots of kids."

"Anything else?"

"Oh, just work stuff. I told her about the latest project I had at work—I wasn't a priest then, obviously. I was an archivist at Myer in their Archives and Manuscripts section, actually the archivist, there was only one, and I was it. I had just started a preliminary list of the papers of a former Senator who had been an alumnus of the college. I remember because it had been a very big deal, the largest collection ever donated to Myer at the time. I told Joan that I realized that day how big a job it was going to be, and that I might be able to get the college to hire an assistant. She told me about her work. She was getting her design business off the ground and had a few clients. She told me about one client of hers who was proving to be a problem."

"Didn't she work at the college?"

"Yes, she was an instructor in the fine arts department. Joan had received her art degree there and they hired her as a part-time instructor. Joan was good—her students loved her, and the department thought highly of her.

The job gave her enough time to work on her business. But she had also hoped the department might take her on as a full-time instructor."

"So, you finished dinner. What happened next?"

I look at her. "After dinner and dessert, it was getting late, so we left."

"Where did you go?"

"We walked back to the car."

Nate stops the camera and looks up. "That's great Father, heard everything loud and clear. What we'll do now is walk down the sidewalk to the parking lot—it's that one over there, right?" He indicates a small lot between the two rows of shops, the one where the restaurant is and the next one with a used bookstore, antique store, and crystal shop.

I nod. That was the parking lot where it all happened. "Do you want to film me walking?"

Before Nate can answer, Katherine says, "No, that won't be necessary." Nate looks irritated.

We get to the lot. It hasn't changed much since that night it seems, but it had been dark and the lot was not very well lit, so I couldn't see much. I look up. There are more lights now, and cameras.

There hadn't been cameras that night. There was no video of what happened. All the police had was my story.

I lead them to the part of the lot where I remember we parked, not too far in from the street. Nate sets up his tripod and camera. After a few minutes he says, "OK, when you're ready."

I nod and he starts the camera.

"We had parked about here," I say. "We took our time walking here, the night was warm and clear. Just strolled together hand in hand. I remember Joan leaning against me, holding me by my upper arm, resting her head on my shoulder. It was late so there were not a lot of cars on the street. By the time we got here, the lot seemed empty except for us."

I pause. Now is the hard part. I say a quick prayer for strength.

"What happened next," I went on, "is foggy. I'm not sure I remember everything that happened. I remember we arrived at the car. We walked around so I could open her door—Joan liked that, she teased me when I forgot, which was quite often. I heard footsteps coming behind us. I looked up, and there he was. Just standing there, holding a gun on us."

"What did you do?"

What did I do? What did I do? "I—I froze. I just stared at him. Joan stared, too."

"What did he say?"

"Nothing. That was the strange thing, nothing. He held the gun on me and grabbed Joan. Started dragging her away."

"What did he look like?"

"I'm not sure. The light wasn't very good. I couldn't make out any features. I could see his eyes but he was wearing a hoodie. A mask maybe."

I stop and stare at the spot in the parking space where my car had been. I am trying to remember what I told the police about what happened next.

"Joan started screaming, hitting at the guy, trying to pull away. But he was too strong. He said something, I can't remember what. I darted after him. I remember jumping on him, trying to wrestle him away from her. He let go of Joan and she ran back to the car, I think. Then he threw me off."

I stop, feeling tears welling up again. "Can we stop for a moment?"

Nate looks up from the camera. Katherine says, "Sure, Father. Take the time you need."

I walk away from the spot. My mind is spinning. I know what happened next. I have lived with the memory every day since it happened. The images swirl through my head every night when I try to sleep. I hadn't talked about what happened to anyone, not since the police interviewed me. Now I am being asked to tell the story again. I close my eyes and say a quick prayer, open my eyes, and walk back to Nate and Katherine.

"OK," I say. "I'm ready now."

Nate looks through the viewfinder. "OK, Father."

I exhale. "He pointed the gun at me. I ran at him and grabbed his arm. I guess I was trying to get the gun away from him. We fought for a minute." I stop and swallow. "Then it happened."

"What happened?"

I stopped. I couldn't form the words in my mouth. I have lost the ability to speak.

"What happened?" Katherine repeats.

"A—a shot," I whisper "There was a shot. He must have had his finger on the trigger. For a second, I thought I had been shot. I didn't feel anything, didn't see any blood. He looked shocked, like he wasn't expecting it." I pause. "Then I looked at Joan."

I close my eyes, tears welling up again. But I can't stop now, I just have to get through it.

"Even in the dim light I could see. Her blouse was white. It was very easy to see the blood. She hadn't screamed or cried out. She just stood there, blood slowly spreading crimson across her front. She began to sway. I ran to her and caught her as she sank to her knees. I started screaming for help. I looked in the guy's direction. He was still standing there. It was like he was transfixed or something. Like he couldn't believe what he had done. I thought I heard him speak, I can't be sure. I was holding Joan, cradling her in my arms, telling her, begging her to hold on until help came.

"Then suddenly, he walked up to me and held the gun to my head. He looked me right in the eyes. I saw—"

"What did you see?"

"I saw—anger, hatred, rage. Murderous rage."

"Did he say anything to you?"

I shake my head. "He just stared at me, pointing the gun right here," I point to my forehead, between my eyes. "I closed my eyes. I thought to myself, at least we'll die together. I won't have to live without her. Then, I heard a click. Then another click. A third click. Not a shot. Just clicks. Something must have happened to the gun. He moved it away from me. I opened my eyes. He was looking at the gun with disbelief. Then he looked at me and screamed, drew his arm back and slammed the gun into my head. I only remember searing pain, then darkness."

"What's the next thing you remember?" Katherine prompts.

My breathing is ragged. "I came to," I say, "and Joan was on top of me." The tears were hot on my cheeks. "I rocked her slowly, talking quietly to her. I looked her in the eyes, willing her to be alive. I held her tight, sobbing, asking God to bring her back. But there was no life in her eyes. They stared blankly into mine. She was gone."

I stop and lower my head, squeezing my eyes tight against the tears that were about to overwhelm my ability to control them. I squeeze my hands into fists, gritting my teeth, using every fiber of my being to control the emotions welling up from inside me. I feel I am drowning in a sea of my own sadness. It is just like before. It hasn't been this bad in a long time.

I shouldn't have done this, I think. *This was a mistake.*

I have lost all awareness of where I am. I am no longer standing in the parking lot, feet from Nate and Katherine and the video camera. I am adrift in a cold void created by the overwhelming pain I have brought back to the surface.

I don't know how long I am like that but the next thing I know, I'm back. I look up. Nate and Katherine are just staring at me.

"That's everything," I say. "That's what happened. That's how Joan was killed."

***

That evening, I kneel in Saint Clare's before the tabernacle. I have just finished Evening Prayer. I am physically and mentally exhausted.

I look at the crucifix, then the tabernacle, comforted by the knowledge that Christ is here with me.

I slowly shake my head. One thought keeps repeating over and over again. It started after we finished filming and I still can't stop it.

It's been fifteen years. You still can't face the truth.

Ten

Sunday's Mass begins as they all do, with me progressing down the aisle behind a ramrod straight Dominic Trent swinging the incense burner—the thurible—by a long chain, sending light gray clouds of fragrant smoke into the space around us. Behind him, the crucifix is held aloft by another teenage boy who I haven't met yet, red-headed with freckles. He in turn is flanked by two younger boys carrying candles. A woman in glasses, wearing a skirt and sweater with her salt-and-pepper hair pulled back into a ponytail—who just happens to be Dominic's mother—carries the silver bound Gospel in front of me, holding it aloft. We all proceed up the steps towards the altar, each bowing in our turn.

I come in last, my eyes fixed on the altar. Today I'm wearing the flowing green vestments of Ordinary Time, trimmed with a tapestry pattern down both the front and the back. My hands are folded in front of me in an attitude of prayer, and indeed my concentration remains unbroken as I genuflect, then walk around the altar, bend, and kiss the marble surface.

I turn to Dominic and take the thurible from his hand, bowing slightly, then turn to the altar. I walk around it, swinging the thurible in small circles. Soon, the entire sanctuary is shrouded in an aromatic haze that smells of a musty pine forest with hints of citrus, spice, and rosemary.

The hymn finishes just as I move to my seat. I adjust the microphone, then spread my arms wide, saying solemnly, "The Lord be with you."

"And with your spirit," comes the response.

"My friends, let us—" I pause for a split second as I catch sight of the young woman with blue hair from the police station. She is sitting in the front row in her wheelchair, dressed in a yellow suit right out of the 1960s, complete with matching gloves and a pillbox hat, with a matillia over the hat.

But in spite of her outrageous attire, she is not what causes me to stumble.

Sitting next to her, in a long navy blue dress made from some sort of wrinkled, sheer fabric, is Helen.

She seems amused by my momentary discomfiture, and I quickly collect myself, continuing, "—acknowledge our sins and so prepare ourselves to celebrate the sacred mysteries."

Mass continues without any further incidents. The closer we get to the elevation, the stronger my focus as I place my hands over the bread and the wine, saying the prayers that turn them into the body and blood of Christ. My eyes fix on the large white wafer as I hold it aloft, barely holding it by the tips of my fingers. A moment later, I elevate the chalice, grasping it with one hand while supporting the base with the other.

More prayers, then it's time for everyone to receive communion. I move about the altar giving plates of communion hosts to the Eucharistic Ministers, taking the big one myself. Throughout the church, people slide out of their pews into the aisles. Helen remains seated beside the young woman as I approach her, always offering communion first to those who might have trouble making it to the front.

I stop in front of the young blue-haired woman and, leaning forward slightly, I whisper to her, "Would you like to receive?"

She has a glazed look on her face. Her lips move as she tries to speak but she only shakes her head, so I ask, "Would you like a blessing?" Wide-eyed, she nods. So, using my thumb, I make the sign of the cross on her forehead. I am a little concerned when she looks like she might pass out.

Still, I move on to Helen. Instead of raising her hands to me so I can give her the host, she folds them together in an attitude of prayer and tilts her head upward, signaling that she wants to receive on the tongue.

Her simple action, taught to children when they are preparing to receive their first communion, hits me like a lightning bolt.

My fingers are still poised above the plate of communion hosts, but my heart is beating so loud it's drowning out all other sounds. I half expect it to leap out of my chest and start running around while a dozen toddlers chase after it. Unbidden comes a flash of a memory of Helen's ruby-red lips in a much different context.

I manage to gain control of myself and take one of the consecrated hosts from the plate. Holding it before her to adore, I say, "Body of Christ."

"Amen," she says quietly. I place the host on her tongue, then go to give the other people their piece of Christ.

By the time Mass is over, I have made up my mind that I need to try to reconnect with Helen and make amends. I greet those passing through the doors briefly, moving them along as best I can. I notice that Helen does not come out the front door, but I assume she went out the side and down the ramp with the young woman in the hat. I step outside into the soft fall day to find them.

At first, I don't see them. I look at the children running up and down the stairs, oblivious to their mother's cries to be careful. Over on the lawn next to the church, where the Rectory is, there's a group of older boys tossing around a ball that someone must have brought from home.

I finally spot them and see Helen speaking earnestly to the woman. I wonder momentarily if she might be part of some sort of program designed to help the differently-abled get jobs.

I walk up to them, but hesitate when I hear Helen hiss, "Gladys! There are children around!"

"I know," the young woman whispers. "So many. Aah." Her expression of ecstasy dissolves into an other-worldly smile.

"Gladys." Helen says, obviously embarrassed. When she doesn't respond, she bends down and speaks directly in her ear. "Gladys!"

She starts and looks up. "Huh? Oh, sorry Chief. What were you saying?"

They both laugh at this and Helen continues. "I was about to ask if you wanted to grab coffee at The Perfect Cup?"

"How 'bout lunch at The Bistro instead?" Gladys says. "My—" she stops in mid-sentence, her mouth open, her eyes filling the frames of her glasses as I approach Helen from behind.

"Good morning, Detective," I say.

She turns. She seems a little flustered but responds. "Good morning, Father," We stand like that for a moment until I hear, "Ahem." The young lady is looking at Helen expectantly, a grin on her face.

"Oh! Sorry, Father. This is Gladys Finklestein. She's the department's forensic data analyst and computer expert."

When I step towards her and extend my hand, Gladys looks like she's going to topple backwards. "Nice to meet you, Ms. Finklestein," I say.

"Nice-ahem-nice to meet you, H—Father Greer," she gushes.

"Your first time at a Mass?"

"Yes. No. I mean. Not in a long time." Then, breathlessly she adds, "Is it always like this?"

This takes me aback a little but I continue to smile, saying, "The Mass itself is pretty typical but with this many kids, it's often loud."

"No," she shakes her head. "That's not what I mean. I mean, is what just happened normal?" At my confused look, she says, "You're kidding? You didn't feel it?"

"What are you talking about?"

"The whole Mass," she says, gesturing back to the church. "It was so . . . the only word I can think of is passionate. Like I was watching the tenderest act of lovemaking I've ever seen. The way you held that wafer so loving and gently and showed it to us. And then, when you touched me with the same fingers that had just held God—I felt . . ." Her eyes close and her mouth drops open slightly. "I've never felt anything—and I mean *anything*—that good!"

I laugh and say, "Well, I hope to see you next week."

"Uh-huh," Gladys nods, still looking at me.

"Gladys?" Helen says firmly, "Why don't you go get us a table at The Bistro? I'll be there in a minute."

"Huh? Oh, sure, Chief, I'll meet you there. Bye, Father," she says, then wheels herself towards the ramp to the sidewalk.

"Is she OK?" I ask.

"Gladys? Oh, yeah, she's fine. But," she turns to me and smiles, "she can be as socially awkward as someone I once knew."

"Oh? And who would that be?"

She sighs. "Just someone."

We both chuckle. "I was surprised to see you," I say. "Especially after the other day."

"I decided to give Saint Clare's a try," she says. "I mean, since it doesn't look like I'm leaving Myerton anytime soon, it doesn't make sense to drive thirty minutes each way when my apartment is less than ten minutes away."

I nod. "Well, I am glad to see you, Helen. I'd like to talk to you sometime, but not here, not now, not like this. Would you be willing to stop by my office sometime?"

"Sure."

"What about this afternoon? I need to get a few things off my chest and I'd like to do it sooner rather than later."

"My, it must be important if you're willing to miss Darlington for it."

I smile at this. She always hated NASCAR, or at least had very little interest in it, so I am curious how she knows about todays' race. As if reading my mind, she admits, "They were talking about the race on the radio when I was on my way over."

"Ah," I say, in spite of myself. "So you still refuse to embrace the one true sport?"

"I suppose so," she says, but guardedly now.

"Could you stop by after your lunch with Gladys? You'll have to pick up your car anyway. I promise I won't take long."

"OK. Sure. I'll see you then." She turns on her surprisingly high heels and walks away. In spite of myself, my eyes linger, but not where most men would. I'm looking at her hair, glistening in the sunlight like the wings of a blackbird, the light turning her black tresses blue as it bounces off.

Recovering, I remind myself of where and who I am and turn resolutely to continue to speak to the people around me.

***

Back at the Rectory, I find myself unable to eat the obviously delicious stew Glenda left for me to warm up. I'm glad she's not here to see me reject yet another of her meals, but I just can't face it.

I know what I need to do, what I want to do, and yet, I am still incredibly nervous about facing Helen and admitting all the ways—big and small, recent and ancient—that I have mistreated her.

I spend the hour or so that passes between when she leaves and when she returns alternatively pacing and flipping channels on the TV. I can't even enjoy the fact that there has been a rain delay and so I won't miss the race.

It's no surprise, then, that I jump when I hear a knock at the door. I rush to answer it with a stupid amount of speed and stop myself just short of snatching the door open.

Helen's standing there on the steps, looking more than she has any right to like—what?

The woman I abandoned? No, that implies a certain helplessness, which was never the case with her.

Betrayed? Again, not exactly that.

Walked out on twenty years ago? Yeah, that's the only way to describe it.

She's obviously less vulnerable than she was then as she says confidently, "I didn't know which door to knock on."

"This one's fine," I say, letting her in and then escorting her through to my office. "Like most priests, I work from home."

I thought this would sound funny but it doesn't at all so we just sit down in wing chairs placed across from each other. Not knowing where to start, I say, "So, what did you think of the Mass? You certainly had a good seat."

She looks uncomfortable at this and rushes to say, "That was never my plan, I can assure you. Frankly, I had planned to sit in the back but there was no room."

"Yeah, those back pews fill up quickly with families with little kids. And I'm sure you noticed there are a lot of those."

"I really could not believe how crowded the church was. I mean, the parish in Frostburg is usually less than half full, and I'm one of the few people there under the age of 60."

"I know. We have a very young congregation, at least at the 10:30 Mass."

"Before I walked in I was afraid I would stick out like a sore thumb. But honestly, I dealt with protests in D.C. as a street cop that were less chaotic."

"Speaking of sticking out, your friend Gladys is certainly . . . exotic? Classic? Odd? In her taste in clothes., I mean."

"Oh, yes," Helen manages to laugh. "Apparently, she watched an old movie to find out what she ought to wear to Mass."

"Well, it's charming to find someone willing to make that level of effort. I wonder, though, where she found that outfit around here."

"Oh, I can assure you, it came right out of her closet and she'll probably wear it to work tomorrow—sans the veil and gloves, of course."

"Really?"

"She does all of her shopping at vintage clothing stores. I doubt she owns anything made after 1965."

"That is interesting."

Our conversation is beginning to peter out, and I realize that I need to get to the reason why I asked her here today.

"Helen," I say, "I want to apologize. I was an ass the other day. I was just upset, when you said the things you said. I thought it was because you were still angry over what happened between us."

"Tom, no, it had nothing to do with that," She shakes her head. "I was just doing my job."

I nod. "I know. I just got angry. And you may remember what I can get like when I get angry."

"You act like a petulant child, if memory serves."

"Ah, yes." I look at her. "No hard feelings?"

"No hard feelings," she says with a slight smile. We just sit in silence looking each other in the eyes.

I clear my throat. "Helen, there's something else. I'm sorry for leaving the way I did. I shouldn't have done that. I was hurt and angry. But it wasn't right to do that to you."

She seems taken aback by this but then says, "You were young. We both were. We were kids who thought we knew everything."

I nod. "Yes. I was a fool. We had something good, and I threw it away."

Helen looks at me, eyes no longer colored by anger or resentment. "Well, Tom," she says quietly "it worked out well for both of us, in the end."

I am suddenly discovering that it is hard when dealing with Helen to find the boundary between priest and former fiancée. I am afraid I have crossed it when I ask, "Were you happy with him? Your husband? Was he good to you?"

Her eyes begin to water as she whispers, "Yes. We were very happy together. You would have liked him."

"I'm sure."

She catches me off guard by asking, "Were you happy with Joan?"

"Didn't you ask me that already?" I ask.

"I want to hear your answer again."

"As Detective Parr?"

She shakes her head. "No. As me."

Now it's my turn to develop moist eyes. "I was. I thought we were happy together. But since coming back, since finding what I found . . ." I slowly shake my head. "I don't know anymore."

I see her arm flinch, as if she was going to reach toward me but then changed her mind. Instead, she says, standing, "This has been very nice, Tom, and I am glad we're friends again. But I really need to go. And anyway, you surely want to catch some of that race."

"Yes, of course." I say, walking her to the door.

She turns to me. "Good-bye, Tom," she says. "I'm sure we'll be seeing each other around town."

"Good-bye, Helen," I say. She starts down the steps. Trying to make my priest-self speak loudly enough to drown out the former lover, I say, "It was good to see you today. I hope you'll come back."

She just smiles and nods, walking down the sidewalk toward her car, a beam of sunlight briefly making her dress transparent.

I step back inside quickly and close the door behind me, subconsciously locking out—what?

Temptation?

Perhaps.

As I lean against the door, I hear the lover ask the priest, *And what will we do if she does come back, Father?*

Eleven

The address Glenda gives me for the sick call is not so much an address as a series of directions which take me out of town and onto a series of left turns, right turns, and curving mountain roads. As I get further from Myerton and into the surrounding mountains, I am struck by how beautiful the fall color is.

I'm not a fan of autumn as a rule—autumn leads to winter, which is my least favorite season. But I do love the fall colors.

Joan and I would drive up into the mountains around Myerton at this time of year to enjoy the color, and there is one overlook where we'd always stop, which has a spectacular view of Myerton surrounded by the mountains, displaying bright splashes of reds, golds, browns, and oranges.

The last time we did that was a couple of weeks before her murder.

I set up a canvas chair and sat a short distance away, reading a book. Every so often I'd look up. Joan was working steadily, stopping every so often to look at the scene, then back to her canvas.

Then, suddenly, Joan began screaming. I looked up to see her stabbing her painting with a pallet knife.

I threw my book down and ran over to her. Grabbing her, I looked her full in the face and shook her. "Joan! Joan! What's wrong?" I cried.

"It's shit!" she screamed at me. "It's just shit! Can't you see it, or are you too blind to see what a pile of shit it is!"

I looked at the remnants of the canvas. I held her close, stroking her hair. "I see it," I whispered. "I see it. It's breathtaking. One of the best things you've ever done."

What I thought would calm and reassure her had the opposite effect. In a flash, she went from leaning against me sobbing to screaming at me, beating my chest with her fists.

"Don't lie to me! You're such a liar! Why don't you just tell me the truth, huh, Tom, why?"

I grabbed her wrists and looked her in the eyes. "I am telling the truth," I say, trying to stay calm. "The painting was—is—great." Then, "What's wrong Joan? Why are you doing this?"

"Wrong? Wrong?" She started beating her chest. "I'm wrong, Tom! I'm wrong! I'm all wrong!" She collapsed to the ground, heaving with sobs as she repeated, "I'm wrong," over and over again. I knelt by her and held her against me as she cried. After a while, I gently helped her get up and led her to the car.

We drove back to our apartment in silence. When we got home, I helped her inside and tucked her into bed. Then I sat in the room, watching her as she slept. I didn't go to sleep for hours, my mind trying to make sense of what had happened. She slept all night and well into the morning.

When she woke up around 11 a.m., she greeted me with a cheerful "good morning," kissed me, and went about her day. She was fine. There was no explanation, not even an acknowledgment that anything had happened.

I decided not to press, to just leave it alone.

As I drive through the mountains fifteen years later, I think how different things might have been if I had.

***

After what seems like an eternity—travel on winding mountain roads always seems to take longer than it actually does—I arrive at the address. The house is a two-story farmhouse, painted a startling shade of reddish-pink that makes it stand out against the surrounding hills. The farm looks like it is still worked, for the fields look as if the corn has just been harvested. In one of the enclosed fields are a few cattle—I can't tell if they are steers or milk cows—and a short walk from the house is a chicken coop and a pig sty. The house has a wrap-around covered porch with three rocking chairs; the porch itself fronted by two beds of flowers struck down by an early frost.

I hear the sound of running feet when I knock on the door. Three children opened the door, two girls and a boy, who look under ten, each with sandy brown hair and hazel eyes. "Hi," I say. "Can I see your mom or dad?"

"Hope, Faith, John Paul," I hear a slightly frazzled voice call from inside. A woman, also with sandy brown hair and hazel eyes comes to the door. "What have I told you about opening the door to strangers—Oh!" she says, when she sees me. "Sorry, Father."

"Hi, um—"

"Serenity," she says, offering her hand. "Serenity MacMillan. Thanks for coming, Father."

"It's my pleasure to meet you, Ms. MacMillan," I say, taking the offered hand. "I'm here for your—-mother?"

"Please, Father, call me Serenity. It's my grandmother-in-law, actually," she says. "She hasn't been to Mass in a few weeks. I've offered to have a priest come to give her communion but she always says, 'Oh, I don't want to bother him, he's too busy,' until yesterday when she said, 'Call Saint Clare's and get the priest over here.'"

"Any idea what changed her mind?"

Serenity shakes her head. "No idea."

I don't have enough experience to speculate. I've heard that people will often call for a priest when they feel the end is near. I assume this was the case, that the person I am there to see can feel she is in her final days and wants to receive the sacraments one last time while still relatively clear. I prepare myself to minister to a frail elderly lady.

"Who is that at the door?" I start at the voice that booms from one of the downstairs rooms, more like a command than a question. The voice of a general or an admiral. I look at Serenity.

"Who is that?"

She smiles. "That's Gloria."

"Gloria? Your—your grandmother-in-law?"

She nods. "She's a force of nature. Always has been."

I have never met a force of nature before, so I steel myself for the experience. Serenity shows me down the hallway to a snug, well-lit room. In the bed, underneath a hand-crocheted afghan, is the force of nature herself, resplendent in a white bed jacket and long gray hair pulled back in a bun.

"Grandma, you have a visitor," Serenity says.

"Well I can see that, silly," she snaps. "Next you'll tell me he's a priest. I can see that, too!"

Serenity looks at me. "I'll leave you two alone. Good luck," she whispers as she slips from the room.

"Ms. MacMillan—" I start.

"Mrs." she interrupts.

"Excuse me?"

"What, can't you hear?" she says. "I say Mrs. Not Ms. Never liked Ms. Never was ashamed of being married to my Harry, though he could be a bit thick at times. Always went by Mrs. Not going to change now."

"OK, sorry, Mrs. MacMillan. I'm Father Greer."

She looks at me as if really seeing me for the first time, squinting through her round wire-rim glasses. She studies me for a few moments.

"You're not Father Anthony," she finally says.

"No," I say. "No, I'm not. I said my name is Father—"

"I heard you just fine, young man, nothing wrong with my hearing, I hear everything worth hearing just fine. Anything I can't hear, well . . .," she waves dismissively.

I smile in spite of myself. Gloria MacMillan is a handful.

"What I mean is, you're the new priest." It is a statement not a question. I nod.

"So, they finally caught up with him, did they?"

"Finally caught up with who?"

"Father Anthony, of course, who do you think I mean?" she says. "I've spent years trying to get someone at the Archdiocese to listen to me about his shenanigans, and I guess they finally decided to take me seriously and do something about him."

I sat down in the chair next to the bed. "What shenanigans?" I ask hesitantly.

She points a bony index finger at me. "Bingo."

I have been with her for five minutes and am totally confused. "Bingo?"

"Bingo. You know, bingo. The game with the cards and the numbers. Bingo."

"What does bingo have to do with it?"

"What does bingo—why, everything young man!" She slaps the bed with her hand.

I look at Gloria MacMillan, convinced she is completely senile. What am I to do with this elderly woman carrying on about bingo?

"For the last twenty years," she goes on, "Saint Clare's has had a monthly bingo game on the last Saturday night of the month. The Knights serve spaghetti—absolutely vile if you ask me, Tim Horton can't cook to save his life—and run the game. They have Father Anthony call the numbers. Guess they figure you could trust a priest to be honest." She harrumphs.

I nod, vaguely remembering Glenda telling me about this when she told me about parish activities. I am dreading having to get involved with it.

"So, Father Anthony," she says, "calls the numbers. I play five or six cards at a time and I always have bingos for the smaller prizes—I've won a slew of backscratchers, don't know why they had so many, I only have one back. The last round of the night is always for the big prize—an electric blanket, a coffee pot, you know, something like that, do you see what I'm saying?"

"Oh, yes, absolutely," I say, when in reality I have no idea what this is about.

"And every month for twenty years, in all that time, I have never gotten a bingo for the big prize." She crosses her arms in triumph. "And now they've got him."

"Got him? For what?"

"For rigging the game, of course! The winner is always one of his favorites. That housekeeper-slash-secretary of his, Glenda, she's won a coffee pot and an electric blanket. I've complained to Father Anthony, but he just smiles and pats my hand and says, 'Well, better luck next month, Gloria.'" She points at me. "So I've written to the Archbishop several times. Never heard anything. Well, I guess they finally listened to me. So young man," she points at me again, "you better be careful. I'll be watching you."

"Mrs. MacMillan," I say, "Father Anthony hasn't been removed for—rigging bingo."

"Oh? No? Why?"

"He's not been removed, per se. I mean, he's still officially the parish priest at Saint Clare's. I'm just temporary. He's had some health issues—"

"Oh, fiddlesticks," she says, dismissing the idea with a wave of her hand. "Health issues? He's younger than I am. They're just trying to cover it up. I promise you," she hits the bed again with the palm of her hand, "I'm going to contact my lawyer and sue the Archdiocese."

"Mrs. MacMillan, please. I didn't come here to discuss this. I don't think you need to sue anyone—"

"But it's wrong, taking advantage of a defenseless old woman like me," she pouts.

I stifle a laugh. I've only just met her, but defenseless hardly describes Gloria MacMillan.

I change tactics and get a serious look on my face. "Mrs. MacMillan, I don't know what has happened in the past. But you have my solemn promise that in the four months I'm here at Saint Clare's, every bingo game will be run with the utmost propriety."

She looks at me. "Really?"

I nod.

"You promise?"

"I promise."

"Well, good. About time." She adjusts herself in the bed, then looks at me.

"So, are you going to give me Communion or not?"

I smile and proceed to do just that.

***

I leave the MacMillans and begin the drive back to Saint Clare's. Just outside of town my cell phone rings. It's a number I don't recognize.

"Hello?" I answer.

"Tom? It's Helen."

I say nothing for a moment. "Helen," I finally say.

"Did I catch you at a bad time?"

"I'm just driving back from seeing a parishioner. What can I do for you?"

"I just wanted to let you know I'm taking another look at your wife's case."

"Really," I say, the amazement in my voice apparent even to me. "Thank you, but I thought you said—"

"Oh, it wasn't my call. I stand by what I said to you the other day." She pauses. "You've been a busy little priest, Father."

I note the sarcasm in her voice. "What do you mean?"

"A reporter called yesterday, started asking questions, wanting a comment for her story. Said she is working with you. I sent her over to Public Affairs, which told her that the investigation was ongoing and we couldn't comment. But since the investigation wasn't really ongoing, the Chief thought it would be a good idea to work on it." She pauses. "So I'm working your wife's fifteen-year-old murder."

"Sorry it's taking you from your bike thieves," I say, immediately regretting it. She is trying to do the right thing, whether she wants to or not, and I shouldn't respond with sarcasm.

"I've begun reading through the file," she goes on, choosing to ignore my comment. "There wasn't much in the way of physical evidence, but what was collected is stored off-site. It will take a couple of days to get it here. I've got some questions about your original statement."

"OK, well what are they?"

"No, not now, not over the phone," she says. "I'd like to do it face to face."

"When would you like me to come down to the station?"

Helen says nothing for a moment and I think the call has dropped. Then she says, "What are you doing tomorrow night?"

"I think I'm free. What time?"

"I thought maybe we could discuss things over dinner?"

I am stunned and don't know what to say for a moment. "Do you think that's a good idea?"

"Why not? Afraid I might attack you?"

"No, of course not, that's not what I mean."

"Look, I just thought a more informal atmosphere would be better." She pauses again. "And I thought we could catch up."

I hesitate, then say, "I don't think that's a good idea, Helen, do you?"

I hear her sigh. "No, Tom," she replies. "I guess not. I'll call you in the next couple of days, arrange a time to meet at the station."

"Fine," I say. "Looking forward to it."

We hang up just as I pull up to the Rectory. My phone rings again. It's Katherine Shepp.

"I hope I'm not interrupting anything," she says.

"Not at all, I'm just getting back to Saint Clare's."

"I was hoping you'd have some time Thursday for an interview."

"I thought we'd already done an interview?"

"No, that was you telling your story," she says. "An interview is where I ask questions and you answer them."

"Oh, OK, what time do you and Nate—"

"Nate won't be there. Just me and a cameraman from the station. For this, I need a little more professionalism than Nate. Is 2:00 p.m. all right?"

"I don't have my calendar with me, but it should be fine."

"Great." She pauses. "This is going to be really good, Father. You'll see."

Twelve

Thursday afternoon arrives and after the Noon Mass, a van with a satellite dish emblazoned with the call letters and logo of Katherine Shepp's television station pulls into the driveway of the rectory. Katherine gets out and walks towards me, her hair perfectly coiffed and wearing a light blue dress. She smiles that same perfect smile I noticed when I first met her.

After we exchange pleasantries, I say, "You're a little early. I haven't even had time to change out of my vestments. We said 2 p.m."

"Oh, I know," Katherine says. "We're going to shoot some B-reel."

"B-reel?"

"Yes, shots we can use to illustrate the report," she explains. "We want shots of the exterior of the church, you walking to the front, of you inside—"

I shake my head. "Not inside, no."

"Really? Why not?"

"I'd have to get permission from the Archdiocese first. There's not enough time."

"Oh, OK." She walks back to the van. "Sam, let's set up at the front to begin with, I'll do my intro standup there. Father," she turns back to me, "why don't you change and come out in about twenty minutes. We'll do some exterior shots of you." She then busies herself with her equipment.

I go back inside the church to the sacristy and get out of my vestments. I then go to my office and lean back in my chair.

After talking to Anna the day before, I am slightly uneasy about agreeing to the interview. Katherine had talked to her, and Anna was not impressed.

"Why did you agree to talk to her?" Anna had asked me. The irritation in her voice came through the phone loud and clear.

"She's interested in Joan's case," I said. "She wants to find out who killed her. I thought you wanted that, too."

"Of course I do, you know that. But Tom, I'm telling you, I don't trust her. Whatever she wants to do, I don't think it's finding out who killed Joan." She had paused. "You need to be careful around her."

"Anna, I appreciate it, but I think you're worried for no reason. I admit she's a little intense—"

96

"No," she had said. "A thunderstorm is intense. Hot sauce is intense. That blond thing is dangerous. Just be careful."

I had promised her I would be, but at the time I didn't really give her concerns too much thought.

Now, however, I begin to turn them over in my mind.

What if she's right? What if Katherine really isn't that interested in Joan's case? And if she isn't really after Joan's killer, then what is she after? According to Nate, she sees a story on Joan's murder as her way of moving up in her profession. What if that is all she cares about?

There's a knock on my office door. I close my eyes and shake my head. There is only one person it can be.

"Come in, Glenda," I call.

The door opens to reveal a very vexed-looking Glenda. "Father Greer," she says, "are you aware that there is a news truck outside?"

"Yes, I am aware of that."

"And," she goes on, "a reporter—I guess that's who she is, though by the way she's dressed it's hard to tell—from one of the Baltimore news stations?"

I nod.

"Why is she here?" Glenda says, walking towards my desk.

I look at her. "She's here to interview me," I say.

"You?" Glenda sits down in one of the chairs in front of my desk. "Why would she want to interview you?"

"She's doing a story about my wife's murder," I say, "and she's here to do an interview. I've already talked to her, but she had some other questions."

The look on her face changes from puzzlement to—something I can't describe. "Oh," she says quietly. "That was about fifteen years ago. The crime was never solved, right?"

"That's right." I have a hard time believing she has not heard.

"So why is she here?"

"I just told you, she wants to do an interview for a story she's doing on Joan's—my wife's—murder. She hopes—we hope—that it will spark interest in what happened. Apparently, it already has. The police have reopened the case."

"They have?" Glenda says, a little too loud. She startles me.

"Yes, they're taking another look at it." I look at her, confused about her reaction.

"Well that's—that's good," she says. She swallows, then draws herself up. "What did the Archbishop say when you told him?"

I get a sinking feeling in the pit of my stomach. "The Archbishop," I say to myself.

"You did tell him about the interview request," she goes on. "To get permission."

"I, ah, well—"

"Father Greer," she says in her typical imperious tone, "You know full well that the Archbishop would not want you talking to the press without his permission."

"I am not speaking as a representative of the Church," I say. "This is a personal matter. I don't believe I need his permission."

"Perhaps not," she replies. "But I would think the Archbishop would appreciate a heads-up, at least."

I have to admit that she has a point. "You're right Glenda. I should have contacted the Archbishop before now. I'll call him after the interview to let him know what's going on."

"I guess that will just have to do," Glenda says as she stands. "By the way, I have to go take my nephew to an appointment. May I leave early?"

"Oh, of course Glenda. How are things going with him?"

She hesitates for a moment, and I see a crack in the stern veneer she hides herself behind. "Fine, thank you," she says curtly, cutting off any more inquiry.

A few minutes after she leaves, there's a knock on the Rectory door. I guess that Katherine is ready for me.

But when I open the door, Katherine isn't standing there. It is Nate, dressed better than I have ever seen him, wearing a white shirt, blue striped tie, and a sportcoat. The fact he's also wearing jeans and tennis shoes is besides the point.

"Hi, Father, am I late? For the interview?"

"No, we haven't started yet," I answer. "Come in, Nate." I show him into the living room and he sits in one of the easy chairs while I take the one opposite.

"I wasn't expecting you," I say. "Katherine hadn't—"

"Oh I know, I know, but I thought since it was my early work that got her attention, she would want to have a few words from me. Also, since we're working on this together, I thought I oughta be here."

"Well, I'm sure since you're here, she'll want to talk to you."

There is another knock. This time it is Katherine.

"OK, Father," she says as she sweeps past me, "we're ready to shoot some footage. What we're going to want you—oh, Nate, you're here." She doesn't sound happy to see him.

"Hi, Katherine," Nate says, grinning from ear to ear.

"What are you doing here?" she says, an even tone in her voice.

"I thought I could help," Nate says with unabated enthusiasm. "Since I started all this, you know."

She smiles. "And I'm so thankful for all you did. It really gave me a place to begin. But," she pats his arm, "why don't you leave this to the professionals?"

She turns to me before Nate can answer, leaving him with his mouth slightly open. "Shall we, Father?" She heads to the door. I look at Nate apologetically as I follow her out. Nate stands in the entryway for a minute then follows.

We spend the next half-hour with me walking back and forth in front of Saint Clare's, standing on the steps looking at the camera, standing with the church behind me gazing into the distance. Several people walking by stop to look at the spectacle. I feel self-conscious and at one point I look in the direction of the Rectory. Nate is still there, standing on the bottom step, his hands in his pockets, looking forgotten and forlorn.

We finish the filming and go back to the Rectory. Katherine and her cameraman spend the next half-hour rearranging the furniture in the living room and setting up lights. I stand by, trying to stay out of the way, imagining what Glenda will say when she sees the parish's furniture rearranged.

"Why don't you sit here, Father," Katherine indicates the better-looking of the two armchairs. She has set the other one up for herself directly across from me, the lights arranged on either side. I have seen enough television interviews to recognize the arrangement.

I sit. "Do I need makeup?"

Katherine looks at me and gives a small laugh. "No, Father, you'll be fine."

She sits up straight and arranges herself in the chair. "OK, Father, here's what's going to happen. I'm going to ask you questions and you're going to answer while looking at me, not the camera. Got that?"

"Sure, I've got it."

"Good," she says. Then she turns to look at the cameraman. "You can start."

The cameraman looks through the viewfinder, presses a button, and a red light comes on.

Katherine turns to me and smiles. "Father Tom Greer," she begins, "Thank you for agreeing to speak to us."

I return the smile. "My pleasure, Katherine." Both the smile and the response comes more from habit than honesty.

"A few days ago," she begins, "I filmed you talking about your wife's murder. That murder, for our viewers who may not be aware of the story, was never solved."

I nod, "That's correct. No one has ever been arrested for Joan's murder."

"And you describe to me what happened in great detail, right?"

"Right," I reply. I'm not quite sure where she is going with these particular questions.

"According to you," Katherine looks down at her notes, then back up at me, "Joan died in your arms."

I swallow. "Yes," I say quietly.

"A very touching story," Katherine says with what sounds like feigned sympathy. "Truly, very touching."

I take out a handkerchief and wipe the beginning of tears from my eyes.

"So Father," she continues, "tell me what happened next."

"Next?" I say. "Well, we had her funeral. Her Funeral Mass was in this church. She's buried at a cematary outside of town."

"Were there a lot of people at the funeral?"

I search my memory. "I think so, yes."

"You think so?"

"Well, it's been fifteen years," I answer, "and I don't remember much about that day."

"You don't remember much about the day of your wife's funeral," she says, "but you remember the details of your wife's murder?"

"It's burned into my memory. What I remember is burned into my memory. Most of the details are hazy."

"But it's been fifteen years. Do you think you may have forgotten some details? Or embellished them, perhaps?"

"No. Absolutely not."

"Hmm," Katherine says. She looks down at her notes again. "So according to my interviews around town, you left town shortly after Joan's funeral. Is that correct?"

"It wasn't exactly shortly after her funeral. It was about six months later."

"OK, six months after her funeral. Why? You had a job at Myer College and had lived here for a number of years—"

"That's true" I say. "I was hired by Myer College as an archivist. That's where I met Joan."

"So you lived here for several years, were married in this church, and your wife was buried here," Katherine continues. "Why did you leave?"

I take a deep breath. "I just—it just became too much. The memories. Joan and I had a lot of good memories here. But I couldn't stay here, not in the town where she was murdered. It was just too much."

There is another reason—one no one except me, the administration of Myer College, and the other person involved knows about—that I pray she doesn't bring up.

"So after six months, you left."

I nod.

"According to your ex-mother-in-law, you didn't tell anyone you were leaving. Is that correct?"

"Not quite," I say. "I resigned from my position. I sent an email to Anna—Joan's mother, my mother-in-law—telling her I was leaving. But I didn't let anyone else know. I just wanted to leave quietly, without a fuss."

"You didn't want anyone to know you were gone," she says.

"No, I wouldn't put it that way."

She looks down at her notes again. "Were you aware that after you left, the police continued investigating your wife's murder?"

"I'm not surprised," I say, "since the crime was unsolved."

"No, I don't mean that," she says. "Were you aware that the police began investigating you?"

I look at her, a little stunned. Anna's warning comes back to me. Slowly, I say. "I only became aware of that after I came back to Myerton."

"Oh, yes," she says, "your sudden and mysterious return to Myerton."

"It may have been sudden," I reply, "but hardly mysterious. Saint Clare's needed a temporary parish priest. The Archbishop assigned me here."

"He assigned you to the parish where your wife's funeral was, in a town you had left fifteen years ago because of the pain you felt surrounding your wife's murder."

"That's exactly right."

"If this place has so many painful memories as you claim," she asks, "why would you ever come back?"

"Would you refuse an assignment from your boss?" I ask. "It was a question of obedience. I had no choice. By my vows, I'm obliged to obey my superiors."

"Still, you can see how odd it is, given the story you tell."

"It's the truth."

"Is it? Is it really?" Katherine looks at me, then back at her notes.

"Let's talk about something else," she goes on. "Were you and your wife close?"

"Yes," I say. "Very close."

"No problems?"

"I wouldn't say that. We were a young married couple. I don't know of a young married couple that doesn't have a period of adjustment."

"Let's go back to the night of her murder," Katherine says. She flips through her notes. "You say you and your wife were having a celebration dinner, right?"

"Yes," I say. "Joan had found out she was pregnant. We'd been trying for a while. We were both happy."

"Really?" she says. "So it was a happy time for both of you."

"Yes, very."

"You laughed, probably toasted each other, talked excitedly about baby things, maybe names for the child."

"Yes," I say quietly.

"All very expected." She pauses. "Does the name Tony Armando ring a bell?"

I think, then shake my head. "No, should it?"

"Probably not, though he was the owner of La Petite Maison fifteen years ago. Retired now, living in Florida." She pulls out a document. "Here's a copy of his police interview. Do you know what he told the police?"

"I haven't the slightest idea." The knot in my stomach says otherwise.

"Are you sure, Father?" she says, a tight smile forming on her lips. "Are you quite sure?"

I stare at her but say nothing.

"Maybe this will jog your memory," she says. She pulls out a small digital recorder. "I located Mr. Armando and interviewed him on the phone. Here's what he said."

She presses play and turns the sound up. Through the recorder's small speaker, I hear an older male voice.

"They had just ordered dessert, I think," Armando says. "All of a sudden I heard her yell at him. I looked over. She had stood up, waving her arms like a mad woman. He was trying to calm her down, get her to sit down. She threw her napkin down, grabbed her bag, and stormed out of the restaurant. He watched her leave."

"Did he go after her?" Katherine's voice said.

"Yeah, he went after her, ran out of the restaurant after her."

She clicked the recorder off. I am feeling hot. Beads of sweat have formed on my head.

"Well?" Katherine asks.

I try to be as nonchalant as possible. "We had a fight. Young couples have fights."

"But," Katherine says, leaning forward, "wasn't it more than that?"

I look at her. "No, just normal young couple stuff."

"Really, Father?" She reaches down and pulls out a stack of papers. I recognize them. They are copies of the emails.

"Then," she goes on, "how do you explain these emails?" She hands them to me. I take them and look through them. They are the emails I had given her.

"These," I say as I leafed through the pages, "are emails Joan received in the weeks leading up to her murder." I look up. "They appear to be from a man who had some kind of obsession with her, who was stalking her."

"Did you know about these emails?"

I shake my head. "No. Nothing. Joan never told me about them. She never told me she was getting unwanted attention from a man and never said anything to me about being stalked."

Katherine sits back in her chair, a look of triumph on her face. "Come now, Father. Do you expect anyone to believe that your wife was receiving these emails, was being stalked, and she said nothing to you about it?"

"It's the truth."

"Or," she says, "isn't the truth actually much different than you've said." She pauses, I suppose expecting a comeback of some kind.

When I say nothing, she goes on. "I have here," she says, showing me another paper, "a copy of a marriage license. Isn't that your wife's name?"

I look and nod.

"But that's not your name, is it, Father?"

"No," I whisper. "No, it's not."

"This license," she says, "shows that Joan Luckgold married a Randy Earl in 1996. I have here," she says, pulling out another piece of paper, "a decree of annulment dated six weeks later. Am I right that you claim you knew nothing about your wife's marriage and annulment?"

"It's the truth," I say quietly.

"What about this?" she says, presenting another document. "This is a document showing that Joan Luckgold was admitted to Gentle Brook Treatment Center six months after the annulment."

I grab the paper out of her hands. It's an admissions paper showing Anna signed Joan into Gentle Brook Treatment Center.

I have heard of it. It is a private mental hospital.

"How did you get this?" I ask.

"I have my sources," she says. "Well, Father, did you know anything about this?"

"No, nothing," I say, handing it back to her.

"Seems there's a lot you didn't know," Katherine says. She looks at me.

"So what really happened that night, Father?"

"I already told you," I say, my voice firm and even. "It's what I told the police fifteen years ago."

"You didn't tell the police about the fight, did you, Father?" Katherine says. "Why?"

"I didn't think it was important."

"Really? Or was there another reason." She leans forward. "Was there really an attack, Father? Was it really a mysterious hooded stranger with a gun?" She pauses. "Or was it you?"

I leap from my chair and snatch the lapel mike off. "Turn the camera off."

Katherine protests, "We're not finished, Father Greer."

I look at her and scream. "I said turn that camera off, now!" My pulse is racing, I can feel heat rising in my face. My chest is heaving. Katherine looks at me, startled, and then smiles.

"Fine, Father," she says. "I have everything I need."

Thirteen

"What I fail to understand, Father Tom, is why you are telling me this now, after the proverbial horse has left the barn!"

I knew it was not going to be an easy conversation when I called Archbishop Walter Knowland to tell him about my interview with Katherine Shepp. I have put off telling him for a week after the interview, telling myself it is in order to find the right words.

In reality, I was avoiding him.

I couldn't foresee how upset he would be. I have never seen or heard the Archbishop angry, and he's always very jovial in our conversations. I have heard rumors of a fiery temper when he is provoked but discounted them.

Standing in the Rectory office with my phone in my hand, I realize that had been a mistake.

I've made a lot of them recently.

"I'm sorry, Your Eminence," I say.

"Don't you think," he bellows, "it might just have been a good idea to ask before you had any dealings with the press? Or are you completely unaware of how the press has treated the Church in the last few years?"

"To be fair, the Church has brought a lot of that on itself."

"Don't get smart with me, Father," he snaps.

"With all due respect," I go on, "this has nothing to do with the Church. This is about something that happened before I even had a notion of becoming a priest."

"Father Tom," the Archbishop says, more patiently this time, "you need to remember that you represent the Church all the time. Even if this interview has nothing to do with the Church or your activities as a priest, people will see you as a priest. Anything you say, anything this reporter chooses to highlight, will be seen by people as being done by a priest of the Catholic Church. I don't mean to come across as hurtful, but no one will care that your wife was killed before you became a priest."

I really haven't thought about that. I have only thought about my situation. I see my life as having two parts. The first part was my life before I became a priest. The second part was my life after I became a priest. For years I have kept my former life in a box, locked away and separate from my life as a priest, or at least I have tried. Coming back to Myerton, I thought I could be here as a priest without having to open up that box.

But that's what I did. I did it in the most public way possible—on television. And I did it without thinking about the impact on my priesthood.

"Father? Father? Are you still there, Father?"

"Yes, yes, Your Eminence," I reply. "I'm still here."

"I asked you how bad it was?"

I hesitate. "Well, it could have been better." Which is the truth. Maybe not the whole truth. But not an outright lie.

The Archbishop does not respond right away. "I could ask you to be more specific, but I don't think I will. Do you want our attorney to intervene? Ask the station not to run the story?"

"No sir, I think that might make things worse."

I hear him sigh. "I suppose you're right. When will it air?"

"I'm not sure. She didn't say."

"Well, we'll just wait and see, I suppose," the Archbishop says. "Maybe it will all be OK."

I hang up. Given what has happened, I can't see how.

Glenda knocks on my door. "Do you have a moment, Father?"

"Of course," I say, indicating the chair.

"My nephew," she begins as she sits. "He needs a job."

I have stopped being surprised by her bluntness. "I thought he had a job working construction at the college?"

Glenda nods. "Oh, he did. They fired him. Got into a disagreement with his supervisor. But he needs work, so I had a thought. There is a lot of grounds work that needs to be done, with all the leaves and everything, and the beds need to be mulched. The parish could hire him as groundskeeper."

"Well," I say, "do you think that's a good idea?"

"Why wouldn't it be?" she says, slightly indignant.

"You just told me he lost a job because he got into a dispute with his supervisor," I say. "Will he do what he's supposed to do? You know, without complaint?"

"You leave him to me," she says. "He'll do what I tell him. He always has."

I think for a moment. It is such a small thing she is asking. And the work needs to be done.

"I'll need to speak to the parish council," I say.

"I already have," Glenda says. "They all say they are fine with it. They just need your say-so."

I look at her with a slight smile. "Well, then, when can he start?"

"He'll be here tomorrow morning," she says, standing. "And thank you, Father. He really is a good boy. You'll see."

***

The next evening, Friday, I am preparing to go into the church to say Evening Prayer when my cell phone rings. It's Anna.

"Hi," I say, answering. "What's up?"

"Tom," Anna says. She sounds strange.

"Is everything OK, Anna? Is something wrong?"

"Why didn't you tell me that woman's report was going to air tonight?"

"What are you talking about? I haven't spoken to Katherine Shepp since my interview. That was over a week ago."

"It's on right now," Anna says. "You better turn it on."

I hang up and run down the stairs to the living room. I turn on the TV.

". . . recently retold the story of that night," the disembodied voice of Katherine Shepp says. On the screen is the video of me recounting the night of Joan's murder. It goes on for about a minute, then cuts back to a shot of Katherine standing in front of the Church.

"That's the story Tom Greer, now Father Tom Greer," she says as a still of me appears in the corner of the screen, "told police. But is that the real story?"

I get a sick feeling in the pit of my stomach.

She holds up some papers. "I-Seven has obtained copies of internal police documents showing that authorities during the original investigation considered Greer a person of interest. The investigators found evidence of financial difficulties between the young couple, and there were reports of arguments between the Greers over money."

The report cuts to Bethany Grable. "Joan was trying to get her business started," she is saying, "and things weren't going well. Tom was constantly bailing her out. Things were tough."

"Police could never find solid evidence tying Greer to his wife's death at the time," Katherine continues, "and did not believe that money was a motive because there was no life insurance or savings that would have gone to Tom Greer in case of her death. So the case has remained unsolved for fifteen years."

I breathe a sigh of relief. It wasn't as bad as I thought it would be.

Then Katherine says, "But this reporter has uncovered new evidence that sheds some new light on this case, light that spotlights one person—Father Tom Greer."

I feel the oxygen leave the room as my photo fills the screen.

The picture cuts back to Katherine. "I-Seven obtained emails that Joan Greer received in the weeks leading up to her death, emails that are from an unnamed man who, by all appearances, Joan had recently ended a relationship with."

The picture cuts to a clip from the interview. There I am, sitting in the Rectory.

I know what comes next. The insinuations. The accusations. My reactions.

I put my head in my hands.

This is bad. So, so bad.

A reporter just accused me of murder on live television.

Katherine Shepp used me. She used my desire to find Joan's killer to further her career.

"That was some reaction from Father Greer," the in-studio anchor is saying. "Any comments from the Myerton Police?"

"Ted, a spokesperson for the department says the case is still considered an open investigation so they have no comment. But a source inside the department tells me that, because of this reporting, they are taking a closer look at the case."

I turn off the TV and stare at the blank screen. I don't know how long I sit there. Time has stopped. My mind whirls. I have not expected this—though I should have from her line of questioning. She had decided that I would make the most likely suspect. Of course, there wasn't much evidence pointing in another direction. All I had were the emails, the fact that Joan had not told me about them, and my vague suspicions.

I also have the knowledge that I did not kill her. But at this moment, that is little comfort.

On the other hand, the one thing I have worried most about, the one thing about that night I have hidden for all these years, the one thing I am most ashamed of, still remains my secret.

Unless, of course, Helen has figured it out.

And while I have no idea what kind of detective she is, I know her—or at least I did. Determined, stubborn, persistent—she is all these things. I fell in love with her because of her stubborn persistence in helping me with Elementary Statistics.

Again, my mind goes back over twenty years.

***

"Tom, you're not paying attention."

She's right, of course; I wasn't. Instead, I was caught up in the scent of her hair: vanilla, like a fresh-baked cookie at my grandmother's house, or the vanilla cola my dad always ordered at the diner. But still, I have my pride so I say, "Yes, I am."

"OK, then what did I just say?"

"That you find me irresistable and want to go out with me?"

"No, that is not even close. Had I said anything so personal, it would have been that I need to leave for Mass in an hour and, while I'm glad to pray for you there, I am dubious about how much it will help if you don't focus."

"Wait, why are you going to Mass? Have I been so captivated by your charms that I've lost a day or two? Did I miss Friday and Saturday entirely?"

"No, doofus," she said playfully, "I try to go to daily Mass during Lent. The church is right on campus, so it's not hard."

"But Helen," I said, trying to cajole but instead whining, "wouldn't saving my grade be of more value to humanity than praying?"

"Actually, no, Tom. You see—and I am going to use little words here so you can understand—God is God and you are, well, you."

I pretend to pout as I said, "I still don't get it."

Then I had an inspiration. "What if I go with you to Mass and then you go to dinner with me. After all, you've got to eat and I sort of owe you for helping me."

She contemplated this for a minute and then said, "All right. I'll do that."

And that's how my 22-year-old self agreed to spend 30 minutes with the God of the universe in return for two hours with a woman.

If they ever perfect time travel, I'm totally going to go back and shake that guy until his teeth rattle.

***

I close my eyes and lay my head back in the chair.

I must have dozed off—when under stress, I often fall asleep, a defense mechanism I learned growing up—because the sound of my phone jars me back to consciousness. I look at the Caller ID.

The first person to call me is the last person I would have thought of.

"Helen?" I say.

"Tom, are you OK?" She sounds worried and angry at the same time.

"I'm really not sure," I chuckle. "I've never been accused of murder on TV before."

"I can't believe you agreed to an interview with her!"

"Look," I say, "I believed her when she said she was interested in Joan's case. It was a mistake. Frankly, Helen, I'm surprised you're not knocking on my door right now."

"Oh, don't be silly," she says. "I'm not about to arrest you for Joan's murder. Unlike a reporter, I actually look at evidence. And the evidence doesn't point to you."

I let out a sigh of relief. "Thank you. So, why did you call?"

"Because I wanted to make sure you're OK," she says. "And also to assure you that bitch did not get that file from me."

I smile in spite of myself. "Helen, I never believed that for a minute. But someone in your department gave it to her."

"And I'm having Gladys check every log-in to our system to see who was the last person who accessed that file. The original's still locked in my office. Just to make sure, I checked."

"You were looking at the original when I saw you," I say. "But the files have been scanned? Why didn't you just look at that?"

"I prefer paper," she says. "I like the feel of it. Also, I could look at you, see your reaction. I couldn't do that if I was looking at my screen."

"Makes sense, actually," I say.

"So when I find who did this to you, Tom, I promise you, I'm going to have their damn badge!"

"Look, I appreciate your position, Helen. You need to find out the person who leaked that file," I say. "But frankly, no one did this to me. I did this to myself. Even if someone hadn't given her the file, she'd have made the same accusations. This is no one's fault but my own."

There's silence on the other end of the call. "Wow," she says quietly. "Tom Greer taking responsibility for something. Never thought I'd hear that."

"I'm not the same person I was back then, Helen," I say quietly.

"You know, Tom," she says. "I believe you're right."

***

Helen no sooner hangs up than my phone rings again.

I'm surprised it took him this long to call.

"Good evening, Your Eminence."

"Father Tom," the Archbishop says. "Can you please tell me how things could be any worse?"

"You saw the news."

"No, no, I was at a fundraiser for the Retired Priests and Religious Fund when it aired. I got a call from Father Wayne about it. I saw it myself online when I got back to the Residence. You were not completely forthcoming with me, were you?" the Archbishop says.

"No, sir, not entirely."

"So you knew when we spoke that this reporter was going to accuse you of murder. On television."

"No, that I did not know."

"I saw the end of your interview—everybody saw the end of your interview! That didn't give you some idea?"

"No, I just thought—"

"No, Father, the problem is that you didn't think. At all. About any of this. You agreed to the interview without consulting me. When you told me about it, you didn't tell me everything. And now, the entire Baltimore-D.C. area thinks the Archdiocese has a priest under suspicion of murder!"

"Your Eminence, the accusation is completely—"

"False, I know, I don't believe it for a minute. But what I think doesn't matter. What the truth is doesn't matter. This is a bad look for the Church. We don't need this publicity, not after—well, everything that has happened over the last several years." He pauses. "I want you to come back. To the Archdiocesan office."

I sit up. "What?"

"Yes," he said, "back here. You don't need to be in the public ministry with this swirling around. I can find another priest for Saint Clare's."

"No, sir, respectfully, no. Your Eminence, don't do this."

"It's for the best, Tom. You'll be no good at Saint Clare's."

"If I leave Myerton now, everyone will think I'm guilty. My friends, my family—they won't know what to think."

"I can't keep you there, Tom."

"Yes, you can," I say. "I need to see this through. Besides, you just mentioned what's happened over the last several years. Do you think moving me will make the Church look good? Right now, this is just about me. I know how it reflects on the Church, but Joan's murder happened before I became a priest. You can argue that it has nothing to do with my position now, that the Church has no involvement, you will let the authorities make the final decision, whatever you want to say. You don't have to say anything about my guilt or innocence. But if you move me, it will look like the Church has something to hide."

There is silence on the other end of the phone. I realize what I have done. I just gave the Archbishop a way out. He can protect the Church by disassociating from me.

And I can stay at Saint Clare's.

"You know," he says slowly, "I could make you. You are under obedience to me."

I nod. "I am aware of that, sir. But you won't. Because you know I'm right."

He is silent for a moment, then says, "All right. You stay at Saint Clare's. For now, Tom, for now. But," he continues, "if anything else happens, you're back here. That will be an order."

He hangs up before I can thank him. I hold the phone in my hand, then toss it on the couch. No other calls come in, and I need to think. I leave the phone on the couch and walk upstairs to my room. I throw myself on the bed fully clothed. I am tired, tired to my bones, even though it is only eight o'clock. I don't want to think, but I know I have to.

I have brought this on myself, I know. I should have left it alone. Joan died fifteen years ago. No one else had found her murderer. I thought I was content with that, that I had found peace. I had my papers and my boxes and my folders and my lists of records. I had my vocation. I had the Lord. Joan was in the past, still part of me, but in the past. Her murder was still a part of me, but in the past.

But it isn't really in the past. And I don't really have peace. Because I know the truth about that night—the whole truth. I have hid the truth from everyone for fifteen years—from the police, from Anna, from our friends. It was easy to avoid the truth when I was away from Myerton.

Then I returned. I found out Joan's secrets. I convinced myself that those secrets had something to do with her murder. I had to find out more, because I thought it would lead to her killer.

Instead, I wound up accused on television of her murder.

Not to mention, seeing Helen again after twenty years has stirred up feelings and emotions I'd buried long ago.

I don't know what to do next.

Fourteen

In my sleep, I hear a pounding.

I wake up with a start. Light streams through the windows of my room. As I sit up in bed, I catch a look at myself in the mirror. I still have on my clothes from the night before, including my shoes. I sit up and run my hand through my hair. I fell asleep without realizing it.

There's a pounding again, and someone at the front door is calling my name. Pulling myself together, I go downstairs and open the door to a very flustered and somewhat angry Anna.

"You pick today not to answer your phone, Tom?" she says, brushing past me.

I rub my face. "Sorry, I left it downstairs. Have you been trying to call for long?"

"Since seven this morning," she says, looking at me with her hands on her hips.

"What time is it now?"

"Almost nine," Anna says. She pauses and looks me up and down. "You look awful."

"Then I match how I feel."

"I wouldn't have come," Anna says, "except Nadine called to tell me no one showed up to celebrate the 8:00 Mass and there was no answer at the Rectory—they called and knocked, too."

I close my eyes and sigh. "I slept through Mass."

"Hmm-hmm," she says. "They were close to calling the police, but apparently someone thought that might be inappropriate considering..."

I look at her. "What are people saying?"

Anna turns around. "Come on, I'll make you some coffee," she says, walking to the kitchen. "Glenda not here today?"

"She doesn't work on Saturday anymore," I say, following her. "About last night," I press, "what are people saying?"

She turns around and crosses her arms, asking "What does it matter what people are saying?" There is an edge of defiance in her voice. Anna is obviously in full mama bear mode.

"Unfortunately, it matters a great deal. It's OK. Tell me."

"Well," she begins. "Look, I really haven't talked to that many people, and the ones I have, well, they really don't know you, and—"

"Anna, please!"

She turns back to the counter and pours coffee into two mugs. Handing me one, she says, "People don't know what to think. Many of the people in the parish weren't living in Myerton when Joan was killed." The ones who were here, on the one hand, know how hard you took it, and on the other how suddenly you left. A few remember the police asking about you." Sitting down with her coffee at the table, she says, "It's mixed, I'd say."

I sit with her and look at the cup. "I had a call last night from the Archbishop."

"I bet that didn't go well."

"You win the bet."

"Mad?"

"Furious." I take a sip of coffee. "He wanted to transfer me out of Saint Clare's."

She stares at me and I look at her. "I told him I wanted to stay."

Anna exhales. "Good, I'm glad to hear it."

We sit in silence for a few minutes drinking our coffee. Finally, Anna speaks.

"You didn't tell me about the emails."

"No, no, I didn't," I say. "I don't even know what they mean."

"What do they say?"

I tell her about the emails, about how they seem to be from a man who had some kind of obsession with Joan. How they were sent in the weeks before her death. How a couple seem to be vaguely threatening. How none of them were signed, only had the email address.

"And you think they're connected with her murder?" Anna asks.

"I wasn't sure, until I got this." I pull my wedding band out of my pocket.

Anna's eyes get big. "Where?"

"In the church." I hesitate before I say, "I left it on Joan's headstone the night I left. Someone picked it up and kept it all this time, then left it where I'd find it."

Anna stares at me. "And you have no idea who?"

I shake my head.

"Why didn't you go to the police?"

"I did, right after I found it. Showed them to Hel—Detective Parr. She didn't seem interested at the time. But they reopened the case when Shepp started poking around."

"Hopefully, she doesn't have you in her sights," Anna says, getting up. Walking to the sink with her cup, she turns on the water to rinse it out.

"I have a question," I say quietly. "Why didn't you—or Joan—tell me about her marriage to Randy Earl?"

She says nothing. She turns off the water and dries her hands. Then, she walks to the table, pulls out a chair and sits. She looks at me, her hands folded on the table in front of her.

"I told her you'd find out someday," she says.

I exhale. I don't know what to say next. I just sit there.

Anna speaks first. "Tom, you have to know, Joan didn't tell you because she loved you."

"Loved me?" I spit out. "Loved me? How could she keep such a big secret from me? Not to mention one that calls into doubt whether or not our marriage was valid in the first place?"

"Now, Tom," she begins, "Everything was handled properly. It was no impediment to you getting married in the Church. We made sure of that."

"But I didn't know. It never came up in our pre-marital counseling."

She nods. "I know, I know. I told her she should talk to you about it. She didn't want to risk losing you. It was a bad time in her life."

"Did Father Anthony know?"

"Yes, he knew. He said that since her marriage was a civil marriage and had been annulled not long after, it was never valid to begin with. It was like it never happened. Joan took that to mean she didn't have to tell you." Anna pauses. "Joan was bad about that, not facing things that were difficult."

"And what about the other," I went on. "She was in a mental hospital when she was sixteen?"

"That wasn't the first time, Tom." Anna sits back. "By the time you two met, Joan had been hospitalized several times. That's where she met Randy. They were patients in the same hospital."

"She never told me that, either," I say. "Why did she hide her illness from me?"

Anna swallows. "You don't understand what it's like, Tom. Not just for the person who has the illness, but for the people who love them. Joan knew the toll her illness had taken on me, and she wanted to spare you that."

"But she could have told me," I say. "I would have understood."

"She couldn't take that chance. She'd told other men about her illness, that she was taking medication and had it under control. But it was always the same story. They'd dump her soon after. When she met you, and you two hit it off so well, she knew you were the one she wanted to marry. And she wasn't about to jeopardize that."

"I would have married her anyway," I say. "I loved her. We would have carried the burden together. She didn't have to do it alone."

Anna sighs. "I told her that. But she wouldn't listen."

We sit quietly in the kitchen for the next few minutes. Finally, I say, "Her father, Drew. What really happened, Anna?"

Anna puts her cup down and folds her hands. "They say there's a genetic component to Bipolar Disorder," she says quietly. "Poor Drew struggled our entire marriage. Hospitals, medication changes, the roller-coaster of manic highs and deep depression. Outbursts of irrational anger. I loved him, Tom. But it wasn't always easy. You say you would have stood by Joan, and I believe you would have. But only a fool or a saint wouldn't consider leaving in the face of all that. In the end, I stayed with Drew. Years later, I still haven't decided which one I am."

I put my hand on hers. "Anna," I ask quietly. "How did Drew die?"

She takes a deep breath and whispers, "Suicide, when Joan was fourteen. Overdose of sleeping pills. I was at work." She closes her eyes as tears flow down her cheeks. "She found him. She called me, said her Daddy wouldn't wake up. I told her to call 911. They were taking him out to the ambulance when I got home. He died on the way to the hospital."

I close my eyes. I was twelve when I came home from school to find Dad dead. That's something you don't just get over.

"Do you think that triggered Joan's problems?"

Anna nods. "She had a major manic episode about six months later. That's the first time she was hospitalized."

"How long was she in the hospital?"

"Oh, only a couple of weeks. Just long enough to get her stabilized and started on her first medications. By the time she left, she seemed better again. She went back to school, and she started seeing a psychiatrist as well as her therapist. There were months of trying to get her medications adjusted so they'd balance out her moods. Her moods, even when she was doing well between episodes, were unpredictable."

I nod. I don't want to remember that about Joan, but Anna is right. When I knew her, her moods could change on a dime.

"So we went on, more or less good, for about a year. Then she had another really bad episode. I don't remember what exactly it was, I think it had something to do with an art competition she entered that triggered it, but it was the first time she tried to harm herself."

"She didn't try to kill—"

"No, no, not suicide. I found out she had started cutting herself, on her upper thigh where no one could see. I don't even remember how I found out. So, another hospitalization for a month because of self-harm."

She gets up and started pacing again. "It was during this hospitalization that she met Randy."

Randy. Her first husband.

"Who was he?" I ask.

Anna smiles ruefully. "Tom, who do you think a patient in a mental hospital is going to meet? I'll answer that—other mental patients. Some as bad off as you are, many worse off. Randy was the latter."

"What was he in there for?"

Anna shrugs. "To this day, I don't really know. Joan told me he was bipolar, but I suspect there was more than that. Maybe some schizophrenia, one of the other disorders, who knows. It doesn't really matter. He may have been mentally ill, but he wasn't stupid. He was shrewd and clever, even charming. And he charmed Joan."

She sits back down and folds her hands. "Joan called him her boyfriend, said they were getting married when they got out of the hospital. I thought she was just being delusional. I should have paid closer attention."

Anna goes on. "So another round of meds, more intensive therapy, and she was released. By this time her sophomore year had come and gone, and she was so far behind that she and I spent the summer doing schoolwork. At first it seemed like things were going OK. Then I found out that she was in contact with Randy."

"How did you find out?"

"I caught her talking on the phone with him at 3 in the morning," Anna replys. "I blew up and we had the first screaming argument we'd ever had. I forbade her to have any contact with him again. She screamed and cried that they were in love and there was nothing I could do about it. She ran to her room and locked the door. I didn't go after her, figured I'd just let her calm down. The next morning she came out of her room, all calm, said she was sorry, we hugged, and got on with our day. I thought things were OK again." She shakes her head.

"About a week later, I went to get her up. She was gone. Joan had left a note, saying that she and Randy were going to get married and live together and I'd never see her again."

"What did you do?"

"I screamed. I cried. I fell on the floor and beat the ground with my fists. I cursed like a sailor. And yes, in the midst of all that, I cried out to God. I asked the Blessed Mother to protect her, to keep her from doing anything she couldn't take back. Then I called the police, reported her as a runaway. I even got in the car and drove around town, hoping I would catch sight of her. But nothing. Every day for two months, I waited for her to call. Nothing."

I just listen to her talk. There is nothing I can say.

"So for two months, I was in limbo," she continues. "I wouldn't do anything except go to work and come home. I'd go to Mass on Sunday, but I dropped out of everything else I was doing. I didn't tell anyone what had happened, I was too ashamed. I told people Joan was off at art camp, that she was doing fine. Looking back, I think people knew there was something wrong, but no one asked me.

"Finally, after two months, I heard from her. It was late one night. The phone rang. She was sobbing, almost hysterical."

"What had happened? Where was she?"

"Baltimore," Anna answers. "I could barely understand her, it took me forever to get her to calm down. She and Randy had had some kind of fight. He had left her alone on the street in one of the worst parts of the city. I later found out they had been sleeping in an abandoned row house for about a month. I still didn't know what they had been doing, what had happened since they left. But I didn't care. She begged me to come get her, to send someone to come get her. Tom, I had no one I could call, so I told her to get to a safe place and stay there, to call me back with the address. I waited for half an hour, scared to death she wouldn't call back. Finally, she called. She was at an all-night diner. The owner had let her call using his phone. I put some clothes on and drove as fast as I could to Baltimore. It was after sunrise by the time I got to her."

She shuddered slightly. "I barely recognized her, Tom. Her clothes were dirty and torn, she had everything in a plastic garbage bag, and smelled like she hadn't bathed in weeks. It looked to me like she had lost thirty pounds, she was almost skin and bones, like she hadn't eaten well. Before we left, I got her something to eat. She downed it so quickly I was afraid she'd get sick. The kindest thing that happened was that when I went to pay, the owner told me it was on the house, that he was just glad to see a girl get back with her family, that it didn't happen often." Anna looks at me. "Made me wonder, how many other Joans were out there.

"I drove her home. She slept the entire trip. She got a shower, and must have stayed in there for an hour. Got some clean clothes on, then crawled into bed. She slept for two days."

"Did you find out anything?"

Anna shakes her head. "Not then. She was too traumatized to talk, and I knew I'd get nothing if I pressed. No, I was just glad to have her back and safe. I knew there would be time enough. I didn't want to push her away by pressing too hard. I also needed the time to prepare myself. She was a mentally ill sixteen-year-old girl who had been, from what I could figure, living on the streets of Baltimore for the better part of two months. You can imagine what I thought had happened. The fact that she hadn't been alone didn't give me any comfort. Randy was worse off than she was, from the little I knew."

By this time it is close to one o'clock. Anna notices the time and says, "I bet you're hungry. I know I am." She gets up and goes to the refrigerator and starts pulling out sandwich makings. I hadn't realized until she mentioned it that I hadn't eaten that day.

I take my wedding ring out and look at it, remembering her smile, the brightness in her eyes on our wedding day.

Was it true? Did she really feel that way? Or was it all a lie?

Anna places a sandwich in front of me. "Tom," she says firmly, "no matter what you learn from me today or anyone else in the future, know this. Joan loved you and was happy with you.

Chewing a bite of sandwich, I say, "Not always."

Anna nods at this and adds, "I know she still struggled. But more often than not, she won."

"So you got Joan back," I say, anxious to get the conversation back on track.

"Once she had rested and eaten some, she was ready to talk. She said they got married and then hitchhiked and walked to Baltimore. Randy had told her he had a job, had friends they could stay with, and Joan believed him."

"He was lying?"

"Not exactly. There were friends they could stay with, but no job. Joan said he kept looking, would work day labor sometimes, but more often than not, he'd just sleep all day. Eventually, he had a fight with his friends and they kicked them out. So they started living on the streets, eating at soup kitchens, sometimes staying in a shelter. Joan told me she wanted to leave after a week, but she was afraid of Randy, afraid that he might hurt her. Then one day, they had a fight and he left."

"And that's when she called you."

"Yes," Anna says. Swallowing, she continues, "She cried while she told the story, cried after the story, cried herself to sleep in my arms. As she lay there, I accepted the reality that she needed to be in a hospital for a while.

"It took a lot of persuasion, but I was finally able to get her to go." She sighs. "She refused to see me the first couple of times I went to see her. Finally, we started talking again. It took three months, but by the time she got out, things were better. They had come up with the right combination of meds, along with the right therapeutic approach. She came home and got her life back on track.

"She got caught up with school, and managed to graduate. Then she got accepted to Myer, in their art program—she and I both wanted her to stay close to home, to make sure that she kept up her treatment." She smiles. "She excelled, she was stable and happy. Then she met you."

I sit back, still trying to absorb what I have heard. "But she never told me any of this," I say.

"I tried to get her to tell you, even after you were married, but she wouldn't listen. She was very careful to make sure you never knew she was on medication. She found a therapist out of town and saw her weekly."

When she says this, I remembered Joan would take a weekly day trip out of Myerton, saying she had to buy things for her clients. It makes sense now.

"And she was on meds through our entire marriage?"

Anna hesitates. "That," she says slowly, "I can't say for certain. She may not have been for the six months before her death."

"Why not?"

"Because she wanted to have a baby—you both wanted to have a baby. She was worried about her meds harming the baby, or that they would keep her from carrying one to term. The miscarriages didn't help. She told me she wanted to taper off them while she was trying to get pregnant. But I don't know."

"If I had known," I say, "We could have done something else. There were always options. We could have adopted. Certainly, she knew it didn't matter to me."

"But it mattered to her, Tom," Anna says. "All she wanted was a normal life, to be a normal wife and mother, to be a normal person. That's all she wanted."

I lean forward and put my elbows on the table, resting my head in my hands and staying that way for several minutes. It has been a long few hours, I am tired and my head hurts. It is a lot to take in but there is one more thing I need to know.

"What about Randy?"

She shrugged. "I never met him, and as far as I know, Joan never saw him again. I think I saw a picture of him once, but I don't think I'd know him if he appeared on my doorstep."

Fifteen

"What are you going to do now?" Anna asks.

I look at the clock. "Take a shower, get some fresh clothes on. I have confessions at 3 p.m. and Mass this afternoon."

"That's not what I mean," Anna says, a tinge of irritation in her voice. "What are you going to do about that—reporter?"

I open my hands. "I don't see anything I can do. You can't unring a bell."

"But you heard what she said at the end of her report. She's going to keep digging into this—into you."

"Oh, she's probably left by now."

"No, she's still at the Myerton Inn."

I am surprised. "How would you know that?"

"Ellie Hooper's son has a part-time job there. Shepp's paying by the week. No, Tom, she plans to stay a while."

"Wonderful," I say.

***

Anna leaves and I decide to get on with my day. I take a shower, put on a fresh set of clericals, and walk up the block to The Perfect Cup for a coffee. The day is bright and clear, cool but not cold, unusually warm for the middle of October. Glenda's nephew is raking near the garage when I walk down the sidewalk from the Rectory. He has done a good job, I think, as I look at the piles of brightly colored leaves dotting the grass. I walk up the sidewalk past the front of the Church towards the coffee shop, passing several people on the sidewalk. Some turn back and stare, apparently recognizing me from the news report.

When I get to The Perfect Cup, the crowded cafe is buzzing with conversation and the sounds of coffee cups and spoons clinking. By the time I get to the counter, the talking has stopped. I don't turn around, but I sense that every eye in the place is on me.

Nate's Uncle Pete is behind the counter. "Hi, Padre, the usual?" he asks cheerfully.

"Thanks, Pete." He hands me a steaming cup of coffee and I hand him a five dollar bill. I find a table in a far corner, sitting so I can see the whole room. When I do, the people in the cafe restart their conversations.

I drink my coffee and look around. People seem to be going about their business, talking with each other or looking at their phones. Occasionally, though, people look over in my direction, then quickly go back to what they are doing. Couples stop their conversations to look, then lean in closer to talk to each other.

Is this going to happen every time I go out in public? Are people going to look at me like I am some kind of sideshow freak, or like I have a scarlet M on my forehead? Maybe the Archbishop was right. Maybe I should leave town. If people in a coffee shop are going to look at me this way, what will people in Church be like?

"Can I get you anything else, Padre?" I look up to see Pete looking down at me, a fatherly smile on his face.

I return the smile. "No, thanks, Pete. I'm fine." I look past him. A be-speckled co-ed is looking at me over her laptop. She catches me looking at her and furtively looks down.

"I seem to be attracting some attention," I say.

"What?" Pete looks over his shoulder. "Ack, don't worry about them. They've got nothing else to do. So they look, and they go on their phones, and they send their Twits, and their Handbooks, and all that social crap. I mean look at them—half of them are sitting with someone they aren't even talking to, they're on their little phones. Now me, I don't have any of that. I've got real friends, I talk to real people."

"Must be nice."

"You Father, you have friends. You used to live here, right?"

"A long time ago," I say. "But everyone knows what happened."

"They think they know," Pete says. He leans over and looks me in the eye. "They don't know the truth. They only know what they see on the news. You—you know the truth. You, and God, and that's all that counts." He stands up. "Stop by on your way out, I'll give you one to go."

I watch him walk away, his words reverberating in my head. *You know the truth. You, and God, and that's all that counts.*

That's the problem.

I know the truth.

***

I leave the cafe and walk back to the church, going straight to the sacristy and grabbing the small purple stole I wear for confession. The church is empty, but it is almost three, and I want to make sure I am in place before anyone comes in. People are nervous enough about confession as it is without there being a chance the priest might be able to place a face with a sin.

I sit in the confessional for a while, waiting for the first penitent. I pass the time saying a Rosary and reading prayers in my Breviary. But no one comes, which is odd, I think. There had been a line the previous Saturday. Are people reluctant to confess their sins to a priest accused of murder?

For the second time today, I wonder if the Archbishop was right. Staying in Myerton seems to be more trouble than it is worth.

After about 45 minutes, I hear the sound of soft footsteps on the marble floor. They get louder as they approach the confessional box. I hear the door open and close and the person sits down.

I say, "Let us begin—"

"Liar."

I stop. I don't recognize the voice.

"Liar," the voice repeats. "You're a liar."

Lowering my voice, I say, "Why do you say that?"

"You know. You know. I saw you on the news. You lied."

"I don't know what—"

"I was there. You lied."

I don't say anything.

"You lied to that reporter," the voice says. "Did you lie to the police?"

I sit quietly.

"You did, you lied to the police about what happened." There is a low laugh. "That's great. So they don't know, they don't know what you did."

"I didn't do anything. You shot Joan, not me."

"Only because of what you did. You know that. You're a liar. Isn't lying a sin?"

I just sit and listen.

"I shot her, but you killed her. That's the truth, Father. You know that."

I hear the person get up and go out the door. Instead of walking this time, I hear the person jog out of the Church.

This time, I don't try to go after them. I just sit. I am having trouble catching my breath.

Staying in Myerton was definitely a bad idea.

Sixteen

After the interview debacle, I fully expected Saint Clare's to be virtually empty Sunday morning.

Boy, was I wrong.

People pack the pews at both Masses. Familiar faces jockey for places with newcomers, most of whom look somewhere between confused and horrified at the chaos of 10:30 Mass. At communion time, most of the new people stay in their pews. I want to believe it's because they hadn't been to Mass in a while and hadn't gone to confession first. But really, they probably aren't Catholic anyway. They're just here to see the priest accused of murder.

Well, at least they are in church. That's a good thing, no matter the reason.

I get through the Mass without any problems, give the final blessing, and begin the recessional. As I am walking down the aisle behind Dominic Trent and the other altar servers, one of the ushers waves at me frantically. I no sooner clear the doors then he grabs me by the arm and pulls me off to one side.

"You don't want to go out there, Father," he whispers.

I look down at his name tag. "What is it, Norman?"

"That reporter's outside. Has a camera set up and everything. I tried to get her to move, but she said something about it being a public sidewalk and freedom of the press."

I sigh. "I think she's right about that. It is a public sidewalk, and unless she steps on church property, we can't ask her to leave." I square my shoulders. "However, I'm not going to cower in here."

Hoping I look more confident than I feel, I walk outside.

Katherine Shepp, camera and microphone at the ready, stands on the sidewalk right in front of Saint Clare's. When she sees me, she actually smiles and waves, calling, "Good morning, Father."

I return the smile. "Good morning," I say before I turn to greet the first parishioners coming out the door. Everyone smiles, shakes my hand, says the usual pleasantries people say to their priest—good Mass, nice homily, thank you—and proceed on their way.

While I am talking to a young couple, I hear a small commotion behind me. I turn around to see Katherine Shepp going from person to person, sticking her microphone in people's faces.

At the sight, something inside me snaps.

I know I should ignore her.

She is, after all, just doing her job.

But this is too much.

I start down the stairs, my vestments flowing behind me. "Ms. Shepp!" I yell. "What are you doing?"

She turns to me. "I'm just trying to get some comments from the members of the church."

"What sort of comments?"

"Oh, just how they feel knowing their priest might be a murderer," she says. A small smile plays on her lips. "You know, the human interest angle."

"No, no, this is too much," I say with an emphatic shake of my head. "You can film all you want to, but I must ask you not to harass my parishioners."

"Harass? Really, Father, I'm not harassing anyone. I have every right as a journalist to ask questions, and they can answer or not. Also, I'm on a public sidewalk, so—"

"Yes, I know you're on a public sidewalk, and I know you have the right, I'm just asking you to respect the privacy of—"

I notice the camera. The red light is on.

"Wait, are you—are you filming this?"

She nods. "It will make great footage in my next report. The accused priest greeting his unsuspecting flock after church. The confrontation with the press. Really good stuff."

"No, no, absolutely not!" I say, lunging at the camera. I manage to grab it out of the cameraman's hand and throw it to the ground. The camera breaks, the lens separating from the rest of the mechanism.

Katherine and her cameraman stare at me. "You—you'll pay for this, Father!" Shepp sputters. "That's station property!"

"Send me the bill!" I yell. "And get out of here! Now! Or the camera won't be the only thing broken!"

I am shaking. The blood rises in my cheeks. My hands clench into fists as I move toward the reporter. Shepp backs up, looking genuinely frightened.

"Father Greer," a familiar but authoritative voice behind me says. I turn. Helen's standing there, looking at the scene.

"Oh, good," Shepp says with a sinister smile. "Detective Parr, I'm—"

"I know who you are, Ms. Shepp," Helen says, crossing her arms. "Now, what seems to be the problem?"

"You saw!" she says. Waving at the crowd of onlookers. "Every person here is a witness to Father Greer's unprovoked attack on me and my cameraman."

"Unprovoked attack?" Helen says, a tight smile playing on her lips. "I saw no attack on you."

"You can't be serious, detective!"

"What I saw was Father Greer asking you to leave his parishioners alone—a not unreasonable request—and to stop filming him. When you did not comply with his perfectly reasonable request, he knocked the camera to the ground while attempting—clumsily—to turn it off himself," Helen says.

"But—But—" Shepp sputters, "He threatened us with physical violence! It's on the tape!"

"I did not hear him threaten anyone."

"Are you deaf as well as blind, detective!" Shepp yells.

"Nooo, my hearing and eyesight are perfect, according to my last physical," Helen says, taking a step towards the reporter. "Father Greer said, and I quote, 'or the camera won't be the only thing broken.'" She shrugs, then adds, "Could have referred to anything, but he clearly did not mention you or your cameraman."

"I want him arrested!"

"Oh, come now, Ms. Shepp," Helen says calmly, breaking into a grin. "You don't want that. I mean, right now you've got a good story. Accused priest loses his temper in front of his entire parish. But if I arrest him, when you have no injuries and no witnesses to back up your claim, how petty will that look, hmm?"

Shepp just looks at Helen for a few minutes. Then finally, she holds up her hands. "OK, OK, we're leaving. Let's go, Pete," she says as she walks to the news van. Pete looks at me, gathers up the pieces of his camera, and follows after her.

I am breathing heavily, my pulse beating in my ears, as I watch the reporter and cameraman climb into their news truck. Helen turns back to me and says, "Are you OK?"

I nod. "Yeah. Thanks."

"I couldn't very well arrest my priest on a Sunday in front of everyone, now could I?" Helen says. "That wouldn't make me too popular around here. Come on. I'll buy you a cup of coffee."

She starts up the steps, and I scurry after her. "I didn't see you at Mass," I say, finally catching up to her just inside the door.

"I was here," she says. "In the back corner. I didn't want to distract you this time."

"You didn't distract me," I say.

"Isn't lying a sin, Father?"

"I wasn't lying. I wasn't distracted, I was . . . surprised to see you."

I walk up the steps to the altar and bow. I head for the sacristy, when I notice Helen's stopped just before the bottom step.

"I, ah . . . I'll just wait here for you, OK?" Helen says nervously.

I smile. "Of course," I say, and hurry into the Sacristy. Shedding my vestments quickly, I emerge only a moment later.

But Helen is no longer alone. Dan Conway is standing with her.

"Dan?" I say.

"Hello, Father," he says nervously. Looking furtively at Helen, he rubs the back of his neck and says, "I—I need to—well, you see, Father, there's something—"

"Of course, Dan," I say. "Hel—Detective Parr, if you'll excuse us. I'll catch up with you at The Perfect Cup."

Helen nods and is about to leave when Dan stops her. "No, Detective—ah, I was going to see you tomorrow morning about this. Might as well rip the bandage off and get it over with."

I walk down the steps and place my hand on his shoulder, aware that Helen's eyes are flickering with something. "How about we go to my office? This sounds like it could take a while."

***

"Well? What do you have to tell us, Dan?"

Dan looks at me, then at Helen, then at his hands. He takes a deep breath, and says, "I'm the one who gave the unredacted case file to Katherine Shepp."

I sit back in my chair, surprisingly calm at this news. Helen, however, sits up straight and yells, "What! Dan!"

"I know," he says, swallowing. "It was a stupid thing to do. I'm ashamed and I'm sorry."

"A stupid thing—ashamed—sorry!" Helen sputters. "Sorry! Dan, you could lose your job over this! It's a violation of department policy, not to mention Father Greer's privacy!"

"I just didn't feel like I had a choice," he says, shaking his head.

Helen's about to yell some more—I remember the look—when I hold up my hand to stop her. "Katherine Shepp told me she had dated someone in college who was now in the police department. That someone was you, right?"

"We didn't exactly date," he sighs. "We slept together a few times. Back then—well, I wasn't always who you see now. God and Miriam are responsible for that. But anyway, yeah, I knew her. She was manipulative back then, too. The other night, she was waiting for me when I left work. She asked me for a drink. I didn't see any harm. I should have just gone home. But we talked about old times, and she reminded me of some things I'm not proud of." He paused. "She threatened to tell Miriam if I didn't get her the information she wanted. I told her to go ahead, that I'd told Miriam about my past years ago. So, she upped the ante."

"She threatened to tell Miriam you'd slept with her that night, didn't she?" Helen says.

Dan nods. "So, I printed the case file out and gave it to her. Oh, Father, Detective Parr, I am so sorry."

"Wait," Helen says. "I had Gladys pull the logs. There's no record of you accessing the Greer file."

"That's because I snuck into your office and used your computer," Dan says softly. "You have a bad habit of leaving your system open, Detective."

Helen's jaw clinches at that. "I see," she says coolly. "Officer Conway, I will be speaking to the chief about this. I don't know what he'll do, but you should prepare yourself for the worst."

Dan just nods. As he stands up, I stand and extend my hand to him. "Dan, I just want you to know," I say, "I forgive you. If there is anything I can do to help, please let me know."

The big man swallows as he wipes a tear from his eyes. "Thank you, Father Tom. That means a lot to me. Detective, I'll see you tomorrow. I . . . I need to go home and have a talk with Miriam."

Dan walks from my office, shoulders slumped in defeat. When the door to the Rectory closes, I sigh and sit back down. "Well, that's one mystery solved."

"Frankly, I'm surprised," Helen says, sitting back and shaking her head.

I shrug. "Dan didn't believe he had a choice."

"No, that's not what I'm talking about. I'm surprised at you. Forgiving him so easily. I mean, Tom, he made things worse for you."

"As I've said, she'd have done it anyway," I say. "He didn't do it out of malice. He was being blackmailed."

She stares at me. "You really aren't the same person, are you?" she mutters.

I smile. "Neither of us are, Helen."

We sit quietly for a few minutes, then I say, "So, what's going to happen to Dan?"

"Well, it's up to the Chief, but he'll probably be fired."

"Oh, Helen, he can't fire Dan. He's got a wife and kids—and another on the way, in case you haven't heard."

"The Chief is not a man inclined to be merciful," Helen says.

"Can't you do something? Put a good word in for him?"

"Put a good—Tom! He broke department policy!"

"Not out of malice."

"Doesn't matter, he still broke the policy."

"OK, then punish him, whatever that looks like. But he shouldn't lose his career over this."

Helen opens her mouth to say something, then stops. She slumps down in her chair. "You know, I happen to agree with you. Dan did something stupid. But he's a good cop. I've seen his record—service in the Marines in Iraq, college here in Myerton, then the State Police, then here. Never even a hint of a problem, not a single civilian complaint—and these days, that's rare. He shows real promise."

"So you'll help him?"

"I'll try, Tom. Maybe I can use my powers of persuasion on the Chief."

I can't help but smile. "If I remember, those were rather formidable."

A wistful look passes across her face. "Not formidable enough in the end, Tom."

That not-so-subtle rebuke hovers in the air between us. Finally, trying to break the tension, I say, "You know, my secretary/housekeeper doesn't work on the weekends, so I usually fend for myself. And I haven't eaten since this morning. How about lunch at The Bistro?"

Helen smiles sardonically. "Well, well, Father Greer. No longer afraid to be seen with me?"

"It's not that," I say. "I just—I don't want there to be any misunderstandings."

"Tom," she sighs. "You're a priest. I know what that means. It's just two old friends eating together."

"Oh, of course," I say. "I agree. Let me run upstairs and change into some regular clothes."

Helen nods and I dash up the stairs to my bedroom. I look at myself in the mirror over my dresser and pull my collar out and place it on the top. I stare at it for a moment. I've always appreciated it as a symbol of my calling. When I wear it, even the most hardened sinner knows who I am.

But until today, I've never realized everything else it symbolizes. Just as a wedding band shows the world I belong to one woman, my collar shows I belong to God, forsaking all others.

"We both know what that means," I say to myself. "We're just old friends. Just having lunch. That's all."

But in spite of that, the former lover whispers, *Yes, that's all. But will it always be enough?*

Seventeen

Ten minutes into lunch with Helen, I have the uneasy feeling I've made a mistake.

After a somewhat awkward walk from the Rectory to The Bistro where I tried to keep at least six inches between us, we manage to find a quiet table in the corner of the restaurant. Not hidden, exactly, but out of easy sight of anyone who might see us and wonder what a priest is doing having lunch with a single woman.

Or any woman for that matter.

It's not like I'm doing something that's forbidden, exactly. We were taught in seminary to be careful with our relationships, to not give any cause for scandal and to avoid the near occasion of sin. But, we were also told we shouldn't avoid friendships, even with members of the opposite sex. We should just take care that they didn't develop into . . . more.

And if Helen were just another woman, close to my age, who happened to be a member of my parish, then I'd have no real reason for unease.

Even if she is a beautiful woman.

But Helen's a beautiful woman who I once loved. Who I was ready to spend the rest of my life with. Who I have very fond memories of, even if how I ended things was horrible.

And she's sitting three feet away from me, chin resting on her hand, looking at me with azure blue eyes that I so often lost myself in.

Yes. I'm definitely in trouble.

"So," she says after we order, "I know what happened to Joan. How did you two meet?"

I chuckle. "We met here, on campus."

"Oh, I know that from interviewing a few people. Your ex-mother-in-law for one."

"Anna? You interviewed Anna? Why?"

"Just part of the investigation. But don't worry. She's a big fan of yours."

"And I of her," I say. "She's been as much of a mom to me as my own Mom—more so, actually."

"Oh, and how is Nola?" Helen asks sarcastically, no doubt remembering our one trip to visit her in my home town of Bellamy, Florida after our engagement.

"She's Mom," I sigh.

"Your sister?"

"The same," I say. "Mom says she's been clean and sober for a while, but . . ."

"I'm sorry."

"Me too." I clear my throat. "Anyway, remember how we met the first time? I was walking along and I ran into you?"

"Yes, I—wait," she says with a grin, "you're kidding me!"

I shake my head. "Nope. I was walking along, reading something, and ran right into her. Only instead of a binder, it was her portfolio. We spent about half an hour chasing sketches and watercolors as they blew through the commons. After we gathered them up, I asked her to lunch."

"Unlike me," she says, "Joan said yes."

I nod. "There was a lot about Joan that wasn't like you."

"Oh? Did she let you sleep with her before the wedding?"

I stiffen. The words are no sooner out than her hand flies to her mouth, a look of horror in her eyes.

I feel my jaw tighten.

This was a mistake.

"Oh, Tom!" she whispers. "I'm—I'm so sorry. I—I don't know where that came from. Please, forgive me. That was horrible."

Looking in her eyes, already filling with tears, I realize I'm not the only one who's changed.

Twenty years ago, Helen wouldn't have apologized for that. She often spoke before she thought, then spent time arguing about how she was right to say what she said.

I take a deep breath. "Helen," I say slowly. "To my shame, I will admit that was one of the things I liked about Joan. She didn't have your . . . concern for the niceties of Church teaching. So, yes. We slept together before we were married. And I've come to regret that, especially recently."

"Why recently?"

I clear my throat as my eyes begin to burn with tears. "Because maybe if I hadn't been so anxious to get her into bed, and then get married . . ." I shake my head.

"I've seen the file, Tom," Helen says. "Your anniversary. Almost a year to the day after we broke up. You didn't waste any time."

I shake my head. "No. I have no excuses."

"You don't need to make any excuses to me," she says quietly.

"No, but I do need to apologize."

"Tom, you've already—"

"No, you don't understand," I say. "When we were together, I put pressure on you to sleep with me. I pretended to agree with you to wait until we were married, but I believed if I kept at it, eventually you'd give in. I didn't respect your wishes. And for that, I am sorry. You were right. I should have listened—really listened—to you."

Helen looks at me with something akin to astonishment. "I don't know what to say, Tom."

"Well, that you forgive me would be nice," I say, breaking into a grin.

"Oh, that goes without saying," Helen says. "I'm sorry, I'm still not used to this."

I nod. The server brings us our food—hamburger and fries for Helen, grilled cheese and tomato bisque for me—and we eat quietly for a few minutes.

Finally, I ask, "What about you and John?"

She stops and looks up at me. With a slight smile, she says, "Well, for one thing, I didn't make him wait."

My heart drops to my stomach. This, I didn't expect.

I take a sudden interest in my soup, even though I'm no longer hungry. "Oh," I say, because I can't think of anything else to say. It's not like I have any right to say anything. After all, I left her, and she met John long after me.

People change. Helen obviously did.

"Tom," she says finally, "let me explain."

"You don't owe me an explanation," I say, continuing to study my soup. It's creamy with crunchy croutons floating on top—not quite as crunchy anymore because of the soup.

"I know," she says quietly. "But I think you deserve one, after everything."

I look up at her. Staring into her eyes, the lover in me is hurt and angry, not to mention jealous. The priest is screaming at me, reminding me I have no reason to feel any of those things.

Oh, lunch was *such* a bad idea.

I should just get up and leave, forget we ever had this conversation, and spend the next few months avoiding her. She can attend Mass, she can investigate Joan's murder—not that she's going to get anywhere—and I can have little contact with her. After all, it's not like I'm going to be part of her life again.

But instead of leaving, I say, "OK. What happened, Helen? You spent our entire relationship keeping me out of your bed. What was it about John? Did you find him more attractive than me? Maybe he was just more persuasive. Was that it?"

Really, really mature, Tom, the priest says. *Watch her slap you again. You really deserve it.*

For just a moment, I think that's what she's going to do. Her eyes flash with anger—not that I blame her—but then she takes a deep breath.

"I can see why you'd think that, Tom," she says quietly. "But it wasn't anything like that. John was a handsome man, yes, but I didn't find him more attractive than I find you."

The lover in me takes note of what she just said.

Find. Present tense.

Don't go there, Tom, the priest says. *A slip of the tongue, no more.*

"Frankly, Tom," Helen says, "I don't have a good reason or explanation. Looking back, I'd become disillusioned with the Church—not God, not even the Mass or anything like that, but the rules. It didn't help that the friends I went to Mass with at Duke didn't seem to care what the Church taught about sex and marriage. Most of them lived with their boyfriends, some of whom attended Mass with them, and they took communion like it was no big deal."

"It was—it is—a big deal," I say.

"I know, I know," she says, "but I reached the point where I didn't care." She pauses. "Then, I met John."

"Was he a student?"

She laughs. "Oh, no. John was older than I was by about ten years. He came down from D.C. my last year of law school to talk about opportunities with his firm. Afterwards, we got to talking, then he invited me out to dinner."

Before I can stop myself, I ask, "Did you sleep with him that night?"

"No," she says. "He was only there for a few days, but after he left, we began a long distance relationship. After about a month of that, he invited me up to D.C. to visit. It was then that we . . . Anyway, he asked me to marry him a few weeks later, and we were married six months after that. I joined his firm, he was already a partner, and we began our brief life together."

She's given me the opening to ask a question I've been wondering about since that day in her office. "What happened?"

Helen's blue eyes begin to fill with tears. Instinctively, I reach across the table and take her hand. I've done it numerous times, with the grieving, with the sick. But this is not the hand of an elderly dying person, rough and worn with age.

It's Helen's hand. It feels exactly as I remember. Soft, with long fingers and manicured but close-cut nails. I used to joke that she had man -hands, and the truth is they are larger than mine. But when we'd walk along together, we'd just . . . fit so perfectly.

She's startled by the gesture, and her expression causes me to pull my hand away.

"He died. On 9/11," she whispers quietly.

"Oh, my God, Helen!" I say with real sorrow. "How horrible. Was he in New York on business, or something?"

She laughs bitterly. "Oh, no. Nothing like that. He was in D.C. just trying to get home to me. I had a bad cold, so I hadn't gone into the office that day. After the plane hit the Pentagon, the firm sent everyone home. I mean, no one knew if there were going to be further attacks that day or not. The office was only four blocks north of the White House, and we lived in Georgetown. So John was trying to get home. We lived in the city, so we either took Metro or taxis.

"Of course, everyone else had the same idea. The roads were gridlocked, the sidewalks packed, buses full to the brim, the Metro running full cars. It was chaos. Everyone was scared."

"Here, the college closed for the day after the first tower fell," I say quietly. "Joan and I were glued to the news. They showed D.C."

"The pictures didn't do it justice. I was waiting, praying for John to get home safe. Hours went by. I tried calling, but cell service was just overloaded. I didn't know anything until around midnight, when I got a call from the hospital."

She takes a drink of tea and clears her throat. "I still don't know what happened for sure, but John was hit by a car while he tried to cross the street. Ironically, he was only about two blocks from our apartment. People on the scene tried to help, but traffic was a nightmare; it took an ambulance too long to get to the scene." She dabs her eyes. "Apparently, he was gone by the time they got there."

"Oh, dar—Helen, I'm so sorry."

She nods. "Well," she sniffs. "After that, I kinda lost it for a couple of months. I didn't go into work. I barely ate. I thought my life was over. I mean, I wasn't even thirty and I'd lost the two loves of my life."

That stabs at my heart.

"But I finally recovered. I started going to Mass again, and gradually got back to work. But my heart wasn't in law anymore. Everything changed that day. Not just for the country, but for me personally. I couldn't see the point in filing briefs about patent infringement or negotiating settlements of class-action lawsuits over defective tricycles."

"So you decided to become a cop?" I say with a smile.

"I decided to become a cop," she says, returning the smile. "Part of me wanted to do something useful with my life. But another part of me thought, if there had been just one more officer on duty for traffic or crowd control that awful day, John might not have died."

She folds her arms. "So, I managed to pass the physical requirements, entered the Police Academy—I was the oldest rookie on the force for a time—became a patrol officer, and eventually made detective."

"And you wound up here."

Helen sighs. "And I wound up here. Not my decision really. It was either accept the job here or be fired."

"What in the world happened?"

She smiles. "Well, you know me, Tom. I can be a little stubborn."

"Oh, really? I never noticed."

"Ass," she mouths. "Yeah, there was a case involving someone rather prominent. I clashed with my superiors. OK, I disobeyed a direct order. Fortunately, the Chief in D.C. owed the Chief here a favor—Lowden saved his life, or something like that—so I was strongly encouraged to accept the job as Chief Detective with the Myerton Police Department, a jurisdiction which included a town of around 20,000 people and the surrounding county."

"So," I say, raising my glass, "we're both here against our will."

She raises her glass in turn. "Well, I've been here a while. I actually like it. I like being a big fish in a small pond. Who knows? Maybe I'll be chief someday."

"I can certainly see that."

"So, you know my story," she says, resting her chin on her hands. "Now I have questions, Tom."

I sigh. "Look, why I became a priest—"

"No, not that," she says, "though I am still curious about that. But I have a more pressing question."

I have a sick feeling in my stomach. I know what's coming.

"It's about the night of Joan's murder."

And, like that, the oxygen goes out of the room. "I've been waiting for you to call me down to the station," I say as calmly as I can.

"Do you have something you want to tell me?"

"You mean, like a confession, that Shepp was right, I did kill Joan in some kind of jealous fit?"

"Did you?"

"No, absolutely not."

Helen crosses her arms. "I really didn't think so, Tom. You learn something about the man you're going to marry. That reporter's full of it, trying to pin the murder on you."

"Thanks, I appreciate that."

"But, I also know when you're hiding something," she says. "Oh, I know you didn't mention the fight, I've known that since I read the file. But that led me to believe that there is something else about that night, something you didn't say at the time, something you've been hiding all these years. So I ask again. Do you have anything you want to tell me about the night of Joan's murder?"

I return Helen's penetrating gaze. There it is. A direct question. A chance to come clean. To tell the truth I've been hiding for fifteen years. To relieve myself of a burden I've carried since that night.

I look at her and she looks at me. I can hear my heart pounding in my head. Can she hear it, I wonder? Can she see my face getting red as a flush runs through my body?

Suddenly, strangely familiar music starts to play, causing me to jump.

Helen blinks. She bends down and digs through what has to be the largest tote bag I've ever seen while her phone continues to play a tune I can't quite place.

She finds it, and as she pulls it out, I recognize the song.

"'Eye of the Tiger'? Really?"

She puts her finger to her lips to quiet me.

"Yes," she says into the phone. She listens to the voice on the other end, then looks at me. "I see. When was it called in?" she asks as she pulls a pen and small notebook out of her enormous tote bag. "Uh-huh, OK. When's the ME going to get there?" She listens to the answer and makes a face. "I know it's a Sunday, what does that matter?" The person on the other end responds, causing Helen to sigh. "OK, start questioning people and keep the scene secure. Call the techs. I'm on my way." She puts her phone, pen, and notebook back in her tote bag.

"What is it?" I ask.

She looks at me and sighs. "Well, Tom, it's a damn good thing we've been together all afternoon. Otherwise, you'd be my prime suspect."

"Prime suspect for what?" I ask, surprised.

"The murder of Katherine Shepp. She was found dead in her hotel room about thirty minutes ago."

Eighteen

"I want to come with you," I say as she pays the check.

"No, absolutely not," she says.

"She should receive last rites."

"She's dead, Tom."

"Her body is dead. I'm concerned about her soul. I need to do this."

"You don't even know if she was Catholic."

"You don't know she wasn't."

We stare at each other. Helen looks like she was leaning towards continuing the argument.

"Look," I say finally, "I wasn't very kind to her the last time I saw her. It's the least I can do. Please, Helen?"

Finally, she shakes her head and holds up her hands.

"Fine. Your guilt wins. But," she points her finger at me, "stay out of the way. Don't touch anything."

"I have to touch the body, for the anointing. But only the forehead."

"OK, but nothing else," she says as we walk out of The Bistro.

***

I manage to keep up with Helen on the way to the hotel, in spite of the fact that she always drives like she's on the road course at Le Mans instead of the quiet streets of a small town nestled in the foothills of the Alleghenies. Somehow, we arrive at the same time.

"You still drive like a bat out of hell," I say.

"And you still drive like an old woman," Helen says.

"There is nothing wrong with my driving," I pout.

"God, Tom," she says, taking a deep breath and marching to the entrance, "just don't do that."

"Do what?" I ask, trotting to keep up with her. But she doesn't answer me.

The Myerton Inn is on the outskirts of town, and markets itself to the families of students at the college and businessmen visiting Myerton. The layout is all interior rooms with one main entrance through the lobby, but stairways allowing exits to the parking lot.

When we get to the scene of the crime—Shepp's room is on the third floor of the five-floor building, halfway between the elevators and the stairwell—there are police in the hallway holding back a few curious onlookers. What strikes me when I get to the hotel is the lack of news people. The murder must not have gotten out yet. But the word will spread, the news will get to Baltimore and D.C., and news crews from both cities will converge on Myerton like locusts.

Like they did after Joan's murder.

"Stay right here," Helen tells me before going under the crime scene tape into the room. "And get these people out of the hallway," she adds to the police officers. They move the onlookers down the hallway and a couple of them turn back to look at me, either wondering what a civilian is doing at a crime scene or, as is more likely, recognizing me from the news reports.

I realize I'm not wearing my clericals. I didn't have time to change at the Rectory, stopping only long enough to get my purple stole and anointing oil. No wonder people are looking at me.

I turn my attention to the hotel room. Helen's looking around the room, following the officer inside as she points at different things. The elevator doors open and a man and a woman in dark-blue jumpsuits carrying cases approach. I have seen enough police shows on television to suspect they are the crime scene technicians.

I move to allow them to pass, but Helen holds up her hand. "Father," she says, "you can come in. Watch your step."

The two technicians look at me puzzled. I dip under the tape and walk into the room.

Suddenly, I realize I can't go any further. The vision of Joan's dead body flashes before my eyes. Here, I am about to see another dead body, another woman violently taken from this life.

I couldn't help Joan then, but I can help Katherine Shepp now.

"Father," Helen says insistently. She looks both irritated and concerned. The irritation is obvious—she wants me to do what I need to do and get out of the way. I have no idea why she is concerned.

I walk slowly around the bed to where Katherine liess. Her body, except for her feet, are covered with a sheet. Near her lies a lamp. The lamp is all white ceramic, except for the base, which is red.

Blood. The red base sits in a blood-soaked carpet.

I squat down by her head and look up at Helen. "May I uncover her head, Detective?"

She nods. "Mike, can you please?" she says to the officer.

The officer bends over and uncovers her head.

I inhale sharply.

I knew there would be blood, but I'm not prepared for what I see.

Katherine Shepp had been a young attractive woman. Thanks to her murderer, she is no longer. They had smashed her head to a shapeless mass of blood, brain, and bone. A wave of nausea washes over me.

I turned my head to look in her eyes. People think it's like in the old movies, where people die with their eyes closed. But no, if someone is awake when they die, their eyes are open. If they die suddenly, violently, you can read their last thoughts in their eyes.

When Joan died, her eyes expressed love and sadness. Katherine's eyes had something different. Very different.

Surprise.

"She didn't see it coming," I mumble to myself. I look at the mass that had been her head. "So violent. More than one hit. Who could you have made that angry?"

I pulled the vial of oil out of my pocket. Quietly saying the rite, I make a small sign of the cross on her forehead, being careful to disturb the body as little as possible.

My work done, I stand up and say to Helen, "Thank you." She nods and motions to the two crime scene techs. They dip under the tape and come into the room. Opening their cases, they get to work.

Helen and I move out of their way. "What do you think?" I ask.

"Too early," she replies.

"I'd think it was obvious. This is somehow related to her story about Joan's murder."

"We don't know that. It could be a robbery gone bad. There's nothing—"

"Helen" I interrupt, "you don't believe that, do you?"

She pauses and looks down at the lifeless reporter. "No, Tom, I don't. She was killed because of what she was doing. And because you were with me, it was someone other than you."

"Joan's killer."

"What? The man who killed Joan? Tom, I know you think he's in town—"

"I don't think," I interrupt. "I know."

"Because of your wedding ring mysteriously appearing at the church?"

"Not just that," I blurt out. Helen starts.

I freeze. I have said too much.

"What else Tom?" she asks quietly.

I shake my head. "I—"

There is a commotion at the door. "I'm telling you I need to get in there now!" I recognize the man arguing with the officer standing guard as the cameraman. He catches sight of me. "You!" he screams and points at me. "You did this. Arrest him!"

Helen walks towards him. "Calm down, sir," she says as she shows him her badge. "Father Greer is here as a priest. Now who are you?"

He stops. "I'm Pete. Peter Rawls. Her cameraman."

"Where have you been?"

"To Baltimore to get another camera." Rawls glares at me. "You'll be getting the bill."

"Baltimore? You've been all the way to Baltimore and back since the incident at Saint Clare's? You made good time." There is more than a hint of sarcasm in Helen's voice. Baltimore is at least a two-and-a-half hour drive.

"Traffic wasn't bad," he says. "I have a bit of a lead foot."

"So when did you last see her?"

"I left about 12:30 p.m. Then she called just before I got to Baltimore."

"Why did she call you?" Helen asks.

"She told me I had to come right back once I got the camera," Rawls says. "I had planned on staying at home overnight and driving back tomorrow. But she said I needed to be back that night."

"Did she tell you why?"

"No. She just wanted me back here, no explanation. My wife wasn't happy when I told her. But that was Katherine. She expected to get what she wanted, and she usually did."

"What time did you get the call?"

He pulls out his phone. "She called me at 2 p.m."

Helen thanks him and tells another officer to take him to get a formal statement. As Rawls is leaving, he looks at the desk. "Wait," he says, rushing toward it before the officer can stop him. "Where's her laptop, her research? All the files?" He looks up. "It was all right here this morning." He looks at me. "What did you do with it?"

Helen places a hand on his chest. "What exactly is gone?" she asks.

Rawls looks at Helen. "All the background research and documents about this story. It's all gone."

Nineteen

After one of the officers takes Rawls to get his statement, I ask Helen, "Do you believe him?"

"It's easy enough to check, but if he's telling the truth, we know when she was killed."

"What do you mean?"

She looks at her notebook. "There was an anonymous 911 call about a dead woman in a hotel room about 4:00 p.m." Helen looks up. "He says he spoke to her around 2:00 p.m. Which means she was murdered sometime between 2:00 p.m. and 4:00 p.m."

"But we only have his word about the call," I point out.

"As I say, easy enough to check." Helen looks at the evidence technician. "Let me see her cell phone."

The technician looks up. She had been photographing the murder weapon. "Cell phone, boss?"

"Yes, her cell phone."

"I didn't bag a cell phone," she answers. "Danny?"

A young blond man pokes his head out of the bathroom. "Yeah?"

"Did you bag a cell phone?"

He shakes his head. "No, not me. Don't think I've seen one."

The other technician looks at Helen. "Sorry, boss, we didn't find a cell phone."

Helen shakes her head and runs her fingers through her hair. "Well, that's great. Whoever killed her took her phone."

"Must be something on there the murderer didn't want us to see," I say.

"You think, Father Brown?" Helen snaps. Then she sighs. "Sorry, Tom. "

I smile. "You still get sarcastic when you're stressed."

She doesn't reply but instead pulls out her phone and places a call. "Gladys, find a judge. We're going to need a warrant to pull cell phone records. Yeah, I'll get the information to you. Thanks." She hangs up and says to me, "It won't be as quick, but we'll find out who she spoke to in the last hours before she was murdered."

I look at the desk, which is empty. "The cameraman says someone has taken her laptop and all her research," I say. "She must have found something the killer didn't want revealed."

"A secret?" Helen says.

I turn to look at her.

"You said something right before Rawls got here," Helen continues. "Something about your ring not being the only thing that makes you think Joan's murderer is in town. What was it?"

I hesitate. What can I say?

"Tom!"

I jump.

"Tell me!"

"All I can tell you is that I know he's in town because I've talked to him," I say quietly.

Helen looks astonished. "What?"

"Yes, he's spoken to me."

"And when were you planning on telling me this?"

"I wasn't."

She goes from astonished to angry. "And why not?"

"Because he came to me in confession," I say. "I can't tell you what he said because it's protected by the seal of confession."

"The seal—Tom, you know you're protecting a murderer. Your wife's murderer. Maybe Shepp's."

"I know," I whisper. "But I can't tell you anything."

She glares at me. Like she used to right before—

"Officer Scott," she calls to the young man guarding the door. "Take Father Greer down to the station."

"What are you doing," I ask, astonished.

"Do you want me to arrest the Father?" the young officer asks, a wary look on his face.

Helen says nothing, but she looks like she's considering it.

"No," she says finally, "just do what I say and put him in an interview room. Keep him there until I get there."

I stammer, "Helen—Detective Parr, I—"

"Don't," she snaps, holding up a finger. "Not a word. Not one little word. You've brought this on yourself, Tom."

***

The officer drives me to the police station and takes me to an interrogation room, with one metal table and two chairs. One wall has a window that looks like a mirror but I know it has to be a two-way mirror.

They haven't taken my watch or my Rosary, I suppose because I'm not being charged. I begin to pray for Katherine Shepp's soul.

Then I pray for the soul of her killer.

Then I pray for Joan's soul.

I don't pray for Joan's killer. I never have, though I know I should. As people so often say to me in confession, and as I have said to my own confessor, I'm working on it.

After several hours, the door opens. Helen walks in, looking perturbed, and stands in front of me with her hands on her hips. She doesn't speak for several minutes but just stands there, looking at me.

Finally, she says, "OK, Tom, you can go."

I look at her. "You mean, that's it? No questions? No interrogation? You've kept me here for hours, Helen!"

"I know."

I wave my hand around the room. "So all of this—"

"Yeah, sorry."

"Sorry? Sorry!" I stop. "Is there anyone behind there," I say pointing to the glass.

"No, it's just us."

"You have me dragged down here for no reason. I've been sitting in this room for hours with no explanation. And you're sorry?"

"Listen," she says, slamming the table with her palm. "I'm doing my job!"

"How is any of this doing your job?"

"You are a witness—a witness who's proven not to be entirely honest."

To my questioning look, she says, "Oh, don't give me that. One, I know there's something you're not telling me about the night Joan was murdered.

Two, you didn't tell me her murderer contacted you in the confessional—wait," she says. "Yesterday wasn't the first time, was it Tom?"

I look at her.

"No, no, it wasn't, was it?" she continued. "The ring. Oh, you found it in the church all right. In the confessional. Am I right?"

"I don't know if it was the same person," I say. "They never spoke."

She put her hands on her hips. "You priests and your damn seal of confession."

"Now wait just a minute," I say.

"No, Tom, you wait just a minute," she points at me. "It's a great phrase, nice and high sounding, but what it really means is you can shield evil people from people like me."

She crosses her arms. "Do you know why John was so non-religious when I met him? Oh, he wasn't always that way. In fact, he was raised a Catholic. He was an altar boy. And you know what? His priest molested him."

I close my eyes. "Oh, my God!"

"Yeah, that's right," she says. "It went on for months before John finally had the courage to tell someone. Then, the priest was just quietly moved. But you know the real kicker, Father Greer? One of the places John was molested by the old bastard was in the confessional."

I shake my head. "That is awful, truly horrific. But it doesn't change the fact that the seal of confession is sacred, anymore than someone being molested in a library means that books should be censored. The seal keeps the sacrament pure. Penitents need to know they can receive absolution without their sins being advertised."

"What about the victims?"

"It gives the priest the chance to pray for them."

"Well, prayers didn't do John much good," she says bitterly.

"You don't know that," I say.

Helen goes to the door and yanks it open. "You're free to go, Father," she says to me as she goes out, slamming the door behind her, leaving me alone in the stark gray room.

***

It is well past two in the morning before I get back to the Rectory. I don't sleep well, but doze fitfully as the events of the past forty-eight hours play in my head. One thought goes through my mind over and over again, like a song on repeat.

That's two people whose blood is on your hands.

I can only hope that the morning will see things begin to turn for the better.

Twenty

After 8 a.m. Mass, I go back to the Rectory. Glenda is there waiting for me with a newspaper in her hand. I recognize it as the daily out of Baltimore. She shoves it in front of me, pointing with her bony finger at a headline below the fold.

INVESTIGATIVE REPORTER FOUND MURDERED IN HOTEL ROOM.

I grab it out of her hand and begin reading it as I walk into the office and sit down at the desk.

Katherine Shepp, investigative reporter for Baltimore's WQDJ, was found dead in her hotel room outside Myerton. Police say the evidence points to murder.

Shepp, 28, was in Myerton working on a story concerning the unsolved murder of Joan Greer fifteen years ago. In a recent story, she confronted Greer's then-husband, Thomas Greer, over evidence that indicated his complicity in her murder. Internal department sources indicate that Thomas Greer, now Father Greer of Saint Clare's Catholic Church in Myerton, was questioned and remains a person of interest.

According to reports, Father Greer had a confrontation with Ms. Shepp after services at Saint Clare's in the hours before her body was found. A parishioner who witnessed the confrontation says Greer was angered that Shepp and her cameraman were stopping parishioners on their way out of the church and attempting to interview them about Shepp's allegations. Greer, the parishioner said, grabbed the camera out of the cameraman's hand and threw it on the ground, then yelled at them to get off church property. WQDJ apparently has video of the confrontation. A spokesman for the network says local police were notified.

A spokesman for the Archdiocese had no comment.

Glenda sticks her head in my office. "The Archbishop called while you were in Mass. He wants to see you. Today."

"You mean he wants me to return his call."

"No," she replies. "He wants you to come to the Residence to meet with him." She pauses. "He said you should plan on staying." She turns and leaves me staring at the empty doorway.

I pick up the phone and call the Residence.

"Yes, Father Tom," Father Wayne, Archbishop Knowland's assistant, says gruffly when he answers the phone. "The Archbishop was expecting your call."

"Good, well—"

"—and he told me to let you know he'll be happy to talk to you when you arrive this afternoon. He'll expect you at 1 p.m."

"But I have sick calls to—"

"He also told me to let you know that he's already assigned a priest to handle your duties at Saint Clare's. He'll be arriving later this morning." With that, he hangs up, leaving me holding the receiver.

Glenda comes back to the office. "So, you'll be leaving?"

I look at her, then get up and walk past her out of the office without saying a word.

"Don't forget to leave your keys," she says as I stomp up the stairs.

Going to my room, I sit on the bed and look around.

For somewhere I didn't want to be in the first place, St. Clare's has become somewhere I don't want to leave.

Not yet.

Not like this.

I guess the Archbishop saw the headline and decided things had gone too far. I am being taken away from Myerton for the greater good of the Church.

I can see that.

I still don't like it.

My phone rings. It's Helen. Reluctantly, I answer.

"Tom," she says.

"Helen."

There is a pause. "Listen, Tom, I'm—well, that is,—look, I was out of line. I just wanted to say I'm sorry."

"It's OK. Look, I understand your feelings, but it doesn't change anything. We'll just have to disagree on this."

"And I want you to know that I understand the seal of confession," she says. "I really do. As a Catholic, I even appreciate it. But as a cop, it's just difficult for me to get my mind around. So, really, we don't disagree. We just have a different point of view."

"Yeah, I guess we do," I muse. "My job as a priest is to show a penitent God's mercy—Saint Maria Faustina actually called the confessional the great tribunal of God's mercy. Your job as a cop is to see that justice is done for the victims of crimes."

"So, Tom," she says, a trace of amusement in her voice, "are we on opposite sides?"

"Oh, hardly," I laugh. "Mercy and justice are two sides of the same coin. You can't really have one without the other. The Cross shows that."

We're silent for a few moments, then slowly Helen says, "How about I buy you breakfast? You know, to make up for yesterday."

A big part of me wants to say yes, to take what might be my last opportunity to spend some time with her.

But another part of me knows, especially after yesterday, that more time with Helen Mason Parr would not be good for me.

I take a deep breath and say, "Sorry, I can't. You caught me right before I started packing."

"Packing?" she asks with—what is that, panic?—in her voice. "Are—ahem—are you taking a trip?"

"Yes, a one-way one apparently. The Archbishop saw the paper."

She says nothing for a moment. "So you're being punished?"

"I guess you could put it that way, yes."

"Do you want to go? I mean, do you want to leave?"

"No, not really."

Helen doesn't say anything for a minute. "I'll call you back," she says, then hangs up.

I look at my phone, shake my head, get my suitcase out and begin to pack. I open the top drawer of the dresser and am clearing out my socks and underwear when my cell phone rings. Helen is calling me back.

"OK, done," she says.

"What's done?"

Just then my call waiting beeps. I check the number.

"Why is the Archbishop calling me?"

"Call me back," she says and hangs up.

I answer the call. "Hello?"

"Father Greer," Archbishop Knowland says in a grave voice.

"Your Eminence, I am just packing."

"Yes, well, about that. I just got a call from a Detective Parr."

My eyebrows go up. "Oh?"

"Yes. She's very—forceful."

I smile. "I've noticed that about her."

"She made it clear that you cannot leave Myerton while the investigation is ongoing," the Archbishop continues. "Detective Parr says because you are a person of interest, you need to stay in town."

"I see," I respond. "So I'm staying at Saint Clare's?"

"No, you're not. I can't make you leave Myerton, but I can remove you from Saint Clare's. Consider yourself on paid leave. I will see you back here when the investigation is over. Until then," he sighs, "try not to wind up in the newspaper again, Tom. Please?"

"I'll try, Your Eminence. And thank you."

"Hmm," he says and hangs up.

I dial Helen back.

"You're welcome," she says when she answers.

"I'm not sure if I should thank you or not," I reply.

"Hey, you told me you didn't want to leave. So, you can't leave." She pauses. "You're welcome."

I sigh. "OK, thank you, I guess. I still need to pack, make room for the new priest."

"Where are you going to stay?"

"Probably with Anna. She has room."

"Do you think she'd have a photograph of Joan's first husband?"

It stings to hear that phrase 'first husband.' "Why?"

"Well, if he's in town, it would be nice to know what he looks like, or looked like twenty years ago. So do you think she has a photo?"

"I doubt it," I say.

"Could she give a description to our sketch artist?"

"She told me she'd only seen him once or twice and wasn't sure she'd recognize him if he was standing right in front of her." I pause. "I can look in Joan's things at her studio. I'll try to get over there today."

"Sounds good. Keep me posted."

Helen hangs up. I call Anna and bring her up to speed.

"Of course you can stay here, Tom," she says. "I'll fix up the guest room."

"Don't go to any trouble."

"Oh, don't worry. It's no trouble. I've got a list of things that need to be done around here that you can help me with."

I finish packing my things and toss the keys on the desk in the office.

As I leave, I pass Glenda's nephew working in one of the beds. He looks up at me. I smile and nod but he does nothing, says nothing, just goes back to work.

I get in my car and sit, looking at Saint Clare's.

***

Later that afternoon, I am in the middle of cleaning out Anna's garden shed when my phone rings. It's Helen, so I say as soon as I answer, "No, I haven't had time to look through Joan's things."

"That's not why I'm calling," she says. "I've been looking into Randy Earl."

"What have you found?"

I hear paper rustling in the background. "Turns out Randy Earl was quite well known in Baltimore twenty years ago, at least among police and mental health professionals. Several arrests for disturbing the peace, assaults, several psych holds. And he was hospitalized for several weeks at a time over the course of several years." She hesitates. "He was definitely in the same hospital Joan was at the same time she was, like Anna told you. That's where they met."

"Where is he now?"

"No idea. Fifteen years ago, he just dropped off the face of the earth."

"Fifteen years ago?"

"Yeah," she says. "Not long after Joan's murder."

"What about family?"

"Mother and father are both dead. No other family listed, either in Maryland or anywhere else."

"What do you think happened?"

"Who knows? He may have left the state. He could be living on the streets and somehow managed to keep out of trouble, though I find that highly doubtful."

"But we know he's in town," I say. "We have to find him."

"We? I didn't realize the department had given me a partner."

"Hey, you called me Father Brown. Besides, I don't have anything else to do right now. Might as well make myself useful."

"Wasn't he kind of a pain?"

"I will do my best not to interfere."

She pauses before saying, "OK, but here's the deal. You don't do anything on your own. You can help, but you can only do what I tell you to. You stay in the background. If I'm interviewing someone and you're there, you don't say anything. Understand?"

"I understand. Where shall we start?"

"Right now, we've got two cases that overlap somehow—Shepp's murder and your wife's murder. There has to be a common factor."

"The same killer."

"Maybe. Or another connection. I think if we find the connection, we'll find either Shepp's or Joan's killer. Maybe both."

"OK, so what do we do?"

Helen pauses. "I've got a lot of evidence from Shepp's murder to go through. We're still waiting for the surveillance footage, but that should come in today hopefully."

Today. Something clicks. "What's the date?" I ask.

"The fifteenth. Why?"

October 15.

"I've gotta go," I say quickly.

"Tom, what—" but I cut Helen off before she can finish.

It's the anniversary of Joan's murder. I have almost forgotten.

There is someone else in Myerton who knows what day it is, and that's what I am counting on.

Twenty-One

The cemetery is just outside Myerton, about twenty minutes from Anna's house. I haven't been here since the day I left. But I know exactly where I'm going.

I park my car not far from Joan's grave. Up a slight rise, underneath the broad branches of a tall oak tree covered in golds, reds, browns, and oranges, is the simple and tasteful white marble headstone. Anna did a good job picking it out. I had let Joan stay buried under the tree, her final resting place unmarked, for two months after her funeral. I couldn't bear to think about it. So her mom had commissioned the stone.

I saw it for the first time when I left.

I walk up to her along the path I'd taken in leaving her fifteen years earlier. Fallen leaves crunch underneath my feet. I can see the top of the hill. I see the tree and the white headstone gleaming in the fall sun.

I look around, hoping I'll see someone by her grave, someone holding a bunch of peppermint carnations, and hoping that person will turn out to be Randy Earl.

But no one is there.

I reach the top of the hill and stand, staring at the headstone, where I had stood years earlier when I said good-bye. I stroke the marble lightly, my finger lingering on the spot where I had placed my wedding ring.

"Hi," I say. It's odd. I pray for her soul and ask for her prayers. But now words fail me.

She isn't really here, I know. Just a dead, lifeless body, more dust than anything else. Her soul is alive. I feel her presence often and reap the benefits of her prayers for me. Still, I feel guilty for not visiting her grave, like I have abandoned her.

"I know you're not here, Joan," I say to the stone. "But I'm sorry I haven't visited." I pause. "It's hard. It's so hard." I feel a lump in my throat as a tear comes to my eye. "I'm so sorry." I pull out a handkerchief and wipe my eyes.

"You OK, Father?"

I turn. The groundskeeper has come up behind me. I hadn't noticed him working.

"Yes, yes, I'm fine."

He points at the grave. "You knew Ms. Greer?"

I look. "Yes, I knew Joan. A long time ago."

He nods. "Yes. Very sad story. She was murdered, you know, died in her husband's arms." He leans on his rake. "The guy was never caught." He shakes his head. "Why would someone do something like that, Father? Do you know?"

I shake my head. "No," I whisper. "I don't."

He shrugs. "Some people are just evil, I guess. Anyway, she must have been a special young woman."

"She was. Very special."

"A woman comes all the time, I guess it's her mom. She comes, talks to her for a few minutes."

I nod. Anna.

"And her husband, once a month, like clockwork," he says as he resumes his raking.

"Her husband?" I grab his arm, a little too firmly. Startled, he looks at me.

"Yeah, Father," he says, looking at my hand on his arm, then at me. Embarrassed, I let him go.

"Her husband visits her? Regularly?"

He nods. "Yeah. Every month. Like clockwork. Brings those puffy flowers, the white ones with the red stripes."

Peppermint carnations.

"What does he look like?" The groundskeeper looks at me. "I knew Joan when we were younger," I say quickly. "I'd like to meet the man she married."

"Oh, well," the groundskeeper shrugged. "He's a big guy, taller than you, dark hair. About your age. A veteran."

"How do you know he's a veteran?"

"Just carries himself like ex-military. Oh, and the cane."

I look at him. "He uses a cane?"

"Yeah, looks like he may have—"

I don't hear the rest, instead I run towards my car. About halfway I stop and turn. "Has he been here today?" I call.

The groundskeeper looks up from his raking. "Today? No, he hasn't. You know, that's odd. What's the date? The fifteenth? Huh, he usually comes in on the fifteenth of the month. Like clockwork."

I thank him and hurry to my car.

I sit behind the wheel and think about calling Helen. I pull out my phone, then put it back in my pocket.

No, I have to check this out myself.

I pull out of the parking spot and turn the car in the direction of Chloe and John Archman's house.

***

I hesitate before ringing the doorbell. The lights are on, and John's car is in the driveway, so I know at least he's home. I hope that Chloe isn't. I need to talk to John, but I'm not sure what I would say or if Chloe knows what I suspect. I'm not entirely sure myself what I suspect.

I steel myself and ring the doorbell. After a minute, the door opens.

It's Chloe, and my courage sags.

She seems both surprised and pleased to see me. "Tom, hi. What are you doing here?"

"Can I come in, please, Chloe?"

"Of course," she says as she stands aside to let me in. I thank her and walk into the hallway. She shows me into their living room.

Sitting down, I ask, "Is John here? I really came to see him."

"He's here, but he's not doing too well," Chloe says. She sits in an armchair opposite me.

"I'm sorry. Has anything happened?"

"He won't tell me, but something had to have to trigger something this bad. It started a couple of days ago, and if it's anything like his other episodes, he'll be fine in a couple of more days. Trust me, Tom, I've been through this enough times. Now," she says sitting back, "what did you come over for?"

I hesitate. "I want to ask John about something." I pause.

"Well?" She asks. "What is it?"

"I just want to ask him why he visits Joan's grave every month on the anniversary of her murder."

The smile disappears as the warmth in her eyes cools. Her brow narrows. "What?" she whispers.

I tell her what the groundskeeper told me and give her the description of the man. "It's John, isn't it, Chloe?"

She stands. "I need a drink, you want one?" Before I can answer, she walks into the kitchen and returns with two glasses of red wine. "Here," she says, handing me a glass. "I don't keep anything stronger in the house, on account of John."

I take the glass as Chloe sits back down and immediately takes a big swig of her wine. She sits the glass on the table and folds her arms.

"Well?" She stares at me. "What do you want to know?"

I think, *What do I want to know? Why do I want to know it? Where to begin?*

"It all began," Chloe starts, reading my thoughts, "when John signed up for one of Joan's classes at Myer."

"I had forgotten that," I say.

"It was his therapist's idea, a way of reprogramming his brain after his injuries. She suggested that he do something creative to develop those parts of his brain he never really used before. So he decided on painting." Chloe takes another drink. "At the time, it seemed like a good idea. Turned out he had some natural talent, no idea where it came from. He took a couple of extension classes, then he wanted something more intensive, he said. So he signed up at Myer. For Joan's class."

"Makes sense, we were friends."

"That's what I thought," she says. A small laugh erupts from her. "If I had only known."

"Now, Chloe, you told me that Joan never cheated on me."

"Oh, Tom," she says, smiling. "No, Joan was always faithful to you. That's not what I'm talking about."

I sit with this for a minute, turning her words over in my mind, slowly realizing what she's saying.

"Was John Joan's stalker?" I ask.

Chloe sighs. "Why does it matter, after all this time, why? Why can't you just leave things alone?"

"Just tell me, please!" I snap. "I'm tired of secrets, tired of people not telling me things. I just want to know the truth!"

"OK, OK." She takes another sip of wine. "It was partially my fault, I guess, looking back. I wasn't the most understanding wife after he got back from Iraq. I was just glad he was still alive. After he was wounded, I just wanted to forget everything that happened. I couldn't understand why he didn't just get on with his life. Things were strained between us. He needed patience and understanding, compassion. I was short of all three, busy carrying the burden of the kids while he healed."

She drinks some more of her wine, then goes on. "He found it with Joan. It started innocently enough apparently, coffee together after her class. But they began to see more of each other, talk for a long time. They'd meet for lunch. John would go to her studio to watch her work. She'd give him advice and pointers with his work. They became very close."

The silence is heavy between us as we look at each other for a while. My wine sits untouched, while Chloe drinks the rest of hers. I am a mix of anger and jealousy and hurt. Joan had let John into her studio, a world she never told me about, a world I never knew existed. And I can't understand why.

"But nothing physical happened between them?"

Chloe shakes her head. "No. Joan swore to me it never went that far."

"She told you about it?"

"Oh, yes, she told me everything after she realized what was happening."

"John was becoming obsessed with her," I say.

"Yeah, he was. Joan told me he was becoming intense, leaving notes at her office in the art department, sending flowers, calling and texting her. She told him firmly to stop, that she only had feelings of friendship with him, that she would never betray you or me."

"He sent the emails and the note, didn't he? You've known this whole time." I am angry.

"Yes, I've known!" she cries. "And I lied when you asked me. I just wanted to forget about it, and I didn't want you to be hurt, knowing it was your best friend."

"Best friend," I spit. "I'm wondering if anyone is my friend in this town. You, John, Anna, all keeping Joan's secrets after all these years. Especially when the secrets may have kept her murderer from being caught."

"I told you that John had nothing to do with her murder."

"But I saw." Chloe and I stand up and turn toward the hallway. John, haggard and disheveled, stands there leaning against the wall.

"I saw," he repeats.

"John," Chloe says, walking towards him. "Go back and rest,"

"I saw what happened that night," he says looking at her. He sways, leaning harder on his cane. "Joan. I'm sorry, Chloe. I loved her."

She nods and pats his shoulder. "I know you did. We all did."

"I did," John repeats. He looks at me. "I loved her, my friend. I know you did, too. But I couldn't believe what I saw."

I stiffen. "What?"

He points at me. "I saw, Tom. I was there. No one saw me. But I was there. I saw the whole thing. I saw. I saw." John sways and pitches forward, falling to the floor in a heap, not moving.

Chloe screams as I rush to John, dropping to my knees by him. "John! John!" I call as I shake him by the shoulders. I lean over to listen.

"He's not breathing," I say. "I can't find a pulse. Chloe, call 911!" I say as I start CPR.

"John! John! What did you do!" Chloe cries.

"Call 911, now!" I order firmly. While I do compressions, I pray for John, that the ambulance will get here before it is too late, and that I'll be able to keep up CPR until they get here.

"They're on the way," Chloe says. "They asked what he took."

"Go see if you can find out," I say. "Come on, John, Come on. Hang in there buddy."

I can feel my back and arms getting stiff. Finally, after what seems like hours, I hear a banging on the door.

"Paramedics," a voice calls.

"Get in here!" I yell, still pumping. I hear the door open and a second later, feel a strong hand on my arm.

"Sir, I'll take over," says the paramedic. He takes over CPR while the other paramedic puts the oxygen mask on John.

"What happened?" the second paramedic asks.

I shake my head. "He was talking, then he just collapsed."

"Is he taking anything?"

"I don't—"

"Here," I hear Chloe say. "He took these. It was a full bottle."

The paramedic takes the bottle and says, "Sleeping pills, just filled yesterday."

Both move quickly. One places heart leads on John's chest and when the screen shows a flatline, the other charges the defibrillator and shocks him, John's body convulsing as the voltage shoots through him. They look at the screen. What had been a flat line now has peaks and valleys, a rhythmic beeping keeping time with the line.

"He's back," one paramedic says.

"He's breathing on his own," says the other. "But his blood pressure is low."

"Let's get him on the bus."

"Can I come with him?" Chloe asks, her worry on full display.

"You can ride with us," one paramedic says.

"I'll follow you and meet you there," I say.

They get him on the stretcher, roll him out of the house, and lift John into the ambulance. The paramedic riding in the back helps Chloe inside; the driver closes the doors and runs around to the front. Lights flashing and sirens blaring, the ambulance pulls away from the curb and races down the street.

I hurry to my car, my mind full of questions. What has driven John to try to take his own life? It wasn't an accidental overdose, it wasn't an overdose of pain meds. He deliberately swallowed a bottle full of sleeping spills. He meant to die. But why now?

Why hadn't Joan told me about John? Why hadn't John told me about things? And what about what John said? He was there that night? He saw what happened? He saw what really happened? What am I going to do about that?

I thought the secret of that night was known only to me and Joan's killer. But no. There is another person who knows.

As I drive, I struggle with what to do next. But there is only one thing I can do.

I am within sight of the hospital when I pull the car over and pick up my phone.

"I was just about to call you," Helen says when she answers.

"We need to talk," I say.

"Yes, we do," she says. "We're finally getting the surveillance footage from the hotel. The camera in the hallway outside Shepp's room wasn't working properly, so the video's going to have to be cleaned up before we can see anything."

"Oh," I say. "What I want to talk to you—"

"But the cameras in the parking lot got something."

I stop. "What did you find?"

"Someone coming out the stairwell exit into the parking lot. It's too far away to see who, but the time is close to the time of the anonymous call to 911. They got in a sedan and left. The camera caught the licence plate. The car is registered to a John Archman."

Twenty-Two

Helen arrives at the emergency waiting room of Myerton General about half an hour later. Chloe is with John in an exam room.

"Any word?" she asks as she takes the seat next to me.

I shake my head. "He was alive and breathing when they got here, but I don't know anything else."

"So tell me what happened again? You didn't get into too much detail on the phone."

So I tell her about John coming out in the hallway collapsing, Chloe finding the empty pill bottle. I do not tell her what John had said.

"Good thing you were over there," she says. "Why were you there?"

"They're old friends of mine, they were in our wedding. John's been having problems since coming home from Iraq. I was checking on him." All of this was true. But I don't tell her what I learned about John and Joan.

I will, just not now.

Helen looks at me. "You know you're a bad liar, Tom, right?"

I feel my face flush but I smile. "What do you mean?"

She points her finger at me. "You know exactly what I mean. You've been lying to me about things. Or at least you haven't been completely honest. And you're lying now. This isn't going to work, Tom, unless you let me know what's going on. Now tell me the truth. All of it."

I hold her stare for a moment. Then I slump in my seat. There is really no sense going on.

"OK, I'll—"

Just then the doors of the Emergency Room slide open and Chloe walks through. We stand up as she approaches me.

"How's John?" I ask.

"Better," she says. "He's stable. They pumped his stomach. Fortunately, not all the pills had dissolved."

"Is he conscious?" Helen asks.

Chloe looks at her, the irritation evident on her face. "Who are you?"

Helen takes out her identification. Chloe looks at it, then me. "Why did you call the police?" she asks me. "Trying to commit suicide isn't a crime."

174

"Technically, it still is in this state," Helen says.

"That's not why she's here, Chloe. It's about something else."

"Oh, what is it?"

I turn to Helen. "Maybe this isn't the best time, Detective."

"I'm sorry, Mrs. Archman," Helen says, "but this is important. Do you know where your husband was Sunday afternoon?"

"What, this past Sunday afternoon? I don't know," Chloe answers.

"You don't know where he was?"

"What, no, of course not. I know where he was."

"Was he at home?"

"No, not in the afternoon. After lunch, he said he needed to go to the hardware store, said he needed some leaf bags, and he wanted to look at snow blowers."

"Did you go with him?"

"No, I had to stay home with the kids."

"So," Helen says, "you don't know if he went to the hardware store."

"Actually, I do know that. He brought the bags back with him."

"Did he stop anywhere else?"

"I don't think so. What's all this about, Tom?"

"Just answer the questions, Chloe."

Helen continues, "About what time did he get back?"

"I think it was around 5 p.m., maybe 5:30 p.m."

Helen and I look at each other.

"Will someone please tell me what this is all about?" Irritation has been replaced with confusion and worry in Chloe's voice. She is not holding up well.

"Maybe you can ask more questions later," I say to Helen.

She shoots me a warning glance. She has no intention of waiting. "I know this is a very distressing time for you," she says to Chloe, "but I wouldn't ask these questions if they weren't important."

Chloe inhales and nods. "Make it quick, please, I'd like to get back to my husband."

"Just a couple more questions, Mrs. Archman. When he got back, did he seem distressed or unusual in any way?"

Chloe gets a serious expression on her face. "Now that you mention it," she says, "he did act like something was wrong. I asked him if he was OK, but he told me he was fine. He suffers from depression, anxiety, and PTSD, so I'd seen him bad off before. But this seemed different somehow."

"Different how?"

"Like something had rattled him," she explains. "Something had upset him. When he couldn't get out of bed the next day, I knew he was having one of his episodes."

"But he didn't tell you anything."

"That was not unusual, Detective. John keeps his struggles to himself, pretty much. Not for my lack of trying. Whatever it was, you'll have to ask him when he wakes up." She looks back towards the emergency room entrance. "If he wakes up."

Helen nods. "One last question, Mrs. Archman. After he got home, what did he do?"

"What did he do?" Chloe repeats. She thinks for a moment, then answers, "Oh, he took a shower."

"He took a shower?" I say.

Chloe nodded. "Yes, he went straight to our bedroom and took a shower. About twenty minutes later, he comes back in a t-shirt and sweatpants."

"What was he wearing when he came home?" Helen asks.

Chloe shrugged. "Khakis and a green polo, I think."

"Where are those clothes now?"

"Why—"

"Just answer her, Chloe," I say, gently placing my hand on her shoulder.

"Those clothes?," she repeats. "In the dirty clothes hamper, I guess." She pauses. "Wait, that's odd."

"What is?" Helen asks.

"I was doing laundry this morning. I'm almost certain that those weren't in there."

Helen and I look at each other, then at Chloe.

"What about the leaf bags?" I ask.

"The leaf bags? I guess they're in the garage. He went there before he came into the house." Chloe looks at us. "Now will one of you please tell me why all these questions?"

Indicating an empty area of the waiting room, I say, "Why don't we sit down over there?"

***

It is the first time I have ever told someone that a loved one is a suspect in a murder case.

I am not entirely prepared for the range of emotions Chloe exhibits: denial, anger, fear, rage, despair—she shows all of them in a matter of moments. She is adamant that John couldn't have had anything to do with Shepp's murder. I don't believe it either, but the evidence shows he had been at the hotel around the time of the murder. Chloe cannot give us a reason why he would be there. I can only think of one, but I can't figure out why John would have killed Shepp.

After Chloe goes back to check on John, I begin to tell Helen what I had started to tell her in the waiting room, about John and his obsession with Joan. About his monthly visits to Joan's grave. About how Chloe told me John sent the emails. I leave out what John says about witnessing Joan's murder.

"Archman was stalking your wife?" Helen says to me as we walk to our cars. Chloe has agreed to let Helen and me search the house. The Archman kids are staying with friends. "That gives him motive."

"I don't see—"

"Shepp was investigating Joan's murder. It's the overlap we keep coming back to."

"Are you thinking now that John had something to do with Joan's murder? Impossible."

Helen stops and looks at me. "I've got a lot of experience with this sort of thing, Tom. One thing I've learned is that when it comes to murder, nothing is impossible."

"But I was there, remember?" I say. "John was my best friend, my best man. I would have recognized him."

"Your own statement says it was dark and he may have been wearing a mask," Helen points out. "Isn't he about the same height as the person you described?"

"Well, yes, but—"

"For that matter, his wife's about the same height," Helen says as she continues walking.

"What, now you think Chloe killed Joan?"

"Jealousy is one of the seven deadly sins, Tom, you know that. She had motive."

I shake my head. "No, I was there. It wasn't her, and it wasn't John, either."

We are at Helen's car. Before opening the door, she turns to me. "I'd have a much easier time believing you if you were being honest with me."

I feel my face get warm. "I'm not sure what you mean."

She points towards the emergency room. "Before Chloe came in, you were going to tell me something. Something about the night of Joan's murder. Something you haven't said before in fifteen years. You kept it from the police that night, and you're keeping it from me now. You know, I can arrest you for hindering a police investigation. Is that what you want?"

"Of course not."

"Then tell me," she demands, but not in her cop voice. "What are you hiding?"

I look at her. She stares at me and then throws up her hands. "You know, never mind. Don't tell me now. Are you coming?"

I nod and turn to walk to my car.

"But this isn't over, Tom," I hear her call after me.

***

I let Helen and myself in using the key Chloe gave us. Things are as we had left them, the unfinished glasses of wine in the living room near where we had been sitting. Helen looks around, not picking anything up.

"If you find anything," she says, "don't touch it. Crime scene will have to photograph and bag it. Where is the bedroom?"

"Back this way, I would think." We walk down the hallway. The house is two stories, with the kids' rooms upstairs. The master bedroom is downstairs, a good-sized room, light and airy. Or it would have been if the blinds and curtains hadn't been drawn. With the sun having gone down an hour before, it is pitch black before Helen flicks on the light switch

The bed is unmade where John had been. An empty water glass and an ebook reader is on the bedside table along with a smartphone. The room is neat and tidy except for the bed.

"What are we looking for?" I whisper.

"His clothes for one," Helen answers in a normal voice. "Other than that, anything that might tie him to Shepp."

I look at the bedside table and pick up the phone. It is fingerprint and pin locked.

"What did I tell you about not touching anything?"

I turn to Helen and smile sheepishly.

"Sorry," I say, putting the phone back, as close as I can, to the same place I found it. She is looking through the drawers while I wander out of the bedroom and down the hall. I want to check the garage to see if the leaf bags are actually there.

The garage has a workbench, garden tools, a lawn mower, and some other yard equipment. It takes me a minute to spot the leaf bags. John had put them under the worktable so I have to bend down to pick them up.

Underneath the paper bags is a stack of neatly labeled file folders and a laptop. They have to be Shepp's.

I pick them up. There is a folder labeled, "Greer, Joan—Background." Another labeled "Greer, Thomas—post-murder." Inside, there is a printout of a page from the Archdiocese website, showing the new seminarians. Each face is young and eager. Except mine.

There are about a dozen folders in all, Shepp's research. The folders had been taken from Shepp's room.

By John.

I open a folder labeled "Myer College." It contains a print out from the Myer College registrar's office listing the students in Joan's class from the summer before her murder. For each student the list has their name, year in school, and email address. I scan the list until I find John's name. Then I find what I already know.

John was "artluver."

I hold the proof in my hands. Shepp had gotten this list from the college, somehow, and found out John had sent the emails.

And John had taken it from Shepp's hotel room.

I close my eyes and let the knowledge sink in.

"Well, I've called the crime scene—what do you have, Tom?" I turn to Helen. She looks exasperated with me.

"I know, but I had to pick them up to see what they were," I say, pointing to the stack of folders.

She looks at them. I hand her the printout and point to John's name. She looks at it and the stack of folders.

"Well, this, along with what I found, places Archman in Shepp's room."

"What did you find?"

She looks at me. "A green polo and a pair of khakis along with a pair of size ten walking shoes buried in the back of the closet. I didn't pick them up, but it looks like blood stains on the khakis. And if I was a betting woman, I'd say it's even money that those shoes match the bloody footprints we found." She pauses and looks at me. "Sorry, Tom, but it's not looking good for your friend."

Twenty-Three

I leave Helen at the Archman home to wait for the crime scene technicians. Once in my car, I call Chloe to find out how John is, but the call goes straight to voicemail. Either she has bad reception in the hospital or she is declining my calls. I don't blame her. I'd be mad at me, too, if I was in her position.

I drive back to Anna's and let myself in. Anna has already gone to bed, and it is after 11:00 p.m. I realize I haven't eaten since lunch, but in spite of that, I'm not hungry. Just tired, tired down to my bones, mentally exhausted from everything that has happened in the last few hours—it is just hours, isn't it? It seems like days. I get to my room, take my shoes off, and collapse on top of the covers.

I must fall right to sleep because I start dreaming. It is the same dream I always have, about the night of Joan's murder—at least, it is the only dream I ever remember. I usually don't remember my other dreams. But this one is different. In this one, I grab the killer and pull his mask off. John's face stares at me. The next thing I know, the mask is back on. I pull it off again. This time, it's Chloe. The mask goes back on again. I pull it off again. This time there is no face, only darkness. From the darkness I hear a voice, the same voice I heard from the confessional. "You should have died. I meant to kill you. It's your fault she's dead." In the dream, I feel the figure's hands grip my throat and squeeze. I can't breathe.

I wake up with a start and sit up. The clock says 12:30 a.m. I have been asleep for an hour.

I collapse back on the bed, not sure I'll be able to sleep and certain that I don't want to.

I lay in the darkness, staring up at the ceiling. I should never have come to Myerton. I should have pushed back against the Archbishop sending me. Nothing good has happened. I couldn't leave well enough alone. Now another person is dead and a friend is a suspect.

I feel trapped.

I need to get out.

I need to leave Myerton.

Twenty minutes later I am in my car, driving east out of town, towards the one place I might have peace.

***

Around 3:00 a.m., I turn off the main road just south of Emmitsburg. I take the narrow paved road deep into the woods of western Maryland, the way illuminated only by my headlights. There are no signs of habitation anywhere.

I finally see what I am looking for. Two stone pillars indicating a driveway, both topped with lights that burn low and orange in the night. I had not thought before I left Myerton that the gate might be closed, as is usual at night.

Tonight the gate is open, inviting me in.

I turn onto a dirt and gravel drive that is barely wide enough for the car. The trees are so close on both sides that if I meet another car coming the opposite direction, I'm not sure what to do. But I also know that possibility is remote. It is rare to see a car leave this place, for this is the kind of place that once you find it, you don't want to leave.

I left, somewhat against my will, but am now finding my way back.

The drive ends in a large open space dominated by a low stone building. It looks ancient, as if it has sprung from the mountain whole. It is old, about two hundred years, I suppose, but men had built it from the stones provided by the earth, men determined to build a sanctuary for God on this mountain where they could serve him through prayer, enriching their souls in the process.

I stop at a small building adjacent to the stone structure, one that is newer by about a hundred years. It is small, more of a cabin than a building, constructed of logs harvested from the forest surrounding the great stone piece. There is a single light burning in the window, a beacon that pierces the darkness, welcoming any visitor who needs comfort, solace, and peace.

I found all of those when I first saw the light, so many years ago. That is why I am there now.

I knock on the door. After a moment, I hear movement, a slow shuffling from inside as someone comes to the door. I also see an orange glow moving through the window. The door opens, squeaking on its rusting hinges. A hooded figure carrying a kerosene lantern stands before me.

If I didn't know who it was, I would run screaming back to my car, thinking I was being chased by the apparition in my earlier dream. But I recognize the kind eyes, the soft features, the gentle smile that greeted me as a stranger fifteen years ago. Older, more wrinkled, but the same person.

He comes a little closer to me, holding the lantern by my head to better see my face. The smile broadens.

"Father Tom," the hooded man says. "I've been expecting you."

I smile. What he says doesn't surprise me. "Brother Martin, you look well."

He beckons me inside. A fire is burning in the stone fireplace in the one room that comprises the entirety of the dwelling. In one corner is a bed that hasn't been slept in, opposite another bed that hasn't been slept in. There is a small table with two chairs, a small desk piled with papers, and a kneeler with a crucifix hanging on the wall over it, on one side an Icon of the Blessed Virgin, on the other an Icon of Saint Joseph.

He closes the door behind me. I hear a click, and light from an electric lamp illuminates the space. I turn in surprise.

"Electricity?"

"A necessary innovation," Brother Martin says. "These days, I order our supplies online. Just as well. My days of going into town once a week are pretty much over."

"Finally gave up driving?" He had been in his early seventies when I first met him, and his eyesight hadn't been the best then.

"Gave up? Nah," he says with a gesture of disgust. "One little three-car accident and Father Abbot ordered me to hand over my driver's license. Said one of the younger brothers could drive me when I needed to go into town. But they wired this place, ran the Internet to the cabin, and got me a computer so it wouldn't be an issue."

The monastery had both electricity and an internet connection to the outside world when I first came there. It was necessary for the brother's business, the production of truly wonderful jellies and preserves as well as books and pamphlets about the Church. But Brother Martin's cabin had neither when I first met him.

"An old Luddite like you?"

"I've adjusted. Sit down and I'll make you some tea." Brother Martin shuffles to a hot plate where a tea kettle has just started whistling. "They also made me give up my wood stove for this thing," he comments as he pours boiling water into two mugs. Dropping tea bags into each, he sets one down in front of me on the table.

"I don't have milk or sweetener," he says as he sits down.

"This is fine, thank you." I absentmindedly dip the teabag in and out of the hot water, letting it steep for several minutes. Brother Martin does the same, neither of us saying anything. The only sounds in the cabin are the crackling of the fireplace and a faint clicking as Brother Martin fingers his rosary beads.

When the tea looks strong enough, I put the cup to my lips and take a tentative sip. It's hot and bracing, herbal, with a hint of mint, burning a little bit as it slides down my throat.

"You say you were expecting me?" I finally say.

Brother Martin smiles serenely. "For some time now."

"I didn't even know I was coming here until about an hour and a half ago. I decided on the spur of the moment. I didn't tell anyone I was coming."

He shakes his head slightly. "You didn't need to. I just knew you'd be coming."

I look at the old monk. Even though he is not one of the cloistered brethren, as an extern and doorkeeper for the monastery, he is by far the most mystical. Had he seen a vision in a dream or in one of his long times of prayer in the nearby grotto?

"No," he says as if reading my thoughts. "I saw no vision, received no inspiration in prayer. I just always knew you'd be back."

"Really?"

"Yes. That and we do get newspapers here, you know."

I chuckle. "So you know what's been going on."

"Only what I've seen in the papers. I wasn't aware you'd been assigned to a parish in Myerton. Why don't you tell me how that came about?"

Over the next hour or so, I tell Brother Martin everything. How the Archbishop had assigned me to Myerton for four months. About Nate Rodriguez and Katherine Shepp. About being contacted by Joan's murderer.

About Helen reopening the case. About Joan, the emails, what her mother told me, about the secrets she had been keeping from me about her illness and her first marriage. It all comes out in a tumble, as if I have been carrying a wheelbarrow piled with stones up a hill, and having reached the top, I dump it out all at once. Hearing everything out loud leaves me exhausted, on top of the fact that it is almost 5 a.m. and a faint pink glow on the horizon shows that dawn is near.

"And that's it. I needed a break. So I left."

Brother Martin leans back in his chair. His smile never softens, but his eyes grow firm. "Just like last time."

I think for a minute before responding. "Yes, I guess it is just like last time."

"You ran."

"Yes."

"But you didn't leave it. You brought it with you." He looks at me over his cup. "Just like last time."

I don't respond. Brother Martin gets up and pours himself another cup of tea. "I used to make my own blend, you may remember. But," he says, flexing his hand, "really can't do it anymore because of the arthritis. So, now it comes in a box from Amazon." He takes a sip and considers for a moment. "Not bad, but not the same either."

He turns to look at me. "I never told you this, but I was not in favor of you leaving."

I look at him surprised. "But at the time you said—"

He cuts me off with a wave of his hand. "I know what I said, and I meant it. A man like you isn't meant for this life, having lived so much in the world and having experienced so much tragedy. You need to serve the Lord out there," he gestures with his cup, "among His people, saying Mass, baptizing babies, marrying and burying, walking alongside them in their darkest times. No, your call is real. It wasn't a figment of your imagination."

It comforts me to hear him say this. I have wondered often since if I had dreamed it all. What I consider my call to the priesthood was so unusual that I sometimes doubt the reality of it. Brother Martin was the first person I told of what I experienced those years ago at the grotto. It had been he who encouraged me to tell Father Abbot. That was the beginning. I went from never wanting to leave the monastery to preparing for a life as a diocesan priest.

"But," Brother Martin continues, "that didn't mean you needed to rush out like you did. I didn't think you were ready. You still had too much of the world you were carrying, too much on your shoulders, too much guilt. And guilt is not a reason to become a priest, ever. You needed more time here for your mind and soul to heal before you were ready to serve others. That's what I told Father Abbot."

"What did he say?"

"Ack, what he always says to me when he thinks I'm overstepping, that I am the extern and the care of the souls in the monastery is his responsibility, not mine. I'm just the doorkeeper, remember?"

I smile. Brother Martin is the monastery's contact with the outside world, but he is much more than the doorkeeper.

"So, I kept my mouth shut and saw you off to seminary," he gestures in the direction of the seminary. "But I always thought you'd be back. Not for forever, no. But you'd be back to finish healing."

"I am healed," I protest.

"No, you're hiding. If you were healed, you wouldn't be here." He sits in the chair opposite me. "You still have the guilt over your wife's murder. Now that's been joined by guilt over that reporter's death and your friend's suicide attempt. Mixed in, too, is your anger over Joan's secrets."

My tea has gotten cold.

"It was guilt that brought you here the first time," Brother Martin continues. "It's guilt that brings you here now. The question is, what are you going to do?"

"I thought I'd stay here a few days, ask Father Abbot for one of the retreat cabins."

"Which he'll grant you, but that's not what I mean." Brother Martin's smile disappears. He leans towards me, asking, "You know why you feel guilty still. You know what you need to do. When are you going to do it?"

I know what he means. Besides being my confessor, Brother Martin is the only person on earth I've ever told what really happened the night of Joan's murder.

I look at him and nod.

Twenty-Four

I finally fall asleep as the sun is rising. Brother Martin prepared the other bed for me before answering the monastery bell summoning the Brothers for Morning Prayer. I am so exhausted I sleep soundly, so deeply that no dreams disturb my sleep. When I wake up, the sun is high in the sky. I check my phone. It is 1 p.m. I am no longer exhausted, but I don't feel rested.

On the table is a covered tray. Brother Martin is not here, so I assume he is off working somewhere else in the monastery. On the tray is a bowl of soup and a small loaf of crusty bread with a glass of water, the ascetic but flavorful noon meal of the brothers. There is also a note in Brother Martin's familiar, but now shaky, handwriting.

Talked to Father Abbot. You can stay as long as you like. Cabin One.

I am hungry, so I eagerly eat the soup and bread. The water is crystal clear and lacks the chemical taste I've grown used to in the city. It is from a natural spring that both feeds the grotto on the monastery grounds and supplies water for the brothers.

After eating, I walk outside. It is a clear and crisp fall day. In daylight, the monastery looks inviting in spite of the fieldstone construction. Except for the parts that have been cleared for the buildings and the paths, the area is surrounded by trees that are still holding on to their brightly colored leaves. The sun shines through their branches, making the colors seem alive. I look down the path which leads to the cabins the monastery maintains for individuals who want to come and make a retreat, either with the brothers or alone.

I'll take the belongings I brought with me there later. There is someplace I want to go first.

A five minute or so walk through the woods, my steps crunching fallen leaves on the path, leads me to the grotto. Some decades before, one of the brothers had discovered a small spring among an outcropping of rocks. He decided to create a reproduction of the grotto of Lourdes, where the Blessed Mother appeared to Saint Bernadette and revealed herself to be the Immaculate Conception. Using only hand tools and manual labor, over several years he created a scale model of the site of the most famous Marian apparition in the world.

In the grotto is a statue of the Blessed Mother as described by the Saint; looking up from the ground, a statue of Bernadette kneels in prayer. Benches have been hewn out of logs. Not many people know it even exists, but the brothers do allow the public to access the site, and every week, individuals and small parish groups come for prayer and to fill bottles with the water that a priest has blessed.

I sit on one of the benches near the front and look at the statue of Our Lady. Her hands are outstretched, a slight smile on her lips, as if to welcome me back. I have a feeling of déjà vu. Everything, including the shadows cast by the trees, reminds me of the day I experienced my calling to the priest-hood. Like this day, I had come to pray and meditate alone for a while.

I take out my Rosary and have just begun the prayers when I hear the sound of crunching leaves behind me. I stiffen, not wanting to turn around. The area teems with wildlife, so I'm not sure what is behind me.

If it is a deer, I have nothing to worry about.

But bears do live in the area.

Whatever it is comes closer, crunching leaves under its feet—or hooves—or claws. Then it stops.

"Thanks a lot for making me drive all this way to bring you back," a woman's voice, heavy with exasperation, says. I turn around to see a very angry Detective Helen Parr standing in the clearing.

"How did you find me?" I ask.

"I'm a detective, remember?" she says as she continues to walk towards me. "I had Gladys ping your cell phone. She says hello, by the way."

"There's no phone reception out here."

"GPS locator still works." Though only of average height, she towers over me, clearly unhappy. "You want to tell me what you're doing here? Why you left town without telling anybody? Against my orders, mind you. I could arrest you, you know?"

"And charge me with what?"

"I'll think of something—hindering an investigation. Answer the question," she says as she sits on the bench next to me.

"I needed to get away, to think."

"You couldn't stay in Myerton and think."

"Everything got to me. It was too much. I needed distance."

"So you left town without telling anyone, just like last time."

"You're the second person in the last 24 hours to make that same comment."

"What is it with you, running when things get tough? I guess *some* things haven't changed." She glares at me.

"I wasn't running," I protest. "I just needed to get away for a few days. I have a lot to put together. I was planning on coming back."

"Really? When?"

"A few days. A week, tops."

"And what did you think would happen in the meantime? That everything would stop until you got your act together?"

"I haven't thought about what would happen while I was gone. I'm not sure I care."

Helen takes her shoes off and rubs her feet. "If I had known I was going for a hike, I would have worn different shoes. I've been walking around here for an hour looking for you."

"Why didn't you ask at the monastery?"

"I did. They said you'd be in one of two places. Unfortunately, I chose the wrong place first."

"Sorry. Why are you here anyway?"

"I tried contacting you, but your phone went straight to voicemail. I called Anna Luckgold and found out you'd left—by the way, she's pissed off at you, too. When Gladys figured out where you were, I decided to come after you."

"But why?"

"Two reasons," she says, putting her shoes back on. "First, John Archman's awake."

"Have you talked to him yet?"

"No, that's one reason I was trying to get in touch with you. I thought you'd like to be there when I do."

"I would. What's the second reason?"

She looks at me steadily. "I wanted to finish the conversation we were about to have at the hospital."

I look at her and sigh. "Right."

"Joan's not the only one who kept secrets. You've been keeping some for a long time. Some you're keeping from me right now."

She stops talking and looks around. "It's beautiful here," she says. "Very peaceful. Lourdes, right?"

I nod and say with a smile. "I used to love coming here, and I came here a lot after I got here. I'd still be here if—" I trail off.

"If?"

I turn to the statue standing in the grotto, showing the Virgin Mary as Saint Bernadette described her. "If I hadn't been called away." I sit quietly for a minute, gazing at the statue.

I look back at Helen. "But that's for another time."

"So," she asks quietly, "are you ready to tell me?"

"No, but I will. You're right, it's time."

I tell her about John hearing Chloe and me talking. About him coming out of the room. And I tell her what he said.

"He said he was there the night Joan was killed," she says with surprise. "Why did he never come forward?"

"You'll have to ask him; he passed out before I could."

"Did he say anything else?"

I exhale, my mouth tightening into a line. I nod. "Yes. He said he saw what really happened."

"And here we are," she says quietly. "What did he mean, Tom?"

I feel tears falling down my cheeks. I have reached the point of no return. I have no choice now. It's time.

"He saw the truth," I whisper, closing my eyes and dropping my head. The tears are coming faster now. I clench my hands together and feel Helen place her hand on mine.

Fighting against the emotions I feel coming up from within me, I raise my head to look at Helen, this woman I once loved. I look into her eyes and see pity, sympathy, and determination.

"Tell me, Tom," she whispers. "Everything."

I know she'll accept nothing less.

So, I tell her.

Twenty-Five

"So," I say quietly, wiping the remaining tears from my eyes. "Now you know."

I don't know when I started sobbing, if it was during or after. But by the time I finished, I was doubled over on the bench, my body wracked by sobs and screams that came from a place deep within me. Years worth of pain and torment, of guilt and self-loathing, burst forth in a flood.

Through all that, Helen held me. She wrapped one arm around me and stroked my head, her warmth and the ever-present smell of vanilla reminding me of another time she held me like this. The time I told her about my father's death.

I needed her then, but not as much as I need her now.

"Oh, Tom," she says quietly. "I'm so sorry."

All I can do is nod.

We sit together quietly for a few moments, then she says, "I need to get back to Myerton."

We stand and walk the path from the grotto to her car in silence.

At her car, Helen says, "You do know I could charge you with making a false statement to police?"

"I know you could."

"Why didn't you just tell the truth at the time? Pride?"

"Pride, guilt, some combination. I didn't want people to know how I failed her."

She starts to say something—probably about the fragility of the male ego—but apparently thinks better of it. Instead, she says. "You'll have to make a formal statement revising your original statement."

"I know."

"And I'll have to mention this to the State Attorney, but," she says, "I'll go to bat for you. I'll make the point you've suffered enough, and in the end, it probably didn't affect the investigation that much. I doubt he'll want to prosecute the husband of the victim of a cold case who's now a Catholic priest."

"Thanks, Helen."

She puts up her hand. "Don't thank me. I'm still mad at you." She gets in her car and starts the engine, then rolls down the window.

"When are you coming back?"

I smile slightly. "I'll be back tonight. I want to speak to Father Abbot first, thanking him for his hospitality, explaining that I won't be staying."

"Then be at the hospital at 10 a.m. tommorrow or I'll ask the State Police to bring you in. In handcuffs." The window goes back up and she puts the car in reverse, turns it around, and speeds down the driveway.

I watch her drive off and then look up at the sun overhead. I close my eyes and smile as I feel the warmth on my face.

Telling Helen has been painful, but for the first time in years, I feel light. I have tossed a great burden from my shoulders. I am no longer hiding from the truth.

"And you shall know the truth," I whisper. "And the truth shall set you free."

"Father Greer?" I turn to see a young brother walking towards me. "Father Greer? Father Abbot would like to speak with you when you're free."

"I'm free now. I was going to ask to see him anyway. Why does he want me?"

"He did not share that with me. He just told me to come find you."

I follow the brother through the entrance to the monastery. I haven't passed through these doors in a long time. The last time, I was on my way back out into the world, into my second life as a priest. I follow him down the hallway to Father Abbot's office.

The brother knocks quietly on the door. "Come in," I hear from the other side as the brother opens the door. Father Abbot Anthony is sitting behind his desk.

"Ah, Father Greer," he says, waving me into his office and pointing to one of the chairs off to the side. "Let's sit over there, so much more comfortable and informal than here." He gets up slowly, grabbing a cane to steady himself. He walks with a slight limp to the other chair.

"Old age," he responds to my questioning look, "nothing more. Arthritis in the hip, in the knees. Some days are better than others. But the Lord has given me a good life in His service, so I try not to complain."

He sits and looks at me. "If I remember correctly, you arrived in the middle of the night the first time you visited us, too."

"And you welcomed me in then, as well."

"Brother Martin has seen to your needs."

I nod. "All of them."

"Yes, Brother Martin has told me of your circumstances," he leans forward. "I'm sorry to hear you continue to suffer because of your wife's death."

"This, I'm afraid, I brought on myself," I reply.

"Perhaps, perhaps. But you're here now and you can stay as long as you need."

"Actually, Father Abbot, I was going to speak with you. I need to go back much sooner than I anticipated. Like today."

His eyebrows go up. "Oh? Well, that's a shame. It kind of negates why I wanted to talk with you. I wanted to ask a favor. Well, I'll still ask, since you're here."

"I'll do anything I can for you. You have been so kind to me in the past."

"It's not really for me, it's for the monastery. You see, the doctors have told me to slow down. They're concerned about my balance. In truth, I have more bad days than good ones. I need the cane all the time just to stand and get around. Which makes saying Mass rather difficult."

He sits back, shifting in the chair to get comfortable. "I've applied to the order for another priest to be assigned, but there is no one available right now. And none of the other brothers here are in holy orders. We have one taking seminary classes up the road, but he won't be ordained for a couple of years. I have been praying for a solution. Then you showed up, and I thought—well, never mind."

"I'd be happy to help if I could, Father Abbot, but I'm under the Archbishop's authority. He'd have to—"

"Oh, I can take care of the Archbishop. It wouldn't be for forever, he'd get you back eventually."

"How long?"

He shakes his head. "I don't know. As long as a year, maybe more, maybe less."

A year in the monastery. Withdrawn from the world, living a life of prayer with the brothers.

At the moment, the idea appeals to me.

"I can't right now," I finally say. "I have to take care of things first."

"Well, I need to get the Archbishop's approval anyway. Is this a yes?"

"It's a maybe. I need to consider this."

"Of course, of course, take the time you need. Pray, seek God's counsel. I will do the same. Who knows, maybe another priest will show up looking for peace." He smiles serenely. "Now let me give you a blessing."

I bow my head while he says the words of a blessing and makes the sign of the cross. I stand up and thank him. "I pray it all works out for you," Father Abbot says as I leave.

I go back to Brother Martin's cabin. He is sitting at the table, drinking a cup of tea and offers to make me one.

"No, thanks. I need to go."

"So the woman detective found you?"

"How did you know—"

"She stopped here first looking for you. Attractive young lady. Seems very smart."

"She's good at her job."

"I'm sure. Just—be careful. Remember who you are."

Brother Martin looks concerned. "I'm not sure what you mean," I say.

"She's an attractive woman."

"Brother, I assure you, there's nothing going on or going to go on. She's just the detective investigating Joan's murder."

"She's a woman who drove over an hour to find you and get you to go back to Myerton. Why do you think she did that?"

"I shouldn't have left, I'm considered a witness, she came to get me."

"She could have sent someone else. She came herself." He pauses. "She likes you, Tom."

"Well, I like her, too." I don't tell him that Helen and I have a history.

"There's more there than you're seeing," Brother Martin says. "Listen, I'm not saying either of you are doing anything wrong or will do anything wrong. Just remember your vows."

Later on the road, I turn over the conversation with Brother Martin in my head. As far as I'm concerned, Brother Martin is wrong.

You are fooling yourself, Tom, the lover inside me whispers. *You know how you feel. You know how she feels.*

"No," I say out loud. "Any feelings I have for Helen, or she has for me, are in the distant past. We are just—well, I don't know exactly what we are. But whatever it is, that's all we are."

Are you really sure about that? the lover asks.

I also think about Father Abbot's proposal. I'm not sure what to do about that either. When I first arrived at the monastery, I was broken. The brothers took me in, and I was healed in their midst. After a few months there, I decided I would never leave. I talked about entering the novitiate to become a full-fledged brother and enter their life of prayer and work.

Then came my call to the priesthood. That call took me out of the monastery and back into the world. But I wasn't really part of the world, not really. I had turned my job at the Archdiocesan Archives into my own little monastery.

Archbishop Knowland knew that. He told me as much when he assigned me to Saint Clare's.

***

"Father," he had said, "do you know what one of my responsibilities is? It is to see to the spiritual welfare of the priests in my charge. That's what I'm doing in your case."

"I don't understand," I said. "My spiritual—there's nothing wrong—"

"I'm not saying you're neglecting your obligatory prayers and Masses." He had leaned forward and rested his chin on his hand, his elbow on the desk. "The priesthood is not a way of hiding from the world." He had slapped the desk with his hand. "No, sir, it is not."

"But, I'm not hiding."

The Archbishop had sighed. "Tom, I know your background."

I looked away from him. It was the first time in our many conversations that he had even alluded to Joan's death. His tone was gentle, father-like.

"I don't doubt the sincerity of your vocation or your devotion to God or the Church. But your entry into holy orders was—unusual." He paused. "The loss you suffered—I can't even imagine. Out of deference to your age and previous

occupation—your skills were needed, there's no doubt about that—Archbishop Gray did not assign you to a parish. Heaven knows I'm not questioning his decision. The more recent records in the Archdiocesan Archives were in horrendous shape and you have done a fantastic job that you are to be commended for."

"Thank you."

"But," he had continued, "I think your position has served you ill. You work by yourself, without any help except for the odd intern or seminarian. It's become your cloister. Your escape from the world. You don't escape from the world when you become a priest. You're called to bring Christ to the world. That's how you serve our Lord. You don't run from the world no matter how bad it is."

***

He had sent me to Saint Clare's to force me to do the work proper for a priest. From all appearances, I have messed that up badly. Maybe—maybe I needed to return to where it all started?

But do I really want to do that? Would I just be running again?

But where do I belong? I'm not sure.

I start to pray for guidance. As I pray, I think more about Father Abbot's offer.

I also think about Helen.

By the time I am at the outskirts of Myerton, I know what to do.

***

It is after 10 p.m. by the time I get back to Myerton. I stopped on the way back for dinner, realizing I hadn't eaten anything except the soup Brother Martin had left for me. I'm surprised to see the light still on and even more surprised to find Anna sitting in the living room.

"So, you decided to come back this time," she says when I open the door.

"I should have let you know I was leaving town. Sorry."

"That's OK. I'm used to you leaving without warning," she shoots back. "At least you didn't wait fifteen years to come back this time. I guess Detective Parr found you?"

I nod. "I needed space to pray so I went to Emmitsburg. She pinged my cell phone, came there and threatened to arrest me."

"Good. She should have brought you back in handcuffs." She turns and looks at the fireplace. I just stand there, not knowing what to say.

Finally, she turns back to me, her expression softer. "Well, you're back now. Do you know how John is doing?"

"Helen—Detective Parr told me he's awake. She's going to question him tomorrow. I'm going to be there."

Her eyebrows go up when I call the detective by her first name. Her brows go up again when I say I'm going to be at John's interview.

"Any idea why he did it? I talked to Chloe, but she is being very vague. Said it had something to do with that reporter's death?"

"We really don't know," I say. "Detective Parr wants to ask him, talk to him about some other things."

"What other things?"

"Just part of her investigation, I don't think I can say anymore."

She looks at me and shrugs. "OK, I guess I'll find out when everyone else does. Oh, why don't you sit down? I'm not going to bite you; I'm not even that mad anymore."

I sit down. "I really need to get to bed."

"So do I, it's way past my bedtime. I just wanted to stay up in case you came back tonight." She takes a seat across from me. "Detective Parr, she seems very competent. A very good detective."

"She is," I say.

"Pretty, too."

"I guess."

"You guess?"

"I hadn't really noticed, Anna."

"You hadn't really noticed?"

I look at her. "What are you implying?"

"Me? Implying? Oh, nothing, nothing. Just making a couple of observations."

Anna holds my look.

"Well," she finally says, getting up. "As you pointed out, it's late. I'll see you in the morning." She leaves the living room, leaving me sitting there looking after her.

I turn out the lights and go to my room. Undressing, I crawl in bed and set my alarm for 6 a.m.

It doesn't take me long to go to sleep. The last thing I remember thinking is one word.

A name.

Twenty-Six

On my way to the hospital the next day, I stop by The Perfect Cup and get a large coffee with a double shot of espresso, cream and sugar, and a chocolate doughnut. I rarely eat breakfast, but I need the extra sugar and caffeine to get going.

As I stand at the counter, I ask the young lady serving me, "Nate's not working today?"

"Nate hasn't been here in a few days," she says. "Not sure what's going on. His uncle says he's sick."

I drive by Saint Clare's. Glenda's nephew is working in the yard, raking more leaves. He's wearing the same sky blue hoodie he always wears, pulled up over his head. He turns in my direction. I am caught short for a moment, realizing I can't see his face. Then I realize it's his beard.

I pull into the parking lot at the hospital a little before 10 a.m. John has been moved out of the ICU into a regular patient room. I find Helen seated in the waiting area, flipping through a magazine.

Closing the magazine and tossing it on the table, she says, "So you did come back."

"I told you I would. Did you doubt me?"

"In a word, yes," she stands up. "Shall we?" She turns and takes a step forward.

"Wait," I say. She turns back, a questioning look on her face. "I never thanked you."

"For?"

"Yesterday. Listening to me. Giving me the opportunity to unburden myself."

"You've told people before."

"Yes, my confessor and my spiritual director," I say. "But not someone outside, out here."

"Well, don't thank me yet," she says. "I still have to talk to the State Attorney and persuade him not to prosecute."

"You said you'd be able to."

"And I probably will. Brian likes me," she smiles. "We've been out a few times. In fact, he even asked me to marry him once."

A flash of jealousy shoots through me. "Oh?"

She shakes her head. "Don't look at me like that, Father. We were only engaged for a few weeks, never even got to the point of picking out a ring."

I blush like a schoolboy.

"He's a good lawyer," she goes on. "He can be a boring conversationalist. His hobby is restoring old furniture. He spent an entire dinner telling me in great detail about an armoire he is stripping. Do you know the difference between a butt joint and a dovetail joint?"

"Not a clue."

"Yeah, well, I do. Come on, let's go talk to your friend." She turns and walks down the hallway, with me following. We stop outside one of the patient rooms. Helen knocks softly on the closed door.

A woman's voice answers. "Yes?"

Helen opens the door. John lays in bed, looking better than the last time I saw him but still haggard. Chloe sits beside him in a chair, holding his hand. They both look at us.

"Mrs. Archman," Helen says, nodding at Chloe. "Mr. Archman, I'm Helen Parr," she flashes her ID. "If you feel up to it I have a few questions."

"Can't this wait?" Chloe asks, the irritation heavy in her voice.

"I'm afraid not, Mrs. Archman," Helen says.

"I can't believe you're having anything to do with this," Chloe says looking at me. "He's your friend Tom. You're his priest."

"Chloe, please," I say.

"It's all right, sweetie," John says, patting Chloe on the arm. "I want to talk. I need to do it."

"But John—"

John shakes his head. "Why don't you run home, get some rest, come back in a few hours? I'll be fine."

Chloe looks at her husband, as if she's afraid to leave him. John knows it, too. "Really, I'll be fine."

Chloe looks at us, then back at John. "Should I call a lawyer?"

"You have the right to do that, Mr. Archman," Helen interjects. "I was going to Mirandize you before we started."

"No, that's OK. I'll talk to you." He turns to Chloe. "Go on."

Chloe hesitates, then stands up and kisses John. Without looking at us, Chloe walks out of the room and Helen closes the door.

John looks at me. "Tom, I'm so sorry."

"Shush, John, you have nothing to be sorry about," I say. "I'm sorry things got so bad for you."

"No, I'm sorry about Joan."

The sentence hangs in the air between us, the following silence thick. Helen breaks through it. "One thing at a time, Mr. Archman—"

"Just call me John," he says, indicating the chair by the bed. Helen sits down. I stand by the wall, in a corner near the window. The shears are drawn, filtering the bright October sun.

"I know you said you'd talk, John, but I need to read you your rights anyway," Helen says, and then does.

"I understand," John says. "What would you like to know?"

"Tell me what happened Sunday afternoon."

"I'll need to start earlier than that," John says. "Late last week—I think it was Thursday—I got a call at my office from Katherine Shepp. She explained who she was, what she was doing. But I knew who she was. She had called Chloe for an interview, but Chloe wouldn't speak to her. I had dreaded hearing from her myself."

"You had been expecting her to call?"

"I knew eventually she'd come across something that linked me to Joan." John looks at me. "I want you to know that I never, that Joan never—"

I nod. "I know John, it's OK."

"Go on," Helen prompts.

"She had been digging and digging, and like I say, I knew she'd come across something eventually. When you found those emails and that note, I just about died. All these years, I thought Joan had gotten rid of them. I thought I was safe. But you found them. And then you shared the emails with Shepp."

"If we can get back to the call from Shepp," Helen interjects. "Please, what was Shepp calling about?"

"What do you think? She had the emails I sent Joan from my Myer College email address. Somehow she had gotten hold of the student list for Joan's class and my records from Myer. I don't know how she got a hold of that. I always thought they're supposed to be private."

"They are. We're looking into that. Go on."

"She wanted to interview me about my relationship with Joan. I told her there was no relationship, I tried to explain. She says I could explain on camera for her story, or she'd run the story without my help. So I agreed to an interview."

"When did it take place?"

"It was supposed to take place yesterday. When I got off the phone with her, I was fine. I had resolved in my mind just to tell the truth. It happened so many years ago, and Chloe knew about it all, I didn't think anyone would care. But the closer Monday came, the more anxious I got, the more scared. I began to think all sorts of things, about how people would look at me differently, whisper things behind my back, how you'd find out," he looks at me, "and what you might say. Then I saw her interview of Tom and knew what I had in store. For all I knew, she was going to say you found out about Joan and me and killed her in a jealous rage, or say I was going to kill you and Joan got in the way. By Saturday night, I realized I couldn't go through with it. I called Shepp and said I was pulling out of the interview."

"How did she react?'

"Not well. She said if I wanted to give up my chance to tell my story in my way, she'd tell it in hers. I pleaded with her not to, but she hung up. I lay awake that night trying to figure out what to do."

"When did you decide to go to her hotel room?"

"After Mass on Sunday, I needed to get out of the house and think. I told Chloe I had to go to the hardware store, but I drove around. I found myself at the hotel. I sat in my car for a while, then decided that I needed to talk to Shepp face to face and plead with her not to run the story. So I went inside to see her."

"Did you stop at the desk to get her room number?"

"She had already given it to me, the interview was going to take place there. I got up to her room and knocked. She didn't answer, so I knocked again, a little harder that time. The door moved, it wasn't completely shut. I opened the door and called her. I stepped in the room. That's when I saw her—well, not all of her, just her foot. I went around the bed and saw her—or, what was left of her. Someone had smashed her head with a lamp. I knelt down and tried to check for a pulse." He pauses and looks at Helen. "She was already dead when I got there."

"Why didn't you call the police?"

"I did."

"Not right away you didn't."

"No, no, you're right. It was my first impulse, then I realized I had no explanation for why I was there. I decided to leave and then call anonymously. Then I saw the files on her desk. I grabbed the whole pile and her laptop and cell phone and left."

"You went out of the hotel by the stairwell at the end of the hallway," Helen says.

John nods. "I called 911 from my cell phone."

"The call came up as an unknown number; they couldn't locate it."

He shrugs. "I'm a tech guy. I disabled the GPS and masked my number."

Helen nods. "OK, what did you do next?"

"I stopped by the hardware store, got some leaf bags, and went home."

"Pretty cool of you. When did you realize you had blood on your shoes and on your clothes?"

"When I got out of the car at home. I hadn't seen it before. I went inside and took my clothes off. I hid the files in the garage—I was going to take them to work, we have a crosscut shredder for classified documents, I was going to put them through there—and the clothes in the back of my closet. Then I took a shower."

"The papers were still in the garage."

"I haven't been to the office," John explains. "The whole thing, seeing her dead, all the blood, it just triggered me, brought back things I'd seen in-country. I have dreams, blending everything together." He looks at me. "I even dreamed about the night of Joan's murder."

"We'll get to that in a minute," Helen says.

"Finally, I just had enough. I was tired, tired of living. So that's when I took the sleeping pills. I didn't leave a note for Chloe, figured it would just make things worse. I was lying in bed waiting for them to work when I heard Tom and her talking. That's when I came out of the room. Talked about being there that night" John looks at me. "I'm so sorry, Tom."

"OK," Helen says. "If you feel up to it, why don't you tell me about the night of Joan Greer's murder? You saw what happened? You never came forward as a witness."

"I couldn't, I couldn't let anyone know I was there. I couldn't let Tom know. I had told Chloe I'd stopped."

"Stopped what?"

John looks at his hands. "Following Joan."

The words hang in the air. "You were following Joan that night," Helen says.

"I was following her every day," John says, "making up one excuse after another to Chloe. I had to see her every day, or my day was just empty. I was obsessed with her. And I was jealous of Tom. I could barely stand to see the two of them together." Looking at me, John asks, "Didn't you wonder why Chloe and I stopped coming over on Saturday nights?"

"Joan said Chloe said you couldn't find sitters."

"That wasn't the truth. I couldn't stand being in the same room with you two together. Chloe knew that, so she made the excuse. I guess Joan believed her, but I don't know. She knew my feelings for her, she had to suspect that had something to do with it."

Joan, I knew by then, was very good at hiding her feelings. She could have known the truth and just decided it didn't bother her.

"Anyway," Helen prompts, "You were following her the night of Joan's murder. What did you see?"

He lays his head back and looks at the ceiling. "I was in my car across the street from the restaurant. I could see Tom and Joan in the restaurant, your table was near the window. I watched you two eat, talk, laugh. You seemed happy. At least most of the time."

I knew what he meant.

"You got a call," John continues "I could tell from your face, that whatever it was, you weren't happy."

It was from a collection agency, about money Joan owed for a design job. She had told me it had been taken care of. I had given her the money to pay the bill. Apparently, she hadn't.

"You got off the phone and said something to Joan. I don't know what you were saying, but I could tell you were angry."

I had asked her about the bill, if she had paid it. She claimed she had, said it must have been an accounting mistake on the company's part. I accused her of lying.

"Joan started waving her arms, banging the table."

Joan had gotten angry and loud. She started hurling accusations against me and saying the most hurtful things. She was nearly hysterical. I went from angry to trying to calm her down.

"I saw you put your hand on her shoulder, trying to calm her down, I guess. She jerked away, got up, grabbed her jacket and purse, and stormed away from the table. You grabbed her arm to stop her, she pulled away."

I tried to stop her, to assure her that we could work it out, that it would be OK. She was beyond reasoning with at that point.

"Why didn't you go after her, Tom?" John says, now looking at me. "I've wondered that for fifteen years."

I had learned it was best just to let her cool off before trying to talk more.

"What did she do then?" Helen prompts.

"She walked out of the restaurant and up the sidewalk," John says. "She was walking really fast, gesturing with her arms. She looked like she was talking to herself." He hesitates. "I did something stupid."

"What was that?"

"I got out of the car and followed her."

"Why did you do that?"

"She was upset, I thought I could calm her down. Besides," he looks at me, "Tom wasn't going after her and it was dark. Something could have happened to her. Something did, didn't it, Tom?"

His words sting.

"Where did she walk to?" Helen asks.

"She walked to the parking lot in the alley by the restaurant. She got to the car and tried to open the door. I heard her curse when it wouldn't open."

I had locked the doors when we parked. I had the key. I had asked for the check and was in the process of paying it while all this was going on.

"I was about twenty feet behind her or so. I had slowed walking when I realized what I was doing. I was trying to come up with an excuse as to what I was doing there—you know, out for a walk downtown, just happened to be passing by. I realized what I was doing was stupid and had decided to just go back to my car when I heard someone calling her name. I looked around and saw a hooded figure standing about five feet behind her."

"What did Joan do?"

"She turned around. I ducked behind a tree so no one could see me. There wasn't a lot of light. The lot had a couple of street lights, so I could see both of them but not a lot else. But I could hear pretty well."

"What did you hear?"

"She asked, 'Who are you? What do you want?' I heard the figure speak and knew it was a man. 'Don't be scared, Joan, it's me.' I saw him lower his hood. 'It's me.'" I saw Joan walk toward him. She whispered something I couldn't really hear, maybe something like 'What are you doing here?' I didn't hear his answer. She started waving her arms, she stomped her foot. 'Why'd you come! I'm married to a good man! I have a good life!' He turned and walked off a couple of paces then turned back. 'Married? How can you be married to a guy when you're already married to me.'"

Helen and I look at each other.

Randy Earl.

"You could hear all that?" I say, ignoring Helen's look.

"They were yelling at each other. Joan said, 'Not anymore. After you left me on that sidewalk, I called my mom, she came and got me, and we got that mistake annulled.' 'No, no, we're still married, you're coming with me.' He grabbed her arm and tried to drag her off. She shook him off. 'Don't you touch me,' she yelled at him. 'Just get out of here. I don't want to see you.' That's when I heard Tom."

When Joan hadn't come back after a few minutes, I left the restaurant and went after her. As I walked toward the car, I heard Joan yelling. I couldn't hear what she said, but I ran towards her voice. I turned the corner.

"You know what happened next," John says.

"Go ahead and finish," Helen prompts.

I lean back and listen to John. While he speaks, I run the scene through my mind.

"I heard Tom call her name. Joan turned away from the guy and started to run towards Tom. The guy said something like, 'Oh, no, you don't!' and grabbed her arm, pulling her back. Joan jerked herself free again and ran to Tom. She grabbed at Tom, Tom held her. The other guy ran up and tried to pull Joan free from him, yelling, 'She's mine not yours!' while pulling on her. He pulled Joan away and started to walk away, pulling Joan behind him. Joan was struggling. Tom leaped on the guy's back, started to hit him. The guy let go of Joan, threw Tom off his back, and turned on him. Tom lunged at him—I don't know what Tom was thinking, the guy was about Tom's size but looked like he had been used to fighting—and the guy struck him across the face, knocking him to the ground. Tom was down, the guy standing over him. The guy reached around back and pulled out a gun—it must have been in his waistband, and pointed it at Tom. He said something I couldn't hear, all I could hear was Joan screaming. Before the guy could fire, Joan grabbed his arm—I think she bit him, I'm not sure—but he screamed. It threw his aim off." John stopped and looks at me. "Tom was lying there, not getting up. He just—he just didn't move."

I heard the accusation in his voice. I have no clear memory of what he described. Just grabbing at the guy I thought was assaulting Joan. Him slamming me across my head. Me going down. Everything else is a blur. Could I have gotten up if I wanted to? Could I have done anything to help Joan, to prevent what happened? Even now, fifteen years later, I'm not sure.

That's the guilt that I've carried all these years.

I had done nothing to prevent Joan's death. I hadn't gone after her when she left. And I hadn't gotten up off the ground.

"What happened next?" Helen says.

"The guy recovered himself, pointed the gun at Tom. I heard Joan yell and saw her run to Tom—then I heard the gun."

John stops talking. I stop breathing.

"What did you see next?"

"I saw—I saw Joan, laying on top of Tom. She—she wasn't moving." John starts crying. "She wasn't moving. Do you realize what she did, Tom?"

I do.

"What did her killer do?"

"He just stood there. I think he was stunned. Then I heard him scream, 'NO!' He walked forward, screaming, 'NO, NO, NO!' He stood right over Tom and Joan and pressed the gun to Tom's head."

I can still feel the cold steel of the gun pressed against my forehead.

"I heard the gun click. Just a click."

There were three clicks. But no bang. No bullet blasting through my brain, exploding the back of my skull.

"I saw the guy back up, look at the gun, look back at them. It was like he didn't know what to do next. Then came the sirens. He looked in the direction they were coming from and ran off."

"What did you do? "

He sighs. "I ran back to my car, drove home, and got drunk."

My eyes snap open. Helen moves towards me, but she isn't quick enough.

Before I know what I'm doing, I grab John by his hospital gown. "You—you were my friend—you said you loved her!" I scream at John, shaking him. "You were there—you saw all this happen—you, you didn't do anything!"

"I couldn't, I couldn't" John pleads. "I was trying to get my life back together, trying to fix things with Chloe, repair my marriage. She would have found out I'd been following Joan."

"You kept this all to yourself, this information from the police, all these years, allowing her killer to stay free!"

"Besides, I already knew he wasn't going to hurt her," he says as he grabs at my wrists, "and I didn't care what he did to you!"

I stop shaking him. John looks at me. "I'm sorry," he pleads. "I wanted you to die. You had her. I wanted her. I thought if you were dead . . ."

John looks away from me. My breathing is heavy, my grip on him firm. I feel a hand on my shoulder. I turn. It's Helen. She gestures with her head for me to move. Letting my old friend go, I throw myself into the nearest chair and stare at the wall.

"When you came back to town," John says, "I struggled with telling you. I tried that day in the confessional."

My head snaps around. Helen asks, "Which day?"

"The first Saturday Tom was here," John says. "I had every intention of coming clean. But I couldn't. I just couldn't."

I look at him. "The ring," I whisper. "You had it."

"Yes," he said. "I've kept it for fifteen years."

"How?"

"I saw you the day you left, at Joan's grave. I saw you leave it there. I had no idea why you'd do that. I took it. You left her alone, Tom, all this time. I made sure she wasn't lonely."

John lapses into silence. No one speaks for several minutes.

"I'll have someone come and take a formal statement—statements, I guess," Helen finally says. She closes her notebook and puts it back in her shoulder bag. "That's all for now. Thank you. We'll let you rest now."

I take that as my cue, so I stand up. John and I locked eyes, then turn from each other.

At the door, Helen turns back. "Oh, one more thing, Mr. Archman," she says. "You say Shepp was already dead when you got there?"

"She was, I swear."

"Did you see anyone in the hallway, maybe going out the exit to the stairway?"

John shakes his head. "No, but maybe Glenda did."

I turn. "Glenda? Glenda who?"

"Glenda Whitemill."

"Wait, who's Glenda Whitemill?" Helen asks, pawing through her bag for her notebook.

"She's the parish secretary and the housekeeper at the Rectory," I answer. "John, Glenda was there? What was she doing there?"

"I guess working," John says. "I was about to get off on Shepp's floor. When the doors opened, there was Glenda with a housekeeping cart. She seemed surprised to see me. I asked her what she was doing there. She said she'd started working there on the weekends, to pick up a little extra money. We chatted for a moment, then she got on the elevator. If anyone knows something, maybe Glenda does."

Twenty-Seven

"Do you believe him?"

We are outside the hospital when I speak.

"About what?" Helen asks.

"Shepp. Do you believe him?"

She thinks and shrugs her shoulders. "I don't know. All the evidence is circumstantial. We don't have any other witnesses. He could be telling the truth. But by his own words, he had motive and opportunity."

"But John's not a killer."

"He was a soldier, right? He's killed before."

"That's different. That was in war. This—he's not capable of cold-blooded murder. I know him."

"Tom," she jabs a finger in my chest. "He was your best friend, but he was obsessed with your wife and watched while you were attacked and she was murdered. He just admitted not caring if you lived or died. Would you have guessed that?"

I pause and shake my head. "No, I wouldn't have." I sigh. "What about what he said about the night of Joan's murder?"

"What he saw of you and Joan at the restaurant matches what you told me, right?"

I nod.

"And," she goes on, "what he says happened after you got to Joan in the parking lot matches up with your account—your account now, that is."

"Yes, it does."

"The only part we don't have any other witness to is from the time she left the restaurant to the time you arrived. And I see no reason he should make it up."

"So it was Randy Earl that night."

"Maybe, Tom, maybe. All we have is John's fifteen-year-old memory of what he could hear."

"But it makes sense," I say. "Earl shows up, wants Joan back. She spurns him. He gets angry. Tries to kill me. Kills her instead. Stunned, he runs away."

"It does make sense," Helen agrees. "But we have no evidence. The only other living person who knows what happened that night is Earl."

"Then we try to find him. We know he's in town."

"I've tried. I can't find any trace, remember? We don't even know what he looks like." She shakes her head. "One murder at a time. I've got to talk to this Glenda person. Where would she be now?"

I check the time. "Now? Probably at the Rectory."

"Come on, let's go," she turns and starts walking.

"Go? Where are we going?"

She stops and turns back to me. "Going? To the Rectory to interview Glenda. You can make the introductions, you know, ease the way."

"She doesn't like me," I say as she walks away.

"I'll meet you there," she calls to me over her shoulder.

***

Glenda doesn't open the door when we ring the bell at the rectory. Instead, a young, redheaded priest answers.

"Yes, can I help you?" he asks.

I smile. "You must be the new priest."

"Yes, I am just assigned to Saint Clare's. I wasn't told I have any marriage counseling appointments." He looks puzzled. "At least I don't think so. Glenda," he calls back in the Rectory, "am I supposed to do any marriage counseling today?"

"There's nothing on the schedule. Maybe it's a crisis," Glenda calls from inside the Rectory.

"Ah," the priest says. "Well, I have time now if you'd like to—"

"I'm Father Tom Greer," I say, extending my hand. "This is Detective Helen Parr." Helen displays her identification to the befuddled young man.

"Oh!" His eyes widen. "Sorry! So sorry!" He grabs my hand and smiles. "Father Greer, nice to meet you. I'm Father McCoy. Leonard McCoy. You're not wearing clericals, and you two look like a couple, so I just assumed—"

"We're here to see Ms. Whitemill," Helen interjects.

"She's here," he says, his smile vanishing. "She's always here."

I try to suppress a smile. "I—I didn't mean that the way it sounded," Father McCoy says quickly. "Glenda is wonderful. Very—very efficient."

"She is that," I say. I pause, then look at him. "Wait, your name's Leonard McCoy?"

The young priest sighs and shakes his head. "Yes, my parents named me Leonard. They were Star Trek fans."

"I bet your childhood was rich," Helen says.

"You have no idea," Father McCoy says as he shows us in. "I'll get Glenda for you." He takes a couple of steps, then stops. "Is Glenda in any trouble?"

"No," I say. "Detective Parr just has some questions for her."

"Questions," he says. "Just questions." Then he whispers something that sounds like, "Pity." In a louder voice, he says, "You know where the living room is, Father. I'll bring Glenda to you."

As we sit down, Helen whispers, "Glenda sounds like a piece of work."

Before I can answer, Father McCoy returns with Glenda. She does not look at all happy.

"Here she is," Father McCoy says. "I'll leave you three to it." He takes a step backwards, gently shoving Glenda towards us.

"Father," Glenda says. "You have sick calls to make. The list is on your desk."

"I know, Glenda, I know," Father McCoy says wearily. "I was just going to attend to them."

"You'd better go to Gloria MacMillan first. She's all the way out in the mountains, and you don't want to be driving those roads in the dark, not your first time out."

"Tell her I said hello," I say to Father McCoy. "You'll find her delightful." He nods, looks at Glenda, then leaves.

"Now," Glenda says, turning to us. "What's this all about? Why do you want to talk to me, Detective?"

"I just have a few questions related to the murder of Katherine Shepp," Helen says.

"Shepp? Shepp? Oh, that reporter," she waves her hand dismissively. "I don't know anything about that. You can go now." She turns to leave.

"Glenda," I say gently. She turns to look at me. "This won't take too long. Just sit down and answer Detective Parr's questions."

She huffs. "Oh, all right," she says and plops herself down in an armchair. Looking at Helen, she says, "Ask."

I see Glenda's nephew outside. He isn't raking leaves or doing any lawn work. He is standing on the sidewalk, looking towards the Rectory. He wears a hoodie, earbud cords snaking into his pocket.

"Were you at the Myerton Inn last Sunday afternoon?" Helen asks.

"Is that any of your business?"

Helen sits on the edge of her seat. "Ms. Whitemill, let me be very clear about something," she says quietly. "This is a murder investigation. The questions I'm asking you are part of this investigation. This can happen in one of two ways. You can answer them here, now. Or I can take you down to the police station, and it will soon get around town." Helen smiles. "You don't want that, do you/ Ms. Whitemill?"

Glenda's imperious expression softens into a tight smile. "Why didn't you just say so, Detective? Of course I'll answer your questions."

Helen smiles. "Thank you. Now, were you at the Myerton Inn last Sunday afternoon?"

"I was at the Myerton Inn last Sunday, yes," she answers.

"And what were you doing there?"

She pauses before answering. "Does that matter?"

"Ms. Whitemill, please answer," Helen says with irritation.

"Oh, all right," Glenda crosses her arms. "I work at the Inn on weekends when they're short-handed. As a housekeeper. The extra money helps." She looks at me. "The parish really should pay me more."

"So," Helen continues, "you were working there Sunday afternoon?"

"No, not in the afternoon. I mean not all afternoon, I finished about 3:30 p.m."

"Did you see Katherine Shepp at all that day?"

"Oh, yes," Glenda nods. "I remember. It was near the end of my shift. Ms. Shepp had called down to the front desk to ask for towels. They asked me to take them to her."

"What happened?"

"I took them up, knocked on the door. She opened the door and I handed her the towels."

"Was she alone?"

"I assume so. I didn't see or hear anyone else in the room."

"How did she seem?"

Glenda shrugs. "Fine."

"She didn't seem upset or afraid or anything?"

Glenda shakes her head. "Like I say, she seemed fine to me."

Helen makes a note, then looks up. "Did you run into anyone as you left the floor?"

"No, no,—wait, yes. I did run into someone."

"Who?"

"Oh, I don't remember the name, he has twin teenage boys, you know the one, Father, I think he's an old friend of yours."

I feel a little sick. "John Archman."

Glenda points at me. "Yes, that's the one. John Archman."

"OK, Ms. Whitemill," Helen says. "Just to review. You brought Katherine Shepp towels, a little before 3:30, right? And she answered the door, you spoke to her. There was no one in the room with her. On the way out, you ran into John Archman coming off the elevator. Does that just about sum it up?"

Glenda nods. "That sounds right, Detective." She stands up. "If that's everything, I have work to do." With that, she turns and leaves the room.

Leaving the Rectory, I see Glenda's nephew again. He is pacing along the sidewalk, his hands in the pockets of his hoodie, watching us.

"What do you think?" I ask.

"That things look really bad for your friend, Tom," Helen says.

"But I'm telling you, John's not a murderer."

She stops. "Now look," Helen says, jabbing me again in the chest with her finger. "I'm not saying he made some kind of plan to kill her. Probably happened on the spur of the moment. He tried to persuade her not to run the story about him and Joan, she refused, he got angry and bashed her skull in. Second-degree murder, manslaughter. With his mental health history, a jury would buy it."

I shake my head. "No, it just doesn't add up."

"Motive, means, opportunity," she counts off three fingers. "He had all three. He's our only real suspect, unless," she points to the rectory, "you think that woman murdered Shepp?"

"As much as I think Glenda's capable of anything," I say, "I admit that's highly unlikely."

"We only have Archman's word that she was dead when he got there," Helen continues. "The word of a man who kept secret what he saw the night of your own wife's murder for fifteen years. A man who's good at lying and keeping secrets. For crying out loud, Tom, it's so obvious."

"So you believe Glenda's story?"

Helen nods. "I believe her story more than your friend's." Then she pauses. "But I will tell you, I got a bad vibe from her."

"She has that effect on people."

"No, I don't mean I found her irritating, which I did. It's something else."

"What do you mean?"

"I don't know. Something just doesn't sit right—who's that staring at us?"

I look. "That's Glenda's nephew. He does yard work around the parish.

"Have you ever met him?"

"Yes."

"Spoken to him?"

"Tried a few times. He's not very talkative."

Helen looks at Glenda's nephew and takes her notebook out of her bag, jotting something down. I try to read her handwriting, but her script is indecipherable. Had she not been a detective, she could have been a doctor.

"What is it?" I ask.

She shrugs. "Probably nothing."

"Are you going to arrest John?"

"Right now? No, it looks bad but I don't have enough. Just two contradictory stories. I need hard evidence. I'm waiting on fingerprints, lab results. These things take a lot longer than they do on TV, you know. In the meantime," she says, looking again at Glenda's nephew, "I think I will look into your parish secretary's background. Just to make sure."

"What about Joan?"

Helen looks at me. "I'll add Archman's statement to the file. Right now, I don't have much else to go on. I'll make some more inquiries about Randy Earl. And besides, we only have Archman's word about what he heard. You know, maybe if you found a picture of him in Joan's things? Aren't you supposed to be doing that?"

I nod. "I'll get back to it."

"You do that."

"I want to be there when—if—you arrest John."

She nods. "OK, I'll let you know."

***

I drive back to Anna's house. There is a bicycle laying in the driveway, so I have to park on the street. I am already in a foul mood, and having to park on the street doesn't make me feel better.

As I opened the door, I call out, "Anna, whose bicycle—", then stop in the doorway.

Nate Rodriguez and Anna are sitting in the living room. They both stand up.

"Tom," Anna says, "thank goodness you're home. Nate—"

"Father Tom!" Nate says as he rushes towards me. He grabs me by the shoulders. "I need your help! I need your help! I—I think I'm in a lot of trouble."

Twenty-Eight

It takes about a half-hour and a couple cups of herbal tea to calm Nate down.

"What happened?" I ask Anna in the kitchen as she makes the tea.

"He got here about fifteen minutes before you. I heard him banging on the door, ringing the doorbell, calling for you. I thought there had been some kind of accident. Nate rushed in when I opened the door. He was breathing hard, saying he needed to talk to you, over and over again, he needed to talk to you. I would have called you but I tried to calm him down first, tried to get him to tell me what was wrong. He just kept saying he needed to talk to you, he is in a lot of trouble. What do you think he is talking about?"

I shake my head. "I don't know. I know he hasn't been at The Perfect Cup for a few days. Maybe he had some kind of falling out with his uncle. I guess I'll find out."

"Well, good luck," Anna says, handing me the tray with a tea cup and tea pot.

Nate and I sit in silence in the living room. I hear Anna puttering around the kitchen.

Finally, Nate looks at me. "If I confess something to you, Father," he says, "you can't tell anyone else, right?"

"The seal of confession is absolute," I say. "I can't tell another living soul on pain of excommunication." Hearing the movement in the kitchen stop, I raised my voice slightly. "In fact, anyone who hears what you tell me has to keep it secret, too." A second later, I hear the whir of the mixer.

"No matter what it is?" Nate implores.

"That's right, no matter what it is."

He swallows. "Even murder."

I sit up. "Yes," I say warily.

Nate exhales. "I—I think I killed Katherine. I'm sure I killed Katherine." He looks at me, his eyes pleading for me to say something.

Outwardly, my face is impassive. Inwardly, I am in turmoil.

"Go on," I say gently. "What makes you think you killed Katherine?"

"Because I—"

222

I hold up my hand. "Slow down, Nate. Why don't you begin at the beginning?"

"The beginning. OK. The beginning." He sits back and thinks. "Since the interview aired, I had been trying to get in touch with her, but she wouldn't answer my calls. I mean, I called, I texted, I emailed. She ghosted me. I mean, not so much as a 'sorry, too busy, will talk to you later.'"

"Why had you been trying to get in touch with Shepp?"

"Because I was angry," he cries. "I mean, I'm the one who started this whole thing. I started looking into your wife's cold-case. I'm the one who got the interview with you. I'm the one you showed the emails to. I'll admit, I wasn't going to get as far as she was, but I deserved credit for something."

"And she didn't give you any."

Nate shakes his head. "Not a word. She aired the footage of our interview without giving me credit on air—I mean, I don't expect overwhelming praise for my work, but honestly, I expected at least an acknowledgment."

I nod. Shepp hadn't mentioned Nate in her report, and the report didn't indicate that the footage of me recounting the events of the night of Joan's murder was made by him as well as her. I can understand his anger.

"But it wasn't just that," Nate goes on. "I didn't like how she interviewed you, implying that you murdered your wife that way. I mean, without any evidence, just conjecture, speculation. It was rotten. An absolutely rotten thing to do. Unethical. I wanted to tell her that."

"How many times did you try to contact her?"

He thinks a moment and shrugs. "I don't know, a couple dozen."

That isn't good. When Helen finally gets Shepp's cell phone records, those calls will stand out.

"So you decided to go over to see her."

"Yes, I had had enough of being ignored. So I went to her hotel room. She wasn't happy to see me. Asked me bluntly why I was there. I told her I thought it wasn't right to air the footage without giving credit, and I wanted it corrected. She laughed—she laughed, Father. She said she wasn't about to do that, that she had told her producer she had filmed the interview outside the restaurant with you herself—"

I hold up a hand. "Wait, wouldn't the cameraman be able to back up your story?"

"Maybe, but she was probably sleeping with him and he was probably married so she had a way of keeping him quiet."

"Oh, I see," I say, mentally adding the cameraman and his wife to the list of possible, though unlikely, suspects.

"She said she'd get fired, and she wasn't about to let that happen, not when she was so close to getting what she wanted. Apparently, she had been contacted by one of the cable news channels and offered an interview. I told her that it was my work as much as hers, and it was important to my career, too, that it was my entry into documentary filmmaking. She laughed more. 'Career? What career,' she said to me. 'Your career is serving coffee in your uncle's coffee shop in this two-bit town. You're not going anywhere. You're certainly not going to pull me down on my way to the top.'"

"But you still have the original raw footage you shot. That would be proof."

"No," Nate said, shaking his head. "I gave her everything I had."

"You didn't keep a copy?"

"Wouldn't do any good, she'd just claimed she gave me the copy."

He slumps back, looking at his shoes. I am quiet for a few minutes. The only sound is Anna in the kitchen.

"After she said that to you, what did you do?"

"That's when it happened," he says quietly, his voice just above a whisper, still looking at his shoes. "I got angry—I never get angry, Father, never did when I was a kid—but I got so angry at her. I grabbed her by the shoulders and threw her to the floor. She must have hit her head on the bedside table or something, because she went down." He looks up, his eyes welling with tears. "She didn't get up. I said her name. I shook her. She didn't move. I panicked. I ran out the door and down the hallway. It took forever for the elevator to get there. I leapt into the elevator when the doors opened and went down to the lobby. I got in my car and drove back to The Perfect Cup. I was supposed to work but I told my uncle I thought I was getting the flu. I went up to my room and locked the door."

"Did you check to see if she was breathing?"

He shakes his head. "No, I thought she was. But then I heard the news. I've been hiding in my room ever since, trying to figure out what to do."

"Do you remember anything else?"

He shakes his head, then says, "Wait. I did hear the other elevator doors open as the doors on mine closed."

I sit back. "Why come to me now? Why not go to the police?"

He extends his hands plaintively. "I don't know, I trust you."

I sit with Nate's story. He looks like he is telling the truth, but he has kept little things from me, so I know that he is capable of lying.

I don't believe he is lying, but something isn't adding up.

He did not mention using the lamp to bash her head in. But that's how Shepp was killed.

Glenda had said she had brought towels to Shepp's room a little before 3:30. So Shepp was apparently alive at that time. Glenda hadn't said anything about Shepp seeming hurt or groggy, but it seems possible that Shepp had recovered shortly after Nate had left and gotten up off the floor.

John said Shepp was dead when he got to the room, which contradicts Glenda's account and makes John look guilty.

Now we have Nate's account.

Something is wrong somewhere.

I look at Nate. "You need to go to the police."

He winces as if I've punched him in the arm. "Can't you just tell them?"

"Me? No, this has to come from you. Besides, I can't tell them."

"Can't I give you signed permission? I can even get it notarized—I know a notary."

"It doesn't work that way, Nate. Even if I could, the police are going to want to hear your story from you."

Nate closes his eyes and swallows. "All right."

I don't have to look at the time to know it's late. I am bone-tired. I haven't slept more than four hours in the last forty-eight and it's beginning to catch up with me.

"Go back to your room," I say standing up. "I'll come by and get you around 9:30 a.m. We'll go see Detective Parr together."

"Will you be in there with me?" He asks.

"You should have a lawyer."

"I don't know any lawyers. One of the baristas dropped out of law school to start a marijuana dispensary. Maybe I can ask her?"

I put my hand on his shoulder. "Maybe not your best plan, Nate. I'll be there."

***

"What do you think?"

Helen and I are in the break room around the corner from the room where she just finished interviewing Nate. He's in there writing down a formal statement.

She looks back in the direction of the interview room. "What do I think? I think he's an idiot."

"That's a bit harsh, don't you think?"

She shrugs . "Maybe. But he's not exactly blessed with common sense, is he?"

On that one, I have to admit she's right.

"But what do you think of his story?"

"Well," Helen puts the coffee down and looks at her notes. "It doesn't really change anything. We know Shepp was still alive after that because we have Glenda Whitemill's testimony. So clearly, Nate didn't kill her."

"Unless Glenda was lying," I say.

She gives a snort. "You really don't like her, do you, Tom?"

"That has nothing to do with it," I say.

"So you're saying you believe Nate killed Shepp?"

"No, I really don't see him as a murderer. His story fits with his personality."

"So what are you saying?"

I shrug. "I don't know, Helen. Something's not right here. I can feel it."

She rolls her eyes. "OK, Father Brown."

"Don't," I say a little more firmly than I mean.

She looks at me, holding up her hands. "OK, OK, sorry." She sighs. "Listen, Tom, I know you don't want to believe your friend killed Shepp, and I admit Nate's story complicates things a little, but we have a witness that says Shepp was alive before 3:30 p.m. And if you're going to tell me that a parish secretary is less credible than a man with known mental health issues and a history of deceptive behavior, then you're the idiot, Tom. Which I don't believe for a minute."

I slump against the counter. "OK, you're right. It doesn't look good. But are you going to check out Glenda's story? We only have her word that she was working that day."

"So what, she lied about working? Why would she do that?" I look at her. "OK, OK, fine. I'll check with the hotel to make sure she was supposed to be there."

We are interrupted by Gladys, who rolls in saying to Helen, "You said you wanted to see this when it came." She turns to leave but then sees me and freezes. "Oh! Oh, hi, Father. How are you?"

"I'm fine, thanks."

Before I can ask how she is, she says with a grin, "Yes, that's obvious."

"Gladys," Helen says tersely, "don't you have something you're supposed to be doing now?"

Gladys looks at Helen a little stunned, then confused, and then defensive, saying "Yeah, bringing you these papers, Chief."

"Thank you, then," she says, nodding toward the door. Gladys rolls away as Helen opens the folder and looks through the pages.

Helen then looks at me and says again, "I'll check on her story. But there's something I need to do first. Come on."

"Where are we going?"

"To the hospital to arrest John Archman for Katherine Shepp's murder. That was the fingerprint report. There were two sets of prints on the lamp—Shepp's and Archman's"

"What?" I say, incredulous. Helen puts her hand on my arm.

"I'm sorry, Tom. Your friend's a murderer."

Twenty-Nine

Chloe is in John's room when we arrive. She starts crying hysterically as Helen arrests her husband and reads him his rights. I hold her as she sobs, her head buried in my shoulder, me patting her back. She doesn't see Helen handcuff him to the bed or have a police officer placed outside his door.

I ask Chloe if there is anyone I can call for her. It takes a while, but before I leave with Helen, she has pulled herself together and is on the phone with a lawyer—their family lawyer—and she is asking for a good criminal attorney.

"I doubt he'll do much serious time," Helen says as we walk down the hospital corridor. "A good lawyer will have him plead down to manslaughter. He won't spend the rest of his life in prison."

"He shouldn't spend any time in prison," I say. "I still don't believe he did it."

She shrugs. "The evidence says otherwise."

"The evidence is wrong." I quicken my pace to pass her.

She stops, grabs my arm, and pulls me back. "Listen, Tom," she snaps. "I know you don't like it, but the evidence is what it is. OK, maybe some of it is cirumstantial, but the fingerprints on the murder weapon are pretty damning if you ask me. Remember, I'm the detective here. This is what I do. I've appreciated the help. I really have. It's been fun, but this case is over."

She pauses, releasing her grip. Then she surprises me by gently rubbing my arm. "As is Joan's murder case."

"What do you mean?" I say as we get on the elevator.

"I probably couldn't make an arrest based on Archman's statement," Helen explains, "But it's pretty clear now what happened. Randy Earl killed Joan and tried to kill you."

I stand staring at the stainless steel doors of the elevator as the numbers count floors down to the ground level. I say nothing. I am processing what she has said.

The doors open and we step into the hospital atrium. "You told me there wasn't enough," I finally say.

"There isn't, not enough to make an arrest. All I really have is his statement. Even your revised statement—which you still need to make, by the

229

way—can't corroborate his because you didn't hear what he did. But I believe his story, and believe he heard what he heard. I have a suspect now."

"A suspect you can't find."

"A suspect I can't find yet. So really, I'm not closing the case. I'm just putting it back in the drawer. Joan's case may never technically be closed," she puts her hand on my arm, "but at least now you know who did it. And why."

I nod. I do know who murdered Joan. And why.

"More importantly, Tom," she continues as we walk, "you can let go now."

I say, "Let go of what?" But I know what she means. .

"Let go of your guilt." She stops as I keep walking. "It wasn't your fault, Tom. You're not responsible."

I stop and stare ahead. Then I turn. "If I had followed her out of the restaurant when she left instead of waiting—"

"Randy Earl would still have been there."

"But he might not have come out if it were both of us."

"True," Helen says, walking slowly towards me. "But then again, he might have."

"If I had just gotten up," I whisper.

"He knocked you down. You were stunned."

"I should have protected her."

"He shouldn't have decided to shoot you," Helen says.

She stands in front of me and places her hands on my shoulders. "Tom, you can continue to blame yourself if you want to. I can't stop you. But from where I stand, there is only one person responsible for Joan's death. And that is the man who shot her."

I look at her. How many times had I heard Brother Martin say the same thing to me? How many times had I heard a fellow priest hearing my confession say it? I hadn't been able to accept them saying it. Would I accept it now, coming from this woman detective? This woman I once loved? This woman I had once planned on marrying?

I don't know.

***

The news of John's arrest for Katherine Shepp's murder makes the evening news that night and is on the front page of the Baltimore paper the next day. I am sitting in Anna's kitchen, reading the story on my phone, eating pancakes that she had made for me. I have just wiped a mix of butter and syrup from my mouth when my phone rings.

"Good morning, Archbishop," I answer.

"Father Tom," comes His Eminence's bass voice over the phone. He sounds a lot more jovial than the last time we spoke.

"I assume you saw the news."

"Yes, yes, I did. Do you know him, this Archman?"

"He was the best man at my wedding."

"Oh," he says . "Well, I am sorry. Sounds like a crime of passion."

I don't blurt out that he didn't do it, that the police have made a mistake, everything I really think.

"Tragic for his wife and family," he continues. "So sad. I will pray for them. And the victim." He pauses a moment. "I suppose you know why I'm calling."

"I've been expecting it."

"With this case over, you're no longer needed in Myerton," the Archbishop says. "Before you protest, I've already spoken with Detective Parr. She says that, while you may be needed for the trial, you're no longer needed as a witness, so you're free to leave."

I listen without saying anything.

"So with that," the Archbishop says, "I expect you back here now."

"Yes, Your Eminence," I reply. "I'll return right away."

"I'm not unreasonable. Take a couple of days to get your affairs in order. But by the end of the week."

"Thank you," I say.

"Of course. Oh," he continues, "by the way. Had a very interesting call from Father Abbot at Our Lady of the Mount. Says he's spoken to you? Apparently you paid them a little visit?"

"Just an overnight one, as it turned out. I had—things I needed to think through. Needed a little solitude."

"That's what he said. Anyway, he asked me about lending you to them temporarily as their priest"

"Yes, he spoke to me about it and said he would talk to you."

"Well, he spoke to me. Has been speaking to me. Father Abbot can be persistent."

I smile. *Not unlike someone else I know*, I think.

"What did you tell him?" I ask.

"Frankly, first I told him no, that I needed you here. But," the Archbishop sighs, "he wore me down. Last thing I told him when he called me yesterday was that I have no objection but I would give you permission to make the decision. He is agreeable to that. So, Father Tom, is this something you'd like to do?"

I think for a moment before answering. "No, Your Eminence, at least not right now," I say. "I need to be available for the trial, and I'd like to be able to visit my friend. I can't really do that from the monastery."

The Archbishop says, "I'll let Father Abbot know."

***

A few days later, I say my goodbyes to Anna.

"You will be back," Anna says, "this time."

"Of course," I say. "To see you. I'll be back for John's trial."

"Have you seen him since . . ."

I shake my head. "No, he's still in the hospital. I spoke to Chloe—well, sort of, she's not too happy with me right now—and she told me he's going to be released from the hospital today, but taken into custody. There'll be an arraignment and hopefully, he'll be released on bail. I'll come back in a week or so and see him then."

She nods. I see her hesitate. I know what she wants to ask me. It was what she has asked me repeatedly since I returned to Myerton.

I smile. "On my way out of town, I promise."

She smiles and hugs me.

***

The trees are bare of their leaves, the victims of a windstorm a couple of nights before. The late October sun shines unfiltered through the gray branches against the crystal clear blue sky. The brown carpet of leaves crunch beneath my feet as I make my way up the slight hill through the rows of white tombstones towards the majestic oak tree.

I stand in front of Joan's grave. I stroke the stone. It feels cool underneath my touch in spite of the sun shining directly on it.

"Sorry I haven't been here," I say.

I pause, thinking about what to say next.

I want to ask her all the questions I have, about everything I have learned about her that I hadn't known when she was alive. It still hurts that she didn't share parts of her life with me.

But I think I am beginning to understand why.

Standing there, looking at her grave, I realize my asking won't give me answers. She took them with her when she died. So I will be left with my questions and no answers. It is the way things have to be.

"I've been away," I say, "but then you know that." I pause. "I need to leave again," I continue, "but I'll visit the next time I'm back."

I pull out my book of prayers and start reading Saint Paul's words from Romans.

"I am convinced that neither death, nor life, nor angels, nor principalities, nor present things, nor future things, nor powers, nor height, nor depth, nor any other creature will be able to separate us from the love of God in Christ Jesus, our Lord."

I finish, saying, "May the love of God and the peace of the Lord Jesus Christ bless and console us and gently wipe every tear from our eyes: in the name of the Father, and the Son, and the Holy Spirit, Amen," while making the sign of the cross.

I stand there for a few minutes in silence, then I bend down and kiss the stone.

"I love you, Joan," I whisper.

***

A couple of weeks later, the Archbishop gives me permission to visit Myerton. A mild October has given way to a chilly November, and the wind whips down Main Street as I drive past the storefronts and Saint Clare's Parish. I make a mental note to check on Father McCoy before I leave. The Archbishop has assigned him to the parish permanently, and I want to see how he is settling in. And by settling in, I meant getting along with Glenda. Before I do that, I have a stop to make.

The county jail is about twenty minutes from downtown, nestled in a small valley between two mountains. From a distance, it looks like a school, or maybe a small hospital. It's only when one gets closer that you see the ten foot fence topped with razor wire. Used to house offenders serving time for minor offenses as well as those awaiting trial, it's where John Archman has been since his release from the hospital.

I park my car and get out. Walking across the lot to the jail, I hear a familiar voice call my name.

Looking up, I see a smiling Detective Helen Parr walking towards me, bundled in a heavy overcoat against the wind, which blows curls of her raven-black hair around her face, causing them to catch the sunlight.

For a second, I'm back in time twenty years to a different windy fall day, in a different place. She's a younger version of the woman I see, same black hair catching the sun, same curls blowing across her face, same smile.

You've got to stop this, Tom, the priest in me says.

It's just a memory, replies the lover.

The priest and the lover begin to argue—again—as I stop and return the smile.

"Tom," she says. "Good to see you."

"Good to see you, too, Helen. I'm surprised. What has you all the way out here?"

"Two reasons, actually," she replies. "The shooting range is almost next door. I come up every couple of weeks to squeeze off a few rounds to keep up my proficiency."

"I didn't know you liked to shoot," I say. "I don't think you ever did when we were together."

"Remember, I grew up in Nebraska as an only child," she laughs. "My dad taught me to shoot. There just wasn't an opportunity in College Park. But, it turns out being able to shoot well is kind of important for a cop."

"Yes, I can see that," I say with a smile.

"Besides," she says. "It's a great stress reliever."

"And what exactly do you have to be stressed about?"

At my question, a wistful look passes across her face. She tilts her head to one side and brushes a curl behind her ear. "My job's very stressful, Tom," she says quietly. "And I've had a lot on my mind recently."

I don't know how to respond to that, but fortunately, Helen continues, "And since I was out this way anyway, I stopped by to get some paperwork. I assume you're here to visit John Archman?"

"Yes, it's the first chance I've had to get away."

"Archbishop keeping you busy, huh?"

"I've got a lot to catch up on," I explain. "How is John, do you know?"

"Sorry," she shakes her head. "I haven't seen him since the arraignment. You know he entered a plea of not guilty."

"I heard. I also heard bail was denied?"

She holds up her hands. "Hey, not my fault, Tom. Bri—the State Attorney opposed and the judge agreed. It's an election year next year. Neither of them want to be portrayed as soft on crime."

I could protest, insist that John isn't a criminal. But I decide against it.

"Well, I need to get going," she says. She stops and turns slightly. "Are you here long?"

"No, just for the day."

"Awfully long drive just for the day."

"The Archbishop is keeping me on a short leash."

"I just thought, well, we—" she stops. "I mean, there is still the issue of the revised statement," she resumes. "I let you get away without it. I still need that, Father."

I shrug. "I should have time this afternoon."

She nods. "Good, I'll see you at my office at 1 p.m. I'll bring lunch." She walks off, stops, then turns.

"Tomato bisque, right?"

I smile. "You remember."

Helen returns the smile, hers small and wistful. "I remember a lot of things, Tom."

***

Because I am in my clericals, the jail staff allows me to meet with John privately. The room has all the charm of a utility closet and is about as large, constructed of cinderblocks. There is one metal table, bolted to the floor, and two chairs. A heavy door with a window is on one wall. The lights are harsh, incandescent.

I wait for a few moments, then John is brought in by one of the guards. I have seen prisoners on TV with wrists and ankles shackled, wearing orange jumpsuits. John wears a khaki jumpsuit and is unshackled.

The guard seats him in the chair. "Father," he says, "I'll be right outside if you need me."

"I'm sure we'll be fine. We're old friends."

The guard looks at me, then at John, then leaves the room, closing the door behind him. He takes his position outside so he can keep an eye on us through the window.

"I'm glad you still consider me a friend," John says, smiling. "I'm not sure I have too many of those left."

"Of course I still consider you a friend," I say. "Nothing's changed. Why would it?"

John rubs his face. "Oh, I don't know, let's start with the fact I stalked your wife. Hid while someone killed her and tried to kill you. Kept secret what I saw for fifteen years. Told you I didn't care if you lived or died. Let's start with that."

"That was a long time ago. You told the truth eventually. The police now know what happened that night."

"Can they make an arrest?" John asks.

I shake my head. "No. They don't know where he is. We're not even sure what he looks like."

"I'm sorry, Tom."

"I didn't come here to talk about Joan," I say. "How are you doing?"

John manages a slight smile. "OK, I guess. It's not as bad as you'd think. Food's not too bad, and they've got a pretty good library. I'm doing a lot of reading. And praying."

"Good. Has Father McCoy been by?"

John grins. "You mean Reverend Bones? Yes, he's been here several times. They let him bring me Communion."

"Reverend Bones?"

He shrugs. "Some of the teens call him that. He's a good priest, nice, but a little stiff. Nervous. Afraid of his own shadow."

We exchange chuckles and lapse into silence.

"What's your lawyer think of your case?" I ask after a few minutes. "You know, the evidence is circumstantial, even though your fingerprints are on the murder weapon, but I'm sure you've explained—"

"I must have touched the lamp when I checked on Shepp," he says. "They found my fingerprints on the folder, on the desk, on the door. I said I was in the room."

"Yes, you were in the room, but you should be able to convince a jury at trial—"

"There's not going to be a trial," John says quietly.

I look at him dumbfounded. "What?"

He shakes his head. "No. No trial. I don't want to put Chloe and the kids through any more. My lawyer's cut a deal with the State Attorney. I'm pleading guilty to manslaughter. In return, the State Attorney will recommend I serve the minimum at the Patuxent Institute over in Jessup." He pauses. "They're taking into account my PTSD and my drug and alcohol abuse."

"John, you didn't do it."

"It doesn't matter," John says. "I don't want to take my chances. And like I say, I can't have Chloe and the kids go through that."

I sit and look at him. "Is there anything I can do?"

"Thanks for coming by. Are you going to be here when I plead?"

I nod. "Yes, I'll come back."

***

After I leave John, I still have about an hour and a half before my meeting with Helen. I decide to go to Saint Clare's to see how Father McCoy is doing and catch the Noon Mass. When I arrive, he is already in the sacristy.

He has his back to me when I knock on the open door. He jumps and gives a little cry, spinning around.

"I told you I'd take care—Oh!" I obviously am not who he is expecting.

"Thought I was someone else?" I ask, unable to hide my amusement.

"What? No, no, yes, I mean—you startled me," sputters the flustered Father.

"She doesn't usually knock, you know."

He grimaces. "I have noticed that. Is there a trick to locking the office door?"

"The trick is there is no lock," I say. "I think she removed it."

"I can believe it," he nods.

"She's not a bad person," I go on. "Glenda is just—intense."

"She's a nightmare," McCoy mutters. Then, realizing what he said, his eyes get big. "Oh, I mean, well, she has many fine qualities."

I decide to put him out of his misery. "Yes, Father, yes, she does." I advance with an outstretched hand. "I just wanted to see how you were doing."

He shakes my hand. "Good to see you, Father Greer."

"Tom, please."

"Tom, it is. Leonard."

"Are you settling in, Leonard?"

"Oh, yes, I suppose," he says. "I wasn't sure I was ready for my own parish when the Archbishop assigned me here. He didn't give me much time."

"It was an emergency," I say slowly. Leonard looks at me.

"Yes, I realize that. Still, to go from where I was to here—I mean, there are just so many people. And children." I think I detect a slight shudder.

"Sunday Mass can be lively."

"Someone is always screaming," McCoy whispers. "A baby or older child."

"Most of the time," I smile. "There is the occasional mom."

He looks at me. "Joke," I explain.

"Ah," he nods. "Don't get me wrong, children are a blessing, and I'm gratified to see so many people open to life and all that, it's just not what I'm used to."

"Where were you before Saint Clare's?"

"I was chaplain at Saints Joachim and Anna's."

I nod. That explains it. Saints Joachim and Anna's Assisted Living is a much quieter posting than Saint Clare's.

"Well," I say, "the children's nativity should at least be—"

"Oh, I've cancelled that," Father McCoy says.

"What?"

"Yes, Glenda explained to me what a bad idea it was, and in this case I have to agree with her."

"She was against the idea in the first place," I say. "I bet the moms were disappointed."

"I've only heard from one," he whispers. "The director. Miriam Conway. She seems like such a sweet person. But she threatened to have me arrested!"

"Her husband is a police officer, though I doubt she'd actually do it."

"Well, that is a load off my mind."

"Anyway, I'm in Myerton for the day," I say, "and wanted to stop by."

"Why are you in town? It's not a short drive from Baltimore."

"I was visiting John Archman."

"Oh, of course. He is a friend of yours. Poor man. I've visited him several times. First time visiting a prisoner. I took him Communion, heard his confession, we chatted. Very nice man. Troubled. I can tell that. His experiences in Iraq. My father was a First Gulf War veteran. Hardly the same, I suppose. He doesn't seem like a murderer."

"He's not," I reply with perhaps a little more force than I mean. McCoy blinks.

"Oh, of course, I didn't mean to imply, it's just that he is going to plead guilty, and the police wouldn't have arrested him without evidence."

"The evidence was all circumstantial," I say. "I understand why he's pleading guilty. But I know the man, Leonard. He didn't do it."

Not knowing how to reply, the young priest says . "Well, as you can see, I am getting ready for the Noon Mass. Would you care to celebrate with me?"

I smile. "I would be delighted."

***

After Mass, I say goodbye to Father McCoy. I still have plenty of time to get to the police station, but I don't want to risk being late.

On my way out, I bump into Glenda.

"Oh, good afternoon, Glenda," I say with a smile.

"Father," she says curtly.

"I didn't see you in Mass."

"Trying to catch up on some parish affairs," she says. "Father McCoy's an adequate priest but has no administrative ability. He'll learn, though. I'm bringing him along."

The vision of Glenda leading Father Leonard with a leash and dog collar flashes through my mind, an image I quickly dismiss.

"Why are you here?" she asks in an accusing manner.

"I was in Myerton visiting John Archman. I have time before another appointment, so I thought I'd come to Mass."

"I see, I see. Well, as a priest, visiting prisoners is your job."

"It is one of the corporal acts of mercy," I say. "We all should."

She looks at me. "Well," she says, "I won't keep you." She turns to leave.

A question pops into my head. "Oh, Glenda?"

She stops and turns around. "Yes?" she asks with a tone of irritation.

"You told the police that you spoke to Katherine Shepp and gave her fresh towels the afternoon of her murder."

"Yes, what about it?" she snaps.

"Did she seem all right?"

"Did she seem all right?" Glenda repeats. "I suppose. I didn't notice anything. I didn't ask about her health, just gave her the towels."

"She didn't seem groggy? You didn't notice any bumps on her head or anything?"

"Oh, what nonsense is this?" she says with a dismissive wave. "I told the police she was alive when I left."

"But I'm just—"

"Wasting my time," she says. She turns around and walks off.

I walk back to my car to drive to the police station. Sitting behind the steering wheel, I think for a few minutes.

I can't shake the feeling that something isn't adding up.

Nate said when he threw Shepp down, she hit her head on the table and was knocked unconscious. As far as he knew, she hadn't gotten up when he walked on the elevator. He said he heard the doors of the other elevator open as the doors of his elevator were closing.

Glenda says Shepp was alive when she gave her towels. But she didn't appear hurt.

Did Shepp have enough time to recover from when she was knocked out by Nate to when Glenda brought her the towels to appear fine? Was it possible that Glenda simply didn't notice if Shepp was hurt?

I shake my head. It doesn't matter. John has decided to plead guilty. The police are satisfied. It isn't my job to try to prove otherwise.

Thirty

John's next court appearance is the first Wednesday in December. Myerton has decorated Main Street with green, gold, and red for Christmas. In the square in front of the courthouse, the town Christmas tree is festooned with lights and large gold balls, topped with a silver star that reflects the early winter sun. In-ground speakers pipe Christmas music through the square to complete the festive holiday scene. There had once been a Nativity scene, but a threatened lawsuit caused the City Council to remove it.

The courthouse itself is decorated with wreaths on the door, a Christmas tree, a Menorah, and a Kwanzaa candelabra in the atrium. I walk down the hallway to Courtroom Three, where John's hearing is scheduled.

The room is crowded, with some members of the press lining the back wall. Two tables are up front. At one sits a man who I assume is the State Attorney, a man about my age in a grey pinstripe suit.

Brian.

Helen's—what? Boyfriend? Former fiancé?

A small wave of jealousy washes over me at the thought of Helen with him.

Stop it! the priest yells at the lover.

I turn my attention to the other table, where John sits with his attorney.

I survey the room, looking for a seat. I see Chloe seated right behind John. I start to walk forward to say hi when I hear my name. I turned to see Helen, indicating the seat next to her.

"I'm surprised to see you here," I say as I sit down. "Your job is done."

"It probably is," she says. "I'm here just in case the judge has a question the State Attorney can't answer."

She swallows and looks away from me. "I also knew you'd be here," she says quietly. "And I wanted to see you."

In spite of myself, I feel a thrill shoot through me. "Oh?" is all I can manage.

She clears her throat and squares her shoulders. "Yes," she says. "I wanted to be able to tell you in person that you're in the clear."

I look at her, puzzled. "The State Attorney decided not to prosecute you," she explains.

I sigh with relief. "I had forgotten about that. Thanks."

"You can thank me over lunch after this is over," she says.

"Are you buying?"

"I bought it last time, remember?"

"All rise," says the bailiff. We stop our banter and stand with the rest of the courtroom as the judge ascends to the bench.

"Please be seated," the judge says, which we obediently do.

It is over in about thirty minutes. John pleads guilty to manslaughter, the State Attorney recommends no more than ten years to be served at Patuxent due to his history of mental illness. The judge accepts the recommendation and formally sentences John. He gavels the hearing adjourned, everyone rises, and he walks out of the room. John turns to hug Chloe, who is visibly sobbing. The guards approach him and quietly lead him away. The crowd begins to thin. Chloe sits down and stares straight ahead.

"Shall we go?" Helen asks, slinging her bag over her shoulder.

"I'll meet you outside," I say. "I want to see Chloe."

She pats my shoulder and leaves the courtroom. I walk to the front and stand by Chloe for a moment.

"Hi, Chloe," I say. She stares straight ahead.

"May I sit?" She turns to look at me and nods.

We sit together in silence for a few minutes. The only other person in the room is a clerk gathering papers from the Judge's bench.

"John told me you visited him," Chloe whispers. "Thank you for that. He really appreciated it."

"It was the least I could do," I say. "He is my friend."

"Yes, your friend. My husband. You know he betrayed us both," she says with a hint of bitterness.

"No, I don't see that—"

"That's because you're blind," she says to me, the anger coming out with every word. "Or too holy now that you're a priest. His obsession with Joan back then betrayed me. Oh, I know nothing happened between them—but emotionally, it was her he wanted and not me. He was too big of a coward to help you that night. Think about it, Tom. Don't you realize that if he had jumped in, Joan might be alive today?"

That thought hit me one day when I was working at the Archdiocese. I felt like someone had punched me in the solar plexus. I felt a boiling rage welling up like a volcano from deep within me, anger I had never felt before. I sat at my desk, gripping the edge. The intern was working quietly at a desk in the corner, oblivious. In my mind's eye, I began to scream, picking up the papers on my desk and hurling them into space, throwing my chair, knocking boxes off the shelf.

With herculean self-control, I left my office, then the building. I walked across the parking lot into the woods. I kept walking until I couldn't see the offices anymore.

Then I screamed.

And screamed.

And screamed.

I don't know how long I screamed. Finally, I ran out of screams. I went from screaming to crying. I fell to my knees in the dirt and leaves and sobbed.

And sobbed.

And sobbed.

"Yes, Chloe, yes, I do," I whisper.

She leans toward me. "Doesn't that make you angry?"

"I was angry," I say. "But I'm not angry anymore."

She crosses her arms. "You're a better man than I am."

I pat her shoulder. "You need to forgive him, Chloe."

I see a tear travel down her cheek. "I know, Tom. I—I just can't right now." She turns to me. "I love him. I'm angry but I love him. Now he's gone from me. Gone from the kids."

"He told me why he pled guilty," I say.

"He pled guilty because he did it."

That stuns me. "Did he tell you that?"

"No," she says. "He still insists he's innocent, that he's just pleading guilty to spare me and the kids a trial. But I don't buy it. I hate to think my husband is a murderer. But he went there because of what she knew about him and Joan. He must have lost control, hit her with the lamp they found his finger-prints on."

"I can't believe that," I say, shaking my head. "I won't believe it."

"Then who, Tom? Who did it, huh? Do you think that woman detective who's attracted to you would have arrested him if she really didn't think he did it?"

"What do you mean, attracted to me?"

"You heard me. I've seen the way she looks at you. You can't be that clueless." Chloe gets up and grabs her bag. "I've gotta go. I'm going to visit John. Where are you going, back to Baltimore?"

"Not yet, I'm having lunch with—" I stop myself.

Chloe smiles. "Tell Detective Parr I say hello. And no hard feelings. I'm trying for forgiveness."

She walks out of the courtroom, leaving me sitting by myself. I shake my head and follow her out.

Outside the courthouse, I meet up with Helen. She is on her phone.

"All right, I'll be right there." She hangs up and looks at me apologetically.

"Problem?"

"No, the Chief wants to see me about something related to a case. I can't do lunch." She sighs. "Raincheck?"

"Of course," I smile.

"When will you be back in Myerton?"

I shrug. "I don't know. I'll probably come back around Christmas, see Anna for a couple of days."

"You're not going to Florida?"

I shake my head. "You remember what it's like when I'm there," I say. "Nothing's changed."

She nods. "I remember," she says as she strokes my arm. "Good to see you."

I pat her hand. "You, too, Helen."

I watch her as she walks away. I think about what Chloe said. About what she sees in Helen. She had said I couldn't be that clueless.

Sadly, I'm not. Not about Helen's feelings.

Or my own.

My phone rings, breaking me out of my daze. It is a Myerton number I don't recognize.

"Hello?"

"Hello, Tom, this is Bethany Grable. Did I catch you at a bad time?"

"No, not at all. What can I do for you?"

"Well, I didn't get a chance to see you before you left the last time, but I am wondering if you could finish getting the rest of Joan's things out of the studio? I don't mind holding onto them, but I could use the storage space."

"Sure, I'll come by and grab some things. I can't take everything today in my car."

"Anything you could do would be great. I'll see you in a bit."

***

Bethany unlocks the door and opens it, reaching around to turn the light on.

"I'll leave you to it," she says. "I have someone coming to look at American Carnage."

I look at her with surprise. Smiling, she says, "Told ya someone would buy it."

She leaves me standing in the doorway, looking at Joan's things in the storage room. I'll take her canvases and sketch books, I decide right away. Her sketchbooks are stacked on the shelf, but I look around and can't find her canvases. I make a mental note to ask Bethany about those; she must have moved them for safekeeping. I go to the boxes on the shelves and lift the lids, peeking inside. Mostly art supplies—paints, brushes, pencils. If they are still any good, I'll tell Bethany she can keep them, maybe donate them to a school.

I look through box after box. Some contain papers that I don't want to go through right away, so I take those off the shelf and carry them to the door. There is one box left on the shelf. Looking inside, I see more papers.

As I lift the box off the shelf, the bottom gives way, the contents of the box falling to the floor.

I utter a scatalogical expletive and toss the remnants of the box to the side. I look around and find an empty intact box. Crouching down, I start picking up the papers—a mix of what looks like scrap paper, pictures torn and cut out of magazines, even entire issues of old magazines. Underneath the pile is a padded binder.

It is a photo album, fallen open to a picture of a very young Joan. She must have been eight or nine years old. She is sitting on a carousel horse, holding a big cone of cotton candy, a look of absolute mirth on her face.

I smile. Our daughter—if it was a daughter—would be older, a teenager by now. I hope she would have looked like her mother.

I slowly flip through. There are pictures of Joan with her Mom and Dad, confirmation pictures, pictures of Joan with groups of boys and girls the same age looking like they were taken at a summer camp. All show Joan happy, laughing, smiling, having fun.

The album is only half full. The last photo shows Joan sitting between her Mom and Dad, blowing out the candles on a birthday cake. From the number, it was her thirteenth.

The last birthday before her father killed himself. She and her Mom are smiling, happy. I look at her Dad's picture. He is smiling, too. Was he really happy, I wonder, or was he hiding his pain, keeping it a secret from those he loved? Is that where Joan learned to keep her pain a secret, that you kept it from your husband to keep from hurting him, so he wouldn't think less of her?

I dismiss the thoughts and decide to drop the album off with Anna on my way out of town. It rightfully belongs to her.

I close the album. As I start to place it in the box, a loose photo drops out and falls face down in the box. I reach to pick it up, then stop.

Written on the back was a month and year. March, 1996. The month and year on her marriage license.

I hesitate, then pick it up. I slowly turn it over. The picture shows Joan at sixteen, looking very different from her birthday picture. Gone is the light in her eyes, the joy-filled smile. Her smile is joyless, her eyes dark.

With Joan is a young man, slightly older looking, with the same expression on his face, a scruffy beard, and longish hair that looks like it hadn't seen a comb or soap and water in a while.

I stare at the man. I bring the picture closer, studying it, looking at the eyes, the shape, the spacing.

In a flash, I know.

Leaving the boxes, I run to my car. On the way, I call Helen's number. It goes to voicemail.

"Helen," I say quickly, "I'm sending you a picture. Call me back as soon as you get this." I take a picture of the photo and send it to Helen's phone.

I get in my car and squeal out of the parking lot towards Saint Clare's.

***

I speed all the way there and blow through at least one stop sign. I park and run to the door of the Rectory. I press the doorbell, and bang on the door.

"Glenda, it's Father Tom," I call, knocking again.

A very irritated Glenda throws the door open. "For heaven's sake, Father Greer," she says.

"I need to talk to you, Glenda. Right now," I push my way inside and spin around to face her.

She closes the door. "You're in a state, Father," she says. "Father McCoy is at the hospital—"

"No, it's you I came to talk to." I show her the picture. She doesn't look at it, and kept her arms crossed.

"What is that?"

"Please look at it," I say. "Take a good look."

"Oh, why should I waste—"

"Just look at the picture!" I scream.

She looks stunned by my outburst, but does as I ask. She brings it close to her eyes. She studies it for what seems like a long time.

"The girl is Joan," I say quietly. "I think you know the boy. He's younger and thinner, but there's no mistake, is there?"

She looks up from the photo. She shakes her head. "No," she whispers.

"It's your nephew, isn't it? His real name is Randy. Randy Earl. Am I right?"

She hands the picture back to me. "Sit down, Father. I'll get us some coffee." She leaves the room.

Before I can sit down, my phone rings. It's Helen's number—not her cell phone, her office phone.

"Did you see it?" I ask as soon as I answer.

"Wait, what are you talking about?" she asks.

"I sent a photograph to your phone. Listen, Helen, I've—"

"I haven't looked at my phone, haven't had time. I have to tell you—"

"Well, look at your phone. It's important."

"So's what I have to tell you," she went on. "Listen, I had an officer go interview the hotel manager. Somehow, we hadn't done it and I wanted to add his statement to the file. The officer asked if Glenda was working that day."

"We know she was. Listen, Helen—"

"No, she wasn't, Tom. In fact, the manager says she doesn't work for the hotel at all."

Stunned, I look to the kitchen. I turn around and walk to a corner of the room. "What?" I say, being careful to keep my voice low.

"She lied, Tom. She lied about why she was there. And there's something else. I've got more information on Randy Earl."

"That's what I've been trying to tell you. I know who he is."

"So do I," Helen says. "Randy Earl isn't his real name. I mean it is his real name, but not his birth name."

"Birth name?" I whisper. "Wait, are you saying he was adopted?"

My mind begins to race. Something is beginning to come together.

"Yes, usually adoption records are sealed, but this was an open adoption. He was adopted shortly after birth by his married aunt, whose last name was Earl. His mother was her sister." She pauses. "You'll never guess."

But I don't have to guess. I already know. It's in the eyes.

"Helen," I whisper, "you need to come—"

"Put the phone down, Father," I hear Glenda say behind me.

I turn around.

Glenda stands in the doorway of the living room, a gun trained on me.

Thirty-One

"Tom, Tom, are you there? Where are you?" I hear Helen say.

"Don't say anything," Glenda says firmly. "Just hang up and give me the phone."

I do as she says. She points to the couch with the gun. "Sit," she says. I take a place on the couch. She sits in a chair, still pointing the gun at me.

"Yes," Glenda says. "It's the same gun. My father's. The only thing he left me when he died."

"He's your son, isn't he?"

"Oh, Detective Parr told you that, did she? Yes, he's my boy. I'll tell you everything. But first." She makes the sign of the cross. "Bless me, Father, for I have sinned," she begins.

"No," I say.

"It has been six months since my last confession." She smiles.

I know what she is doing. Making sure I can't say anything. Anything she says is now under the seal of the confession. I am pretty certain now that she'll let me live, but if she does, she doesn't want me to be able to tell anyone what she told me.

"It won't work," I say. "They already know you lied about working at the hotel."

"This is my confession, Father," she says. "Shut up and listen."

I settle back. And pray.

"You're right, of course," Glenda begins. "Randy is my son. I got pregnant at 15—I was troubled, I'll admit that, I am a later-life child and I'm still not sure my parents really wanted me. I got drunk one night at a party and some boy, I don't even know who, well, took advantage of the situation. I didn't tell my parents at first, but after I missed a period and started throwing up every morning, I had to tell them. The doctor confirmed I was pregnant."

"How did they react?"

She shrugged. "Not too badly, I suppose. My mother was mainly upset with herself for not putting me on the Pill. They were Catholic, but not too Catholic—mainly just Christmas and Easter, making sure I had all my sacraments so they could check the boxes. They were Catholic enough not to have

251

me get an abortion. In fact, they saw my situation as a solution to another problem."

"What problem was that?"

She frowns, her eyes grow darker. "My older sister," she says bitterly. "The good one. She and her husband had been trying for a baby for five years, but had had no luck. After several miscarriages, her doctor told her she might never be able to carry a baby to term. So, they all sat down and agreed that when I gave birth to my baby, my sister and her husband would adopt him or her and I'd become Aunt Glenda."

"How did you react to that?"

"I was fifteen," she says. "I didn't want a baby. It made sense to me at the time. I'd have the baby, my sister would raise it, and I'd go on to have a life. Besides, I thought I'd get married and have other babies." She paused. "It didn't work out that way, though."

"What happened?"

She exhales slowly. I think I can see a tear welling up. "I went into labor about a month early. I started bleeding. They had to do an emergency Caesarian to save Randy. They wouldn't let me hold him. They couldn't get my bleeding to stop, so to save my life, they had to give me a hysterectomy." She sniffs and wipes away a tear. "So there would be no more babies."

I feel a tinge of sorrow for young Glenda.

"I was only sixteen, Father, and I'd never have children. The only child I would ever have would never be mine." She shakes slightly. "I lay in that bed for days, knowing I would never have a baby of my own and hating my sister and my parents for taking mine away from me. I never forgave them for that," she whispers.

"Did you tell them how you felt? Maybe they would have changed their minds."

"You didn't know my parents," she laughs. "No, they were determined to have no single moms in their family. They brought me the papers to sign and I signed them. I put a smile on my face and kept it there. Over time, I buried my anger deep inside until I wasn't even aware it was there. I played the role of the dutiful younger aunt, seeing Randy as often as I could in the early years. After a time, I grew used to it and didn't see him as much. I went off to the university and got my teaching degree. That's how I wound up here, in Myerton. I took a job at one of the high schools in the county. I started attending Saint Clare's, I even began to date—though I knew I would never marry."

She looks so sad. If she hadn't been holding a gun on me, I would have felt pity.

"I'd still see Randy occasionally," Glenda continues. "Christmas and birthdays."

"He never found out you were his mother?"

"No, dear sister did a good job of keeping that from him. It wasn't until much later. Anyway, time passed. Then I began to hear about Randy."

"He was beginning to act out," I say.

"Very good, Father, you know the lingo and everything. Yes, my sister started telling me about his episodes, the mania, and depression, the uncontrollable rages, all of it. It began when he was thirteen or fourteen, I guess. They had to hospitalize him after he tried to kill himself the first time. After that, he was in and out for a couple of years before they put him in a special residential school in his senior year."

"That's where he met Joan," I say.

Glenda shrugs. "I suppose. I didn't know about her until much later, about them being together."

She pauses for a long time. "At first, I blamed myself. I thought that it was my fault he was sick, that it was because I gave him up and somehow deep inside, he knew. Or I thought I gave it to him, that I have it in my genes, or the guy who made me pregnant was that way and gave it to him. The anger returned." She smiles ruefully. "About the time he graduated from that school—he was, he is a very bright boy, Father—I was fired from my job at the high school."

"Why?"

She looks at me and smiles. "One day I got tired of my students not paying attention. So I sprayed my class with a fire extinguisher." She laughs. "I didn't hurt them and it got their attention. But the principal thought it was a bit excessive, especially after the parents sued the school district. My going was part of the settlement."

I just sit quietly, taking it all in. From the way she is talking and from what I am seeing, I have no doubt where Randy's illness comes from.

"So, I was fired," she goes on. "I couldn't get another teaching job, so I just remained in Myerton. I was able to get a couple of administrative jobs—glorified secretaries and office clerks—so I got by."

"What was Randy doing at this time?"

"Well, he graduated from the school, he was eighteen and a legal adult. But he really couldn't handle keeping a job. He lived with his parents and tried to work. Occasionally, he'd leave home for months at a time, go back to living on the streets, pick up odd jobs. His medication kept his bipolar disorder under control, but he still wasn't well. Frankly, I doubt he ever will be. This went on for several years. Then, his parents died in a car accident."

"Where was Randy at the time?"

"Let's see, I think he was living at home. They had gone out to dinner, it had snowed, and the temperature had dropped. They hit a patch of ice and slammed into a tree. My brother-in-law was killed instantly. My sister lasted for a few days at the hospital. I visited her before she died. The last thing she said to me was, 'take care of Randy.'" She pauses, looking at me over the gun. "So that's what I've done."

"He came to live here with you. When did he find out you were his mother?"

"That happened by accident. He has this habit of rummaging through things. One day he was in the basement and he started going through a box of old photos. There were several of me pregnant, with my sister who obviously was not. Like I say, he is very bright. He figured it out."

"How did he react?"

"He accepted it, started calling me Mom almost immediately. He was doing well those first few months." I see a shadow creep over her countenance. "That's when he saw her."

"Joan," I say.

She nods. "I remember him coming home, excited, talking a mile a minute, saying over and over again, 'Mom, I saw her, I saw her, she's here, she's here, she's come back to me.' It took me forever to calm him down. Then he told me the story, about how he and Joan had met at the school, how after he had graduated and she had left, they had run away together to get married, and how she had just up and left him a couple of months later. He was so excited."

"She didn't leave him," I say. "He left her alone on the streets in Baltimore."

She shakes her head. "That may be what she said, but my Randy wouldn't do that. Such a good-hearted boy."

Looking at the gun, I decide not to press the point. "Where did he see her?"

"I'm not really sure about that, I couldn't get a clear answer from him. I think he saw her just walking down Main Street one day when he was working on a construction job or something. It's been so long, I don't remember." She sighs. "After that, Joan was all he'd talk about. He lost that job because he couldn't focus. He started roaming around Myerton, looking for any chance to see her."

"He didn't attend Saint Clare's with you? We attended once in a while."

"No, he didn't want to go and I wouldn't make him. I couldn't tell him you and she even attended Saint Clare's. I didn't know myself until that first Sunday you were here. Well, eventually he saw her again and he followed her." She looks at me. "He saw her with you one day, I guess you were walking together arm in arm. He came home devastated; he cried for two days. I really thought he was going to kill himself. Then he pulled himself together. But that's when he started stalking her."

She exhales. "He somehow figured out where she worked and where you two lived. He started following her everywhere she went. He'd stay out all hours, sometimes all night—I think he'd sleep outside where you lived. That went on for weeks. Then it happened."

The room is quiet. "So you knew," I whisper. "All these years."

She nods. "I didn't realize until it was too late that he had gotten Daddy's gun. He came home late that night in the worst state I'd ever seen. He just kept repeating. "I didn't mean to do it, it's not my fault, it's his fault, I didn't mean to do it." It took me forever to calm him down to get the whole story."

"Why didn't you call the police?"

"And betray my boy!" she cries. "I couldn't do that, not again. I had betrayed him when he was born. No, I needed to help him. It wasn't his fault anyway."

"He shot her, Glenda. He had the gun."

"He didn't mean to shoot her. He meant to shoot you. She got in the way. If she had just gone with him, like he wanted, she'd still be alive. So Father, it really is your fault, not my boy's."

I look at her, dumbfounded. She really believes what she is saying.

"Once I got him calmed down," Glenda continues, "I had to come up with a plan. I had to get him out of town, somewhere far from Myerton until everything settled down. He didn't want to go, but I was able to get him to do it. I knew someone who was looking for men to work the Bakken shale oil fields in North Dakota—the boom was just starting, and they were desperate for men. It was perfect for Randy, hard work outdoors, he'd learn a skill, and it was far from here. So a couple of days after the incident, I put him on a bus to Bismark." She sighs. "It broke my heart to send him away, but I had to do it. To protect him."

"You stayed here, knowing the whole time."

She nods. "I had no problems with what I did. I was protecting my son. Doing what any mother would. I hadn't been a mother to him when he was growing up. It was the least I could do. It was a great plan. And it worked. They never figured out it was him."

Glenda smiles, pleased with herself.

"It would have gone on working, too, if you hadn't come back," she says bitterly.

"When did Randy come back to Myerton?"

"Only about six months before you did," she says. "You may know, the oil boom in North Dakota went bust about three or four years ago. He was laid off, and he wasn't able to get into another job. That triggered his symptoms. He had been doing fine, keeping on his meds and everything, without a major manic episode. He lost his job, he lost his health insurance, and couldn't afford his medication. He wound up in the hospital again."

"What happened?"

"He tried to kill himself again. Didn't succeed, really didn't even hurt himself, but it was enough. It was the start of a cycle. He was in and out, when he wasn't living on the streets, for a long time. And North Dakota isn't a place you want to live on the streets."

"Did you know what was going on?"

She shakes her head. "Not really. He'd call me occasionally, write some. There were weeks—months—where I wasn't sure where he was. I would have gone and looked for him, but that wasn't practical. No, all I could do was pray, so I did a lot of praying. I found real comfort in prayer."

The irony of a woman holding a gun on a priest while speaking about prayer is not lost on me.

"Eventually, he was stable long enough to work and earn money for a bus ticket back here. Like I say, he got back about six months before you did. People had forgotten about the murder, so I thought it was safe for him to stay. I got him a construction job, which he lost after six weeks, then another job, which he held onto for a little bit longer, but mostly he slept a lot and played video games." She sighs. "It wasn't easy. I had forgotten how high maintenance he could be. But he's my boy and I am so glad to have him back. And everything was fine. Until you arrived."

"He recognized me that first Sunday," I say.

"Yes. He had come to meet me after Mass when he saw you standing outside greeting everyone. Somehow, he recognized you immediately. It really sent him into a panic."

"You were trying to calm him down, weren't you? I saw you talking to him."

"He wanted to talk to you," she says. "I don't know about what. I told him to go home. It took a lot of persuasion. But he did what I said."

"He did talk to me later, you know," I say. "Did he tell you that?"

"Oh, yes, he told me. I am so angry with him for doing that. Everything was getting stirred up again. It was bad enough when that waiter was running around wanting to do his video about the case and that reporter started poking around. Then you had to get involved and do that interview. I had to do something."

"Why did you kill her?"

She blinks. "Why? To keep her from figuring out what happened."

"You knew the police were looking into it."

Glenda dismisses my statement with a wave of her hand. "They hadn't figured it out in fifteen years. No, she was the danger. I knew it when she waved around those emails."

The emails. The ones that John had written. "You thought—"

"I just knew Randy had written them," she says, "and it'd only be a matter of time before she figured that out. I had to get them from her."

"They were just copies. I have the originals."

"I'd figure that out later," she says. "No, she was investigating. She was beginning to put two and two together."

"Did Randy tell you he'd written them?"

"Oh, he denied knowing what I was talking about. But I knew he was lying."

"But he wasn't lying."

"No," she admits. "No, no, he wasn't. I know that now."

"You pretended to be a housekeeper at the hotel so she'd open the door. Did you plan on killing her?"

"No, I don't think so. I was just going to find those emails and steal them. If I had to, I'd knock her out or something. I am really clever. I grabbed a cart from another floor, put gloves on—no one pays attention to staff—so I was confident no one would take notice of me.

"But when I got to her room, the door was cracked. I called out that I was housekeeping and opened the door. I found her lying on the floor, face down, moaning and trying to get up." She shrugs. "Seemed like an ideal opportunity. So I picked up the lamp and bashed her head in."

"But Glenda," I say. "You left the emails."

"I couldn't find them," she says. "I started looking for them on the desk, but I thought I heard someone in the hallway. I had to get out of there."

She stops. We look at each other for a while.

"Where is Randy now?"

"Oh, he's at home."

"You know the police are going to figure it out."

"We'll be gone. Our bags are already packed. As soon as we're done here, I'm going and we're leaving Myerton for good."

"They'll find you."

"No, I don't think so, not where we're going."

I look at her. "What about me? Are you going to shoot me?"

"Oh, don't be ridiculous, Father Tom. I'm not going to shoot you. I'm not a killer. No, this is what's going to happen." She leans forward. "We're going to finish here, you're going to get up from that couch, and leave. I know you can't reveal to anyone what I told you. So I have nothing to fear from you."

"You need to turn yourselves in, Glenda, you and Randy."

"No, that's not going to happen."

"Aren't you the least bit sorry for what you've done?"

"Hmm, no, not really. I did what had to be done. To protect my boy."

"If you have no contrition," I say, "I can't grant you absolution."

She raises the gun a little higher. "Oh, I think you can, Father. You will. Do it now."

I look her in the eyes. Slowly, I shake my head. "No."

She stands up and takes a step forward. "Do it now, Father," she screams, "or I will shoot!"

Suddenly, I'm back in the parking lot. Joan is dying in my arms and the gun's to my head.

What if it hadn't misfired? What if she hadn't jumped in front of me? I'd be with her now. We'd be together again, with our child, the little one I've never held. Maybe Glenda would be doing me a favor. After all, "to be absent from the body is to be present with the Lord."

Justice would be served, and all this pain would be gone.

It's not a suicide. I am just standing firm for my vocation.

I'm thinking about this when I hear the Rectory door quietly open.

I am afraid that Glenda will hear it, but she doesn't react. I've noticed before that her hearing is not really good.

Behind the crazed woman, Helen steps quietly into view, training her gun on Glenda. I try not to look at her, but keep my eyes fixed on the woman in front of me.

"You're wasting time, Father!" Glenda screams.

Helen is close now and I give in to the temptation to look at her. Her eyes meet mine. They radiate confidence—and something else.

Suddenly, I realize that I want to live.

I do want to be with Joan and to meet our baby, but not yet.

"OK, Glenda," I say, trying to buy Helen the time needed to get across the room. In my best priest's voice, I say firmly, "Bow down for the blessing."

As I expected, this elicits an automatic response. As Glenda drops her head, Helen steps forward and places the gun against the small of her back. In a firm, calm voice she says, "Give me the gun, Glenda. It's all over."

After only the briefest of hesitations, Glenda drops her hand and Helen takes the gun. She hands Glenda off to another officer and looks at me, asking, "Are you all right?"

I nod. "It took you long enough."

"Hey, I've told you these things don't work as fast as they do on TV." She offers me her hand. "Come on, let's have the paramedics look you over." I take her hand and she pulls me up.

I wind up standing very close to her—not touching, but close enough to smell the scent of vanilla in her hair. We look into each other's eyes. Again, I'm captivated by hers, a deep azure blue. Her hand is so soft in mine. Her hair—oh, her hair, so black. There's a curl dangling down. I resist the urge to brush it behind her ear.

Helen's lips part as if she is about to speak.

"What in the name of—what is this?"

We turn to see a very confused Father McCoy standing in the doorway. "Father Greer, what are you doing—what, what are all these police cars doing?"

"Father McCoy, you remember Detective Helen Parr? She'll be glad to explain everything to you." I incline my head. "Detective, I think you wanted me checked out by the medics?"

She nods, with a slight smile. "Yes, Father Greer, that's right."

"Well, I'll go do that," I walk towards the door. "Oh, Father McCoy?"

"Yes?"

"You'll need to hire a new parish secretary."

***

"We're getting the prisoner now, Father. It will be a couple of minutes."

I thank the guard. After he leaves, I stand a moment, looking around the room. It's the same one in which I visited John.

A couple of minutes later, the door opens. The guard brings the prisoner in, clad in a khaki jumpsuit, hands and feet shackled. The prisoner shuffles along the floor, hampered by the ankle cuffs. The guard helps the prisoner to the table and fastens the handcuffs to a metal loop on the stainless steel surface.

"I'll be right outside, Father, if you need anything," the guard says.

"Thank you, we'll be fine."

He nods and then takes his place guarding the door, though he looks through the window instead of at the hallway.

I look at the seated figure. The prisoner is an image of despair. Shoulders slumped, head down. Helen told me they haven't gotten much since the first night, that the prisoner has spent most of the time in the cell staring at the wall.

"You can visit if you want to, Tom," she had told me on the phone. "I'll clear it. But don't be surprised if you're the only one doing the talking."

"That's fine," I said. "I just need to say a few things."

Now, sitting across from the prisoner, I'm not quite sure where to begin. So I decide to keep it simple.

"Hello, Randy."

Randy Earl doesn't look up, but stares at a spot on the table.

"Are they treating you well? I hear the food isn't bad."

He continues to stare at the table.

"I want to thank you for seeing me. We've never really had a chance to talk." I smile. "That day in the confessional, you did most of the talking."

I pause and look for a reaction. Nothing.

"When you killed Joan," I say quietly, "you ripped my heart out. I didn't—I wasn't sure I wanted to go on. I loved her so much, and missed her so much, that I could hardly stand it."

I pause and take out my handkerchief, catching the tear that's beginning to make its way down my left cheek. "I couldn't eat. I couldn't sleep. I could barely work. I cut myself off from everyone. I made one really bad decision that cost me the little I had left. I left Myerton and didn't come back for fifteen years."

I stop and clear my throat. "I left her here because I didn't want to remember. I thought I could run away from my pain. But it was with me wherever I went. They say time heals all wounds, but they're wrong. It's not time. Do you know what heals, Randy?"

Randy stares at the table.

"Forgiveness," I say gently. "God's forgiveness and man's forgiveness. My problem wasn't that I couldn't forgive you—though I'll admit, I couldn't do that. I couldn't forgive myself."

I take a deep breath and slowly blow it out. "You told me it was my fault she is dead, that I am the one who should be dead. That's what I believed, too. And I carried that guilt with me, not forgiving myself and not being able to forgive you."

I stop and look for any kind of reaction from Randy, but there is nothing. He just sits quietly. I'm not even sure he's listening to me.

"But now, I can," I say. "I'm here to tell you that I forgive you, Randy. And that God will forgive you too. But you also need to forgive yourself."

I reach out and put my hands over his shackled hands. "I know you didn't mean to kill Joan. I believe you loved her, and that killing her was an accident. And it's eaten you up since that night. I can forgive you, Randy. But God, through his forgiveness and infinite mercy, can help you forgive yourself. And help you heal."

I sit with him for another minute, looking for some kind of sign. His hands are still beneath mine. There's not a flicker of movement.

I squeeze his hands and remove mine. "I just wanted to tell you that, Randy. I will be praying for you." I stand and walk to the door.

"Father?"

I stop and turn back. Randy's looking at me.

"Will you hear my confession?"

I smile and go back to the chair. I get out my book and my scapular, kiss it, and place it over my shoulders.

Randy's looking across the table at me now, his eyes filling with tears.

With a smile, I say, "Let us begin."

Epilogue

April has grown sunny and mild after a cold and rainy March. The sun is bright in the cloudless sky. Birds sing, and the flowers in the planters lining the sidewalk along the grounds of Myer College are beginning to put forth their blooms. I walk down Main Street past storefronts, past The Painted Lotus Gallery, where a sign advertises a show of new works by the creator of "American Carnage," past a small yarn store that is having a two for one sale, and past the used book store.

I'm in sight of The Perfect Cup when I see Helen seated at a table.

I take two more steps, then stop.

She isn't alone.

Sitting with her is Anna.

I pick up my pace again and walk up to the table. "Well, hello."

They look up at me. "You're late," Helen says.

"Really?" I check the time. "Sorry, I got delayed."

Anna finishes her coffee. "Well, I need to get back to Saint Clare's. I've got to arrange things for Father McCoy for the Parish Council meeting tonight."

"I take it you're settling into the parish secretary's job?" I ask.

"Yes, but I only agreed to do it on a temporary basis until they could find someone else. He's conducting interviews this afternoon. I really like one of them; she's a young single woman, really active in the parish. Pleasant personality. I think it will be a nice change of pace for Father. I don't think he's fully recovered from the shock of having the last parish secretary arrested for murder."

I laugh. "Well, he's lucky to have you."

She looks at me. "Can you stop by on your way out of town?"

"I probably won't have time. I'm expected at 3:00 p.m. and it's after noon now. I've just got time for coffee."

She nods. "Well, I'll see you when I see you," she kisses me on the cheek and gives me a hug. "Don't stay away too long. Promise me."

I nod. "I promise."

She breaks the hug and turns to Helen. "And I'll see you on Sunday, right, Helen?"

"See you then, Anna."

As Anna walks off I sit down across from Helen. "You two have become friendly," I say. "I didn't know you knew her."

"Well, I met her when I interviewed her after I re-opened Joan's case," Helen says. "It was a tense conversation, to say the least. But she brought cookies to me the week after the arrests to thank me. We got to talking, and she wound up inviting me to Christmas dinner at her house with a bunch of other single people from the church. I was the youngest one there, as it turned out, but still it was nice to meet some other people from the parish. She's made me feel welcome."

"Anna's a mom at heart," I say. "She tends to adopt us strays."

She laughs. "Well, I'm not sure they know what to make of me, yet. A woman my age, not married, with no kids. It is taking me a while to get used to all the kids."

"You don't like children?"

"I like children fine. Just maybe not so many all in one place. But I will say, Officer Conway's kids are amusing. Especially that Catherine."

The mention of Dan's name leads me to ask, "I never found out, what happened with Dan?"

"Well," Helen says. "I was able to persuade the Chief not to fire him. He was suspended without pay for a month, which he's already served. He's still on the force, back out on the streets instead of behind a desk. I'll be honest, Tom, I've had my eye on him for a while. He's a good officer. He made one mistake. Now, he gets a chance to prove himself."

"Well, I'm glad to hear that," I say. I pause for a moment, looking for the right way to ask a question I have on my mind. "Um, Helen, does Anna—"

Helen shakes her head. "No, I haven't told her about us."

Nate Rodriguez brings me a cup of coffee, heavy cream and sugar. I look at him. "How's it going?"

"Great," he says. "You caught me on my last day."

"Oh, you have another job?"

"I've sold the documentary," he says, "About Joan, about the investigation. I'm going to New York to sign the contracts."

"You're moving to New York?"

"Oh, no," Nate says. "I'm coming back to Myerton. I'm just not going to work here anymore."

He leaves us alone. I look at the sun reflecting off her hair. A years-old memory flashes through my mind, one I quickly pushed out.

"How's Glenda?" I say.

"Difficult, from what I hear."

"She confessed to Shepp's murder and pled guilty to second-degree murder," I say. "When is she going to be sentenced?"

"It's coming up soon. With no criminal history and her age, she'll probably get the minimum." She takes a drink of her coffee. "I was surprised you weren't here the day John Archman was released."

"I couldn't get away, but I am glad your boyfriend supported his motion to withdraw his guilty plea."

"First, Thomas Jude Greer," Helen says somewhat testily, "Brian Dohrmann isn't my boyfriend. We dated. We were engaged briefly. But that's over. Our relationship is strictly professional. "

"Sorry," I say. "I didn't mean—"

"Second," continues Helen, "he really didn't have much choice."

"Randy's competency hearing is coming up too, isn't it?" I ask, trying to get the conversation back on track.

Helen nods. "End of May. Considering he knew what he was doing when he confessed to everything the night we arrested him, I'm not sure his public defender will succeed in getting the confession thrown out. That's good, because the only thing we really have to tie him to Joan's death is the gun Glenda used on you. He'll probably enter a plea of not criminally responsible. I doubt he'll spend any time in prison. Probably the state hospital, maybe for the rest of his life."

"That's probably the best thing for him," I say.

Helen sits back. "So what are you going to do now? Go back to Baltimore?"

I trace the rim of the cup with my fingers. "No, I'm not. I have a new assignment."

She sits up straight. "Oh?"

I look at her. She looks at me with expectation.

I shake my head. "No, not Saint Clare's. The parish is in good hands with Father Leonard."

She slumps a little. "Maybe, but he's no Father Tom. So, where are you going?"

I tell her about my new assignment. Her eyes widen.

"Well, that is a change. Does that mean you're never coming back?"

I laugh. "Oh, I'll be back. Anna's the only real family I have. Joan is here." I hesitate, then add, "I have friends, too."

She smiles. "I hope you consider me one, Tom."

I nod slowly. "Yes, Helen. I do."

She leans forward and looks at me. "Tom, I want to ask you something. If you say no, I understand, given our history together and your position now. But could we stay in touch this time?"

I take a deep breath. "Helen, I—"

"It's OK," she says, shaking her head. "I understand."

"No, I wasn't going to say no," I say slowly. "I'd like that. But it'd have to be email. Where I'm going, the cell service isn't great, and talking or texting—I just don't think that's a good idea."

"OK, sure, email's fine. You can send things to my work email."

"And," I add, "because of my position and our past relationship, anything we send to each other, I'll show to my spiritual director. I want you to understand that."

She smiles slightly. "Of course. Tom. Keep everything proper and above board."

"Exactly," I say. I don't add, *because I'm afraid of what I might say otherwise.*

"Well," Helen says, gathering her tote bag, "I need to go. And you need to be getting along, too, I suspect."

"Yes," I nod. "I do."

She looks at me, then leans down and kisses me on the cheek.

"I'll miss you, Father Tom," she says. "Don't stay gone too long."

I look at her as she walks off, my heart beating rapidly.

It's a good thing I'm leaving Myerton.

But I will be back.

***

I turn off the main road onto the gravel drive, making my way through the open gate. I follow the drive up the slight hill, twisting through the woods with trees casting deep shadows from the green leaves that had burst forth with the coming of spring.

I pull up to the hand-built cabin. I get out of the car and look around. I walk to the door of the cabin. I knock softly.

It opens.

"Welcome, Father," Brother Martin says with a smile. "We've been expecting you."

The End

About the Author

Susan Mathis was born in and grew up in an extremely small town in Alachua County, Florida where her family has lived for more than 100 years. When Susan was still very young, James (J.R) Mathis was born in a somewhat bigger small town about 100 miles south of where she lived. Within a decade, James' small town would become part of Orlando, the biggest tourist destination in the United States. He was not amused. That is how, while Susan was running barefoot, swimming in lakes full of alligators and feeding chickens, James was sitting in his bedroom reading books faster than his father could bring them home from the library.

Were James and Susan to write their love story, it would definitely be an enemies-to-lovers trope. They met in the library where he was working. He found her demands for books that he had to pull and bring to her so unreasonable that he actually turned her into the head librarian. She in turn was so anxious to drive him away that when some friends secretly set them up she laid out an entire speech about how miserable her life was (she is typically very upbeat). Little did she suspect that he had a passionate attraction to misery and they were married just over a year later.

Fast forward 26 years, three children, four grandchildren and 20 years of James working for the Federal government. He was diagnosed with a highly treatable but still very scary form of cancer. As so often happens, this brush with mortality inspired him to do something he'd always wanted to do, write a novel. After the publication of the second Father Tom Mystery, Susan joined him as coauthor. As far as the Mathises are concerned, writing together is the most fun a couple can have sitting at a computer.

Read more at https://www.facebook.com/groups/J.R.MathisAuthor/.